D0291391
Clockwork
II Planet
Yuu Kamiya & Tsubaki Himana
Illustration: Sino

"Ooh?! A swimsuit that suits you? Gah, how difficult!"

An idiot stared at the mannequins in the window of a store next to the station, groaning happily.

"This one... wait, actually... the swimsuit pales in comparison to the fine specimen it's intended for! Shouldn't it be the other way around?! Am I supposed to pity it?!"

"It appears that is the case, Master. Swimsuits are designed with consideration for those with disappointing figures, so as to supplement them. When it comes to someone shaped as perfectly as myself, it is all the more difficult to find something worthy of adorning me."

Immediately after, the two legendary automata clashed.
"——'Bloody Murder'——"

"——'Mute Scream'——"
RyuZU pinched up the hem of her skirt and curtsied, while AnchoR simply dropped down onto all fours upon the ground. Like a wedding vow and a cry of despair respectively, they spoke the most heretical, blasphemous words in this world:

Naoto Miura
RyuZU
Marie Bell Breguet
AnchoR
Vainney Halter

contents

Clockwork Planet

CLOCKWORK PLANET, VOLUME 2

Cover illustration by Sino

First published in Japan in 2013 by Kodansha Ltd., Tokyo. Publication rights for this English edition arranged through Kodansha Ltd., Tokyo.

Follow Seven Seas Entertainment online at sevenseasentertainment.com.
Experience J-Novel Club books online at j-novel.club.

TRANSLATION: fofi
J-NOVEL EDITOR: Andrew Hale
COVER DESIGN: Nicky Lim
INTERIOR LAYOUT & DESIGN: Clay Gardner
COPY EDITOR: Cae Hawksmoor
PROOFREADER: Jade Gardner
ASSISTANT EDITOR: Jenn Grunigen
LIGHT NOVEL EDITOR: Nibedita Sen
EDITOR-IN-CHIEF: Adam Arnold
PUBLISHER: Jason DeAngelis

ISBN: 978-1-626928-17-6
Printed in Canada
First Printing: June 2018
10 9 8 7 6 5 4 3 2 1

Clockwork Planet

Presented by

YUU KAMIYA *and*
TSUBAKI HIMANA

Illustrated by

SINO

Clockwork Planet

THERE IS NOTHING ETERNAL in this universe.

That is the truth. It is a great and fundamental principle that will never change.

I'm not talking about something abstract here.

"If there's a beginning, then there will be an end."

Actually, calling this simple fact a truth might be a bit over the top.

Just like how we're born meaninglessly and die worthlessly, this fleeting universe will someday burn out.

Expanding faster than the speed of light, it will consume an unfathomably enormous amount of energy to reach an end referred to as the heat death of the universe. Contrary to what you might expect from the name, it's said that the greatly expanded universe will eventually approach a temperature of absolute zero.

It's inevitable that we'll meet our demise someday. Whether it be Man or the universe, all changing things meet the same end. This is one of the fundamental roots of thermodynamics. It needs no proof, as it is a completely self-evident relationship of cause and effect.

However, can't you think of it this way?

If it's true that nothing can be eternal, then even that truth, in itself, cannot last forever.

Most likely, that's what *he* thought.

Followed by: *If that's the case, we only need to restore it.*

The world allows for contradictions. All phenomena that seem subjectively inconsistent are nothing more than the result of two contradictory truths. Science is a scripture that continually updates its text by adopting the newest conjectures—it is nothing but another form of religion. The real problem is on a whole other level: Our universe is actually completely illogical. At the very least, *he* thought the universe was incomplete, the study of physics flawed, and so...

If that's true, then what harm could there be in tampering with this absurdly enormous base mechanism and turning it into a series of completely different moving parts?

Wouldn't doing that make the universe continue to turn uneventfully on a set of physical laws completely different from the current ones, just like how non-Euclidean geometry was established without any contradictions?

There were many who mused on such things through the course history. Yet, unbelievably, what made those musings a reality was just a single, stupidly talented person.

His name was "Y."

The Earth had reached the end of its lifespan and was about to succumb to heat death. Y was the aberrant genius who rebuilt the planet out of gears. The ultimate clocksmith who created this Clockwork Planet. With a joke of a theory, he accomplished a feat so prodigious that nothing that came before or after could ever match its greatness. It was a legend that couldn't even become a myth; it was simply too outlandish. However, reality could not be denied. The Earth, which had died, was now kept alive by gears.

Click, clack, click, clack—like turning the hands of a clock. A thousand years later...

● Prologue / -- : -- / Sweeper

THIS CIGARETTE TASTES TERRIBLE.

Squinting his mechanical eyes, the man pursed his lips. Even in the dark, the unlit room seemed as bright as day thanks to the light-catching function of his artificial eyes. Gazing at the glowing ember of his cigarette, which was particularly bright, he quietly exhaled the smoke.

He was a man in the prime of life. Possibly thirty—at least, that was how old his cyborg body looked. It was a power-type body: thick skeletal frame jam-packed with muscle gears, over which he wore a black rubber suit made of synthetic resins. His name was Vermouth. It wasn't his real name—just a code name. He was a covert operative who belonged to a certain corporation. A man who had screwed up in his youth and lost both his human body and his old upstanding life.

"..."

He exhaled a breath mingled with purple smoke. If Vermouth were to abide by the tenets of a spy, he wouldn't be smoking during an operation. Not only did a cigarette stand out in the dark, it left a scent behind. As for any health concerns, in Vermouth's case, that wouldn't be an issue.

Ignoring the risks, Vermouth puffed away. That was his quirk. He'd silently lit his cigarette, deeply inhaled its smoke, and savored its release. He then determined the taste of it with a body that was crammed full of gears. Vermouth divined his fortune by its flavor. *It tasted terrible.*

"...Amaretto. I don't remember waiting here until morning being part of our job." Where his eyes pierced the darkness, there was a silhouette crouching by a steel door.

"Could you not rush things so much, Vermouth-senpai?"

Amaretto's voice was sarcastic. He was a slender young man also wearing a black rubber suit, so the only part of him revealed by the distant light gear's white glow was his face. He spoke without turning around, working with the countless tools in his hands. "It takes time to make this frigid padlock moan. Premature ejaculators aren't sexy, you know."

"This cigarette tastes terrible, Amaretto." Snorting, Vermouth shook his large body. "When my cigarette tastes bad, more often than not, our feet have already caught fire. If we don't hurry and finish this, we'll end up with muzzles shoved up our asses."

"...I just don't get it. Vermouth-senpai, what is the point of a full-body cyborg like you smoking cigarettes? It's not like you can taste them, am I wrong?"

"Are you an idiot, or am I the idiot for trusting my back to an idiot like you? Cigarettes aren't savored by the tongue, they're something a man experiences with his spirit. That guy's a virgin who sold his soul to the gods. He's not a ma—"

Vermouth stopped in midsentence and drew his gun from his waist faster than the blink of an eye. There was no way to tell from his stone-cold face that he had just been bantering. His gaze was sharp as he pointed his gun precisely at the ceiling. Amaretto placed his back against the wall and drew his gun. He hadn't sensed anything, but Vermouth, his senior, had done so, and that was reason enough.

There was no room for doubt. The two of them stared vigilantly through the darkness and readied themselves for a battle that could break out at any moment. And then—*snap*. The sound came from a duct near the corner of the ceiling. The mesh lid came off, and a woman poked her face out. She was a female cyborg with short silver hair, wearing a black rubber suit, the same as them.

Vermouth let out a sigh and lowered his gun. Amaretto grabbed hold of the padlock and resumed work. The woman descended to the floor with slippery movements, like squeezing fresh cream out of a piping bag.

"How was it, Strega?"

"Ain't good. As expected, the space 'yond this door is isolat'd." The woman, Strega, brushed the dust off of her rubber suit. "Its walls're on the level of a nuclear bunker. Even the sonar device couldn't produce a proper image of the interior. I tried gettin' in through the ducts, but its ventilation system's separate from the rest of the building. Forget a mouse, ev'n a fly wouldn't be able to get in."

"Hmm," Vermouth nodded.

Strega continued, "They must've somethin' they really want to keep hidden here. This security ain't somethin' made on a whim for show. Very least, I can't see it bein' just a regular factory... well, that's why we're here right?"

"Another fishy job, huh? Goddamnit... no wonder my cigarette tastes like shit."

Their mission was to investigate a certain ammunitions factory. Factories of unknown affiliation, run by dummy corporations, weren't rare. When you considered the holdings of the Five Great Corporations, places like this were a dime a dozen. However, a factory that consumed the power and resources of an entire city was a different matter. Who ordered it built? What was being made there? For what purpose? They had to confirm what was inside by any means necessary.

This job wasn't just about the interests of their corporate employers. It was necessary for maintaining a robust emergency management and security protocol in line with their everyday duties. Using camouflaged short-distance resonance gears, the three of them conversed through encrypted transmission signals.

"On the surface, it's a major factory that the military sold off," Vermouth sent, lighting his second cigarette. "But when we actually came here, it turned out to be guarded by a PMC with a security system on the level of a central reserve bank. We haven't been able to grasp even a bit of its background, even after infiltrating this deep. I get that it's something big, but you've gotta be kidding me."

"...Only ones who could've made a facility like this are the Five Great Corporations, or the military."

"Yeah, and it can't be our family, since they're the ones who sent us here."

"The ones I'm seein' most likely to do somethin' like this are the Vacherons," Strega muttered suspiciously. "But..."

"Do they really have that kind of time right now?" Amaretto replied. "They just took a blow from the Breguet princess and are bleeding out their asses, you know?"

"It's true then? That crazy rumor that the Breguet princess is actually 'live and been the one exposin' the dirty secrets of the Vacherons, the military, and Meister Guild to the public?"

"If nothing else, she's undoubtedly dead on record." Vermouth shrugged. "They even held a company funeral, you know. I was there. Casually slipped in. It was a touching ceremony with eulogies that got tears out of the president and the first daughter. They couldn't possibly say, 'We made a mistake,' at this point."

"G'ess that means that they can't complain if someone up'n kills her a 'second' time, then. She's ain't long for this world."

"That's not necessarily true," Amaretto butted in, "There's no evidence that Marie Bell Breguet was involved in that terrorist information leak. But then, that's obvious, since she was already 'dead' by then."

"How's that related to anythin'?" Strega asked, pouting, "Yer makin' no sense. Circumstantial evidence's plenty for those in our line of business."

"Of course, she's guilty. The problem doesn't lie there. That she managed to do all that without leaving any evidence behind—that's what's important."

"...Whaddya mean?"

"She pulled off that stunt like a ghost. That by itself suggests she's still deeply connected to, and receiving support from, her family—the Breguet Corporation," Vermouth elaborated. "If you kill her, that would automatically make you an enemy of the Breguets. Even if they can't protest publicly—no, in fact, that just makes things all the more dangerous."

"Make you an enemy? Aren't they the ones askin' for a fight?"

"That's not necessarily true," said Vermouth. "The incident at Kyoto may have been instigated by the Vacherons and the military—but the remaining three corporations, in essence, endorsed them with their silence. Since we were unable to stop them, we're just as guilty."

"Ya sayin' that was all within the realms of retribution? Ev'n if that's the case, didn't they go too far?"

"It was unprecedented," Vermouth agreed. "Many of the bigwigs involved were forced to step down... but, at the same time, that means the classified information that *was* revealed was only worth so much."

"Only worth so much ya say...?" Strega widened her eyes.

"The truly classified information... the information that would destroy those organizations, was not revealed," Amaretto explained. "If it were, society would topple. What got out was only 'open secrets,' so to speak."

"...Isn't that all they knew?"

"Could be true," Vermouth said, exhaling, "But it could be false, too. What if they *purposefully* ended the information leak when they did—in other words, what if that was nothing but a warning?"

Amaretto nodded with a bitter smile. "I wouldn't want to provoke a princess who raises that kind of hell just from having her butt felt up a little."

Strega cast a cold gaze on Amaretto. "It'd be good for the world if ya were stabbed just once."

"Enough chatter, open it up already."

"Yes, yes—it's open now. Thank you for your patience," Amaretto replied in his natural voice.

A heavy sound rang out as the steel door slowly slid open.

"All right, wake Sambuca up. We're breaking in."

Vermouth wound the spring of the support-type automaton sleeping in the corner of the room to start him up, and they advanced into the depths beyond the door.

• • ● ● ● • •

And then they saw something they shouldn't have.

"You can't be serious," Vermouth gasped, voice dry. "Wh-what is this? Are they insane...?"

He shook his head. What he was seeing was simply unbelievable. The gigantic vault that they had gone through the trouble to open...was empty. The manufacturing area was a large and empty space.

Had it already fulfilled its purpose? Countless tools, equipment, and the gigantic cranes and ladders that must have been used to make *something* now all looked lonely in there. Like they were abandoned in a hurry. They snuck past that empty manufacturing area to where, deep in the back, was what appeared to be a research office lined with bundles of documents and computers. Information had been left behind. Reading only a small portion of it was enough to make them shiver.

Amaretto was the first one to regain his composure. "If all of this is true, the sacrifices won't stop with just one or two cities. In the worst case, the Clockwork Planet itself could be... in any case, let's make some copies and get out of here, Vermouth-senpai. We can study the information all we want to afterwards. What's important right now is to bring it back without a hiccup. Otherwise..."

It might have been that just by looking at such dangerous information, Amaretto could see right away that this case was beyond them, but...just as Vermouth and Strega came to their senses and were about to start photographing the documents, the three cyborgs felt something.

"...?!"

It was the illusion of a sensation. They shouldn't be able to experience it through their artificial skin. There was no other way to describe it: they felt goosebumps. The three veteran spies froze in terror. They felt a presence. Outside the room, in the thick darkness, "something" was definitely there. It was small, so small, and yet it had the scent of extraordinary violence. Without uttering a word, the three of them scattered, so desperate to hide themselves in the shadows of the room that they looked like they were on the run from something. Without having agreed on it beforehand, they all drew their Coil Spears instead of their guns.

Coil Spear—a bayonet that vibrates at ultrahigh frequencies. Able to change into a pistol, a shotgun, or a grenade launcher with just a swing of the arm, Coil Spears were the best weapon a single person could carry in terms of both adaptability and firepower. If you mastered their use, a person could fight against both human soldiers and automata. For three combat cyborgs, it was an armament—a multifaceted weapons system—that would allow them to challenge just about any enemy, even if that enemy was a heavily armored automaton. However, being the product of cutting-edge clockwork technology, it couldn't be manufactured by anyone other than the Five Great Corporations. As such, there was a risk that their affiliations could be exposed by the differences in company technology.

For those whose most important job was to remain undercover, simply having to use it meant that they had failed in their mission. Even so, they had decided to use their Coil Spears without a moment's hesitation. There was only one exceptional case in the mission regulations that would authorize the use of a Coil Spear. When returning alive without using it became hopeless, and when there was a significant reason to prioritize survival over death. Being pros, the three of them determined that this situation fit the bill.

No, that's just an excuse. Vermouth laughed silently as he acknowledged his own shaking hands. The fact was, whoever was outside the room had made them, three combat cyborgs, draw their most powerful weapon in fear. Vermouth analyzed the situation with his body's light and sound focusing functions.

We are in a cramped room that lies deep in the facility. There's only one exit. The owner of the presence is standing still outside the door. She's...alone. If we throw Sambuca at the enemy to buy time, it should be possible to forcefully break through even in a worst case scenario.

The support-type automaton that accompanied them, Sambuca, looked at first glance like an ultralight-armored automaton. It was using civilian parts procured locally to conceal its affiliation. That said, having been modded by the three of them (all Geselles), its performance capabilities were powerful enough to fight against even a military automaton. Vermouth mentally went through the escape plan they'd put together for this kind of situation. With no need for words or transmissions, the three exchanged glances and nodded.

The door rattled as it opened. Vermouth stuck his head out of the shadows to visually confirm the enemy and execute the plan... however, upon seeing the enemy, his thoughts froze. The presence they had sensed standing in front of the open door. The one who had pierced their hearts with unspeakable terror was...

A...child?

It was an automaton. One with the body of a young girl. She looked like a prized doll. Her dainty arms and legs were covered with an ominous-looking chain of plates that gave the impression of both armor and, strangely, restraints. Her hair fell all the way

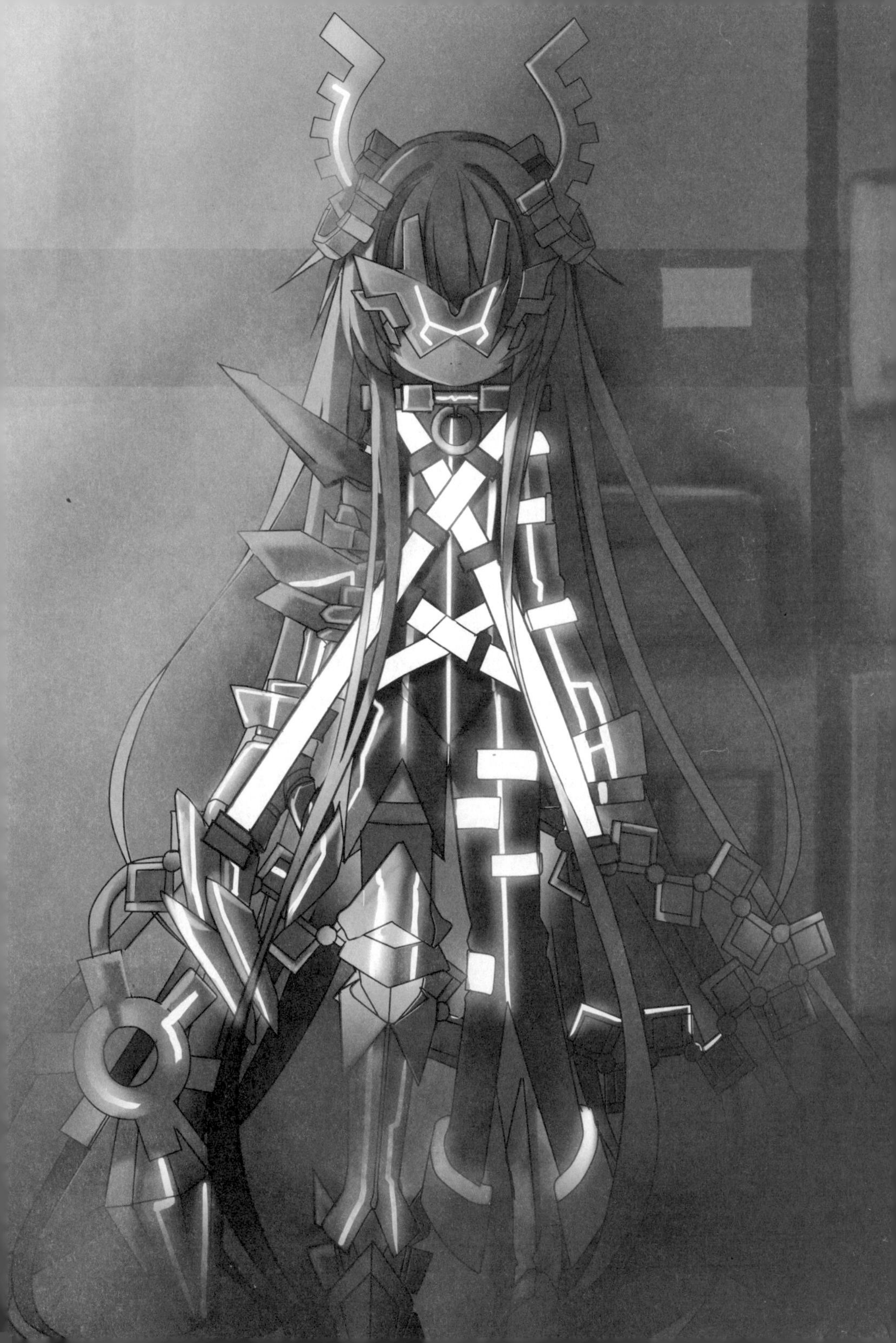

down to her feet, as deep a red as blood. An ominous mask covered her young, innocent face. Through her mask, their gazes met. Vermouth felt it. His intuition screamed to discard the plan and eliminate the enemy in front of him immediately.

"Sambuca! Execute Code D3! Stop that thing!!"

Code D3—restrain the current target even if it means self-destruction. To that order, Sambuca rushed forward without a sound. He was a support automaton that ran on silent mechanisms and wasn't originally designed for direct combat. However, if he grappled the target, he could at least keep her from moving momentarily. Just a second would be enough. If Sambuca could restrain the enemy, then the other three could riddle them both full of holes with the focused fire from their Coil Spears. However...

A cube made up of solid black gears floated beside the automaton that looked like a little girl. And those black gears...twisted.

Like a towel being wrung out, the cube rippled as it transformed into two cones with a brief sonorous sound. Faster than their cyborg sensors could detect the hum, Sambuca's body...vanished, along with a part of the floor.

"Huh?!" One of them shouted, dumbfounded.

The masked girl glanced at the faces of the remaining three. Seeing her nonchalant and inorganically cold gaze, Vermouth understood.

We can't win. With a shiver, he acknowledged that fact.

"Break the walls!" He shouted fiercely without turning around. If there was an enemy like that blocking the only entrance, they had no choice but to increase the number of exits.

"I'll hold'er back! Gimme cover!" Strega booted up her double-speed gear. Emerging from the shadows, she kicked off against the wall and then the ceiling in a flash. She wielded her Coil Spear like a blade. Vibrating at ultrahigh frequencies, it was sharp enough to easily cut through standard building materials. If she diced the ceiling, the falling rubble could be used as cover. Then maybe they could escape through the opening. In any case, she could buy them time.

Vermouth instantly realized Strega's intention and pointed his Coil Spear at the automaton girl, preparing to shoot. He chose armor-piercing, high-carbon steel grenades. With those, he could provide a barrage of covering fire while Amaretto blasted a wall with high-powered explosives. If a hole opened up, they should be able to escape from there as well. That would have been the plan...if, upon loading the shell into his Coil Spear, Amaretto's entire upper body hadn't been vaporized without leaving behind a single strand of dust.

"...?!"

"Yer kiddin' me..."

The floating cube made of black gears twisted into cones and hummed. This time, it was Strega who exploded into scrap iron mid-air with a thunderous roar.

What the hell is going on?! Vermouth's reason screamed. Both Amaretto and Strega were cyborgs armed with the latest technology, to the point where leaving their bodies behind was as forbidden as using their Coil Spears. But right now that was the least of Vermouth's worries. Both of his allies had been *annihilated* without a trace. Even if the enemy was a heavily armored automaton, she shouldn't have been able to render them so overwhelmingly helpless. But regardless of his protests, the reality of Vermouth's situation wouldn't change. Ironically enough, the presence of this unbelievable monster explained everything.

The concealed nature of this facility and the gravity of the information they had found here. The security left to a measly PMC that was all too weak. And then, out of nowhere, this demon...

There was no longer any room for doubt. What was this place? The answer was simple: it was Hell.

There's no doubt! The silent operation that rendered their detection capabilities useless. The overwhelming firepower that outclassed them to the point of absurdity. The automaton with the form of a young girl that shouldn't have existed. The enemy that stood before his eyes. This god of death was...

"You must be one of the Initial-Y Series!!"

The enemy didn't respond. Without even changing her stance, she focused her mineral gaze on Vermouth.

I'm gonna die. Trusting his screaming instincts, Vermouth hit the ground. Above his head, an unknown blast eroded everything in its way as it shot right over him. His left arm, unable to get out of the way in time, was taken by the unperceivable attack. He ignored the screaming signals that reported the damage to his brain.

Adjusting his posture to compensate for the missing weight of his left arm, Vermouth kicked off the floor. He swung his Coil Spear, and the loaded grenades changed to something else. He fired. An anchor shot out and pierced the wall and, for an instant, there was a roar of gears turning at high speed. A cloud of dust billowed from a portion of the wall, crumbling from the ultrahigh frequency vibrations. Vermouth barely managed to leap into the opening before the girl vaporized the space where he had just been.

• • ● ⬤ ● • •

Think!

Vermouth fled, just barely evading the incoming attacks from the god of death that pursued him. Every time a blast came, he'd try to react as he lost yet another piece of his body. He had only been able to survive up to this point because of his intuition. He discarded the information his sensory devices fed him and ignored all tactical theory. If his instinct told him to dodge, he would dodge. If it told him to run, he would run. In this manner, he managed to survive for a little over five minutes. You could call it a miracle. However, it was about to come to an end.

The room that Vermouth had just dived into was a dead end with nowhere to hide. Worse, everything below his right knee had been vaporized by a blast that had detonated when he'd thrown himself in here. Vermouth's honed instincts were useless if he couldn't run. He had lost his Coil Spear, too. The only thing that he had left was a hand grenade that wouldn't even scratch his enemy.

While his body felt hot enough to catch fire, his reason was thoroughly cold and clear. He concluded that, given things had reached this point, his death was inevitable. His life had gone awry ever since he screwed up twenty years ago. Today just so happened to be the day he screwed up again, nothing more. An idiot who should have died twenty years ago would finally kick the bucket. That was all. It was nothing worth fussing over. The problem was...

"Obediently handing my life over to the reaper like this... no matter how I think about it, it grates on my nerves, damn it!"

Footsteps. Mixed among the damage reports flooding his brain, the sound of death approaching. The god who had destroyed his two colleagues like they were nothing.

"Haaaah."

Fumbling a cigarette with a hand missing fingers, Vermouth gently lit it. Such was his job. Neither Amaretto nor Strega were really his friends. He didn't even know their real names. What colors they liked, what kind of music they listened to, their family, friends, and lovers, if any—he knew none of it. He had never asked about their past and frankly, he didn't care. After all, even without asking, he was sure that they were scum just like him. Vermouth had no reason, out of duty or friendship, to mourn their deaths.

However, what *they* were trying to do... that he knew. Vermouth felt a long forgotten zeal. It wasn't from a sense of justice. He wasn't moved by cheap feelings of humanity, nor was he attempting to finish the job out of a spy's respect for his profession. It was simply a pure and primitive emotion that came from his gut.

"Kicking the bucket without being able to even deal one blow to that damn monster *really pisses me off*."

Such was the petty pride of the man known as Vermouth.

"Think...!" Vermouth groaned as he exhaled, spewing out smoke.

There was no meaning in facing off against this monster. He had neither the skill nor the power to do so. The most he could possibly do would be get the information he was carrying outside by any means necessary. The problem was: how?

He didn't hope to return alive, nor did he care about exposing his background. Compared to the weight of this information, such things were as important as scraps of paper. Before all else. At any cost. He had to tell someone about what had happened here. That was enough.

"That's right. I won't hope for anything else, so...!"

Think. How can I contact the outside world from here?

This area is completely isolated. We couldn't find a single communications room, even though we made a sweep of the entire area. There's no way to contact someone through a line. If there were a way, it would have to be a simple message sent through the primitive telegraph device equipped inside my body. But what point would there be in doing something like that? What kind of crackpot would pick out meaning from such a random message?

"Pft, bwa ha ha ha ha!" Vermouth burst out laughing.

Someone like that does exist.

There was just one person he knew that would care about such a meaningless message. Someone whose actions no one else could predict. The smartest, biggest fool on the planet. Vermouth stifled his laughter and tuned the frequency of his telegraph device. As for where he addressed his message...

"The only ones who can do something about this insane plot are people who are insane themselves."

If it's her... if it's the princess who dealt a mighty blow to the evil in this world, then maybe...

The footsteps stopped. Death was standing right before his eyes, but Vermouth's heart was strangely peaceful.

There's no problem. I've done what I could. I can leave the rest to those who come after. With this, our deaths won't be in...

"Hmph."

A thought had arisen, unnoticed, in the back of his mind. It was something that Vermouth hadn't yearned for in a very long time. That the efforts of someone like him would be *rewarded*. It was an innocent desire that he had left behind somewhere, in a time that he could no longer remember...

"What a mess I am..." Scoffing at his naivety in this final hour, Vermouth cracked a bitter smile. He puffed on the cigarette in his mouth.

I've borne the ill will of many people, but I've never thought anything of it. I always thought that was just the way things were. That's why the world's shit. But I think I get it now. In this world, there are truly evil scum that can't be forgiven even if they pay with their lives.

He didn't come to that conclusion with fastidious reasoning, nor a juvenile sense of justice. It was something simpler, a hot emotion that boiled up from the bottom of his gut. He just didn't like this. It pissed him off down to his very core. So, if there was a way to hinder this monster, even just a little...

...What kind of idiot wouldn't take revenge? If, in return for our lives, we can expose this nauseating scheme, then I say we blow every last bit of it to hell!

Vermouth breathed in the ample smoke. For a moment, he almost thought he could taste it, but that couldn't have been possible.

"Ahh," Vermouth sneered. "How delicious... ha ha ha... watch and see what happens, you bastards."

Before he could exhale, Vermouth's body was annihilated, along with the space it had once occupied.

· • ● ⬤ ● • ·

...I'm getting sleepy, the girl thought, her mind covered in a dense fog. She could faintly tell that she was in a dreamlike state. She was forgetting something important, but she couldn't gather her thoughts. Her footing felt soft and somehow unstable, her eyelids were beginning to droop...

"Hmm... a short-wave transmission sent by a telegraph, huh."

She could hear the voices of human men, although she couldn't tell who they were. Beyond the fog in her mind were voices that she felt she'd heard somewhere before...

"I can't imagine anything important was sent with something like this, but...I can't help wondering which organization these rats belonged to."

"She erased them. I don't think there's any hope of identifying their bodies."

"She's unable to hold back. It's her flaw...but well, the deftness of their infiltration, and the professionalism they showed in paying for this information with their lives...those are like dog tags in and of themselves."

"The Audemars? Or the Breguets? In any case, they're directly affiliated with one of the two, surely."

"Is that short-wave transmission traceable?"

"I'm already on it. Though, I can't imagine they would lead us to their employer..."

How boring. Quickly losing interest in the men's conversation, the girl became dejected. She hated complicated discussions. She didn't like cold-hearted schemes or scary stories, either. *Crushing, breaking, smashing, jumbling, and cleaning up?* The girl couldn't understand the fun in such things at all.

Could it be, she thought, *that these people are idiots? Even though there are any number of fun things to do, they're always talking about the same boring, meaningless trifles. Singing, dancing, playing, laughing, and cleaning up...* Why didn't they do those things instead? The girl couldn't understand it. No matter who was involved, or what time of day it was, they should be allowed to do fun things.

"AnchoR." The man called her by name. The girl—AnchoR—raised her gaze. The man smiled. "You did well. That was a magnificent victory. You must have worked hard."

Victory? AnchoR tilted her head. In her mind, at least. In reality, she simply continued looking up at the man's face without batting an eyelid. *As I thought, this person really is just a dummy, isn't he? Calling mere cleanup a victory—is that why he's boring? Or is he like this because he's boring?*

"We'll take care of the rest. You can return to base and receive maintenance."

AnchoR nodded silently, unable to come up with the answers to the two questions whirling inside her head. *I suppose it doesn't matter...*

The Fourth of the Initial-Y Series—AnchoR, "The One Who Destroys." As she turned to make her exit, the consciousness of the eternal, indestructible, and strongest automaton sank into a daze once more.

Clockwork Planet

• Chapter One / 14 : 30 / Goober

LIFE IS WORTHLESS, but it isn't meaningless.

I'm sure there are objections to that statement and even rebuttals—but regardless, it is a truth that no one, not even God, can deny. After all, even if one's worth is acknowledged by others, the meaning is determined by yourself. That's why everyone lives out their lives trying to find their own meaning. We all try to do so, in our own ways, because I'm sure everyone knows *that* is where true happiness lies. Even if you are poor, or orphaned, or homeless, or your looks or brains leave something to be desired...finding meaning in your life, acknowledging it, and living life for its sake, is surely the greatest happiness you can achieve. Naoto Miura was certain of it, because he had found that meaning for himself.

"I'm sure you understand what you should do when you've discovered your calling," Naoto Miura said as he made a fist and dug his feet firmly into the ground. In spite of his scrawny body, Naoto's chest was puffed up with determination. He knew the meaning of his birth. What he was willing to die for. At this critical juncture in his youth, he'd already found a destiny worth betting his life on.

"If you're human… no, if you're a man!" Naoto's gray eyes lit up feverishly. "If a man hears there's a super cute automaton girl somewhere, then whether she's at the North Pole or Mar de Ajó, no, even if she's on the other side of the universe! To dash to her at full speed would be his manly duty—no! It would be his fate!"

He thrust his fist upwards with this shout. As if galvanized by Naoto's energy, the older man standing before him nodded slightly.

"…And so?"

"Right! As such, I'm announcing that I'll be absent from school for a bit due to personal circumstances compelling me to charge towards Tokyo." With that, Naoto Miura presented his leave of absence form with a face full of smiles.

His homeroom teacher beamed. "Ah, I know what you are, Mr. Naoto Miura." The old teacher thrust a different paper in front of Naoto's eyes. It was a sheet of scrap paper with a "0" written in red ink—Naoto's answer sheet. "You're an idiot aren't you?" Seeing Naoto's smile freeze, the homeroom teacher continued cheerfully. "Just shut up and take your supplementary lessons. If you fail the follow-up test again, forget a leave of absence, I'll make you fill out a withdrawal form, and while I'm at it, I'll introduce you to a good brain surgeon, too. Got it?"

And so Naoto Miura's grand destiny and profound resolve to fulfill his life's purpose were mercilessly crushed without any further room for discussion.

Naoto had no other choice.

There was an anomaly in Tokyo.

It'd been confirmed that RyuZU's little sister—another Initial-Y Series—was there as well. Naoto had resolved to depart immediately upon learning of that information, but... while being watched with the shining eyes of the girl who was his everything...

"Master Naoto, if you manage to fall to an even lower social rung, even if nothing about you has actually changed, society will at long last brand you more worthless than an amoeba. As my master, I would greatly appreciate it if you could do your best to avoid becoming so pitiful that I would no longer be able to look you in the eye."

The girl's smile let Naoto know that she harbored not even a bit of malice.

Her heartbeat that let Naoto know that she was simply worried for him.

It really was meant to be a well-intentioned lecture, but any hint of the girl's kindness had been pruned by her actively abusive verbal filter.

Seeing the automaton worry lovingly for him, Naoto simply had no choice...

"And thus, the history of human warfare ended a thousand years ago." The bland voice of the history teacher was the only thing ringing in the nearly empty classroom.

"The Earth had been mechanized with exceedingly advanced technology, and humanity was not foolish enough to engage in warfare while atop an instrument that was essentially as delicate as a finely tuned clock. Eventually, an international treaty was signed, limiting the military force of all nations to only the amount needed for the defense of their municipal grids. Furthermore, the public use of older technology which threatens the survival of humanity today—in particular, the kind known as electromagnetic technology—was nearly entirely banned..."

The teacher continued the lecture by simply reading aloud the contents of the textbook and jotting down some key points on the blackboard every now and then. Bored, Naoto propped his chin on his hand and asked the silver-haired girl sitting next to him, "Hey, RyuZU. What's 'electromagnetic technology'?"

"Long ago humanity, in its greatness, tried to fathom the unknown with their childish brains. Electromagnetic technology is the remnants of that effort."

The girl he had asked—RyuZU—deepened her bewitching smile. Her voice, high and clear as a music box, rang clearly through the classroom.

"It is probably accurate to call it a futile labor that even monkeys would sneer at. In the modern day, such things are just worthless antiques of little significance. Considering the capacity of Master Naoto's brain, learning about electromagnetic technology would simply squander the little memory resources that you have left."

"Ah, In other words, it wouldn't be a problem in the slightest if I didn't know about it?"

"It's nothing that a member of the elite like yourself would need to be expressly informed about on your day off, Master,"

RyuZU answered with a blooming smile that would put even a flower to shame. Her eyes, however, were filled with malice—a pair of knives at the ready to murder some hated enemy.

Prickled by RyuZU's sharp gaze, the teacher continued in a trembling voice, "Th-this is mandatory knowledge that is taught in elementary school, you know! B-because electromagnetic force causes gears to become misaligned—excluding the 'planet governor,' the magnetic field deployed from the North and South Poles to protect the Earth from solar radiation—its use and research has been completely banned."

"Did you hear that, Master? The teacher has just courteously informed us that, in the end, all he knows how to do is regurgitate what he has memorized from the textbook."

The teacher trembled at RyuZU's immediately snarky response. Naoto tilted his head looking perplexed.

"Why do you say that?"

"If both the use of and research on electromagnetism were banned, then there is no way he actually learned about it. Everything he has said for some time now has been, word for word, what's in the textbook. Are modern lectures just public recitals? I must say, if that's the case, then lectures are a waste of time. It would be more efficient to read the textbook at home yourself."

"Well...yeah, but if it weren't for lectures, I wouldn't learn anything. I never study on my own," Naoto sighed.

RyuZU deliberately folded her arms.

"To begin with, who was it that committed this act of utmost insolence by summoning *my* Master Naoto to school on the weekend? Would it be that venerable pig over there, fat and ready for the slaughter? This swine who has only been equipped with a textbook recital function?"

The teacher's face stiffened at RyuZU's sharp tongue. Naoto let out a bitter sigh and covered for the teacher.

"You've got it wrong, RyuZU. It's my fault for being so close to failing this class that I have to take remedial lessons."

"I see." RyuZU gave a big, theatrical nod in such a human way that, for a moment, even Naoto forgot that she was an automaton. RyuZU continued with an unchanging smile, "In that case, who could be the person that judged my Master Naoto would fail? Where is the self-professed all-knowing and almighty person who is in reality at the apex of incompetence? Surely it is not that person over there whose regrettable head has been left wanting in terms of both brain and hair?"

Naoto gave a sidelong glance at the teacher. He was trembling all over. Naoto shook his head.

"No, RyuZU, the reason he said I would fail the class is because I failed the final exam."

"I see. In that case, which monkey was it that came up with the blasphemous test questions that made *my* Master Naoto fail? Could it be that baboon at the podium who's trembling for some strange reason? The one who is so apparently adequate *down there* that he exchanged *pleasantries* with his neighbor's wife last night?"

"H-h-h-how do you know that?! Er, no, wait! That's not what I meant!" the teacher shouted, clearly flustered and with tears in his eyes, "I'm simply trying to fulfill my duties as a teacher! It's not like I have it any better. I'm working on a weekend just for Naoto, you know! Can't you have some consideration for this futile endeavor that I'm obligated to undertake, RyuZU?"

RyuZU continued smiling despite the teacher's pained appeal.

"Yes. Receiving a lecture from a flea is surely a waste of time, so I have been politely *requesting* with the utmost discretion and sincerity that you let Master Naoto go home accordingly, but...it appears that you will not understand unless I speak in a flea's language."

There was no way that RyuZU would accept these remedial lessons, set up on the assumption that Naoto would likely have to repeat a year. Already, on the second day, she showered the teacher with abuse that endlessly chipped away at his ego.

RyuZU was completely unaware of her words herself—what she said was simply the result of her properly functioning abusive verbal filter. She wasn't trying to be rude. In her mind, she really was making a polite and courteous request with full sincerity. However, there was no way that anyone aside from Naoto, who could hear her operational sounds, could understand that.

Thanks to the artistic insults that RyuZU mercilessly spewed throughout these remedial lessons, the teacher's spirit, having endured until now, was about to collapse.

I've done my best up to now, so it's fine if I just end it all here, right? Just as the teacher's heart and knees finally began to fold...

The school bell rang.

"I-I've had enough... enough I tell you! Mr. Naoto Miura! Tomorrow is Sunday, so the next remedial lesson will be on Monday. From Monday onwards the teacher will be for a different subject, so show up with that in mind! Principaaaaaaaaaal! I'll have you know I'm going to apply for overtime pay *and* mental therapy for work-related injuries!!!"

The teacher ran shouting from the classroom. Naoto looked up at the ceiling while RyuZU, unaware of her own wicked tongue, simply tilted her head, looking puzzled.

"Has he finally become aware of his own imbecility and resolved to visit a hospital for treatment? Although his intellect is less than that of a flea, if he learns some modesty after having become aware of that, I feel I can respect him for his self-reflection."

"Right, what should I say?" asked Naoto, holding his head in his hands. "Make sure to apologize to him so that his anger at being unduly abused isn't directed at me, all right?"

They left the school together.

I guess I should come up with some countermeasures before the new victim shows up on Monday...

• • ● ● ● • •

Marie Bell Breguet had no experience of going to school.

Well, that was a little misleading. After all, she had graduated valedictorian from several prestigious universities overseas. But if we were to speak of how Marie felt on attending Tadasunomori High School in Kyoto—this was her first day of school.

As the daughter of the president of the Breguet Corporation, one of the Five Great Corporations that ruled the world economy, Marie had been given a superb educational befitting her enormous potential. A wealth of talented tutors. An abundance of funds. The very best equipment. What reason would someone like Marie have to go to school?

Even the greatest educational institution in the world couldn't hope to match the Breguet family's educational environment. As such, the reason that Marie entered college was neither to study nor to do research. It wasn't even to expand her social network—something that being the daughter of a respected family demanded. It was for proof.

Something that would make the talent and capability of Marie Bell Breguet obvious at a glance.

It had all been for that purpose. As such, from Marie's perspective, she couldn't say that she had ever gone to school. She had simply spent a bit of time taking the necessary exams to acquire a few certifications. That's all it had been.

Her thought process wasn't much different from a job-hunting graduate filling in the qualifications section of an application.

On the other hand, here at Tadasunomori High School, it went without saying how the educational environment compared—the level of the teachers and the students were child's play in comparison to the universities that Marie had graduated from.

There was absolutely nothing that Marie had to learn here after all her experiences working on the front lines as a Meister, not even as an independent study of society.

However, in spite of that considerable gap, there was something that Marie had just witnessed for the first time. That something was...

"I see now that a failing mark is a real thing..." Marie muttered earnestly with a matcha dumpling in her mouth.

Halter looked down at the girl with an indescribable gaze.

Marie had brilliant golden hair and pale, ethereal skin. She was as beautiful as a porcelain doll, but a powerful will resided in her dazzling emerald eyes—squinting in annoyed disbelief. She was wearing a standard midday uniform with an orange parka. Despite that, she exuded an air of such class and ardor that her outfit did nothing to mask her regal aura.

"Just for the record, you really didn't know?" Halter asked in a suspicious tone.

"I knew of the phrase, but I thought it was more of a theoretical kind of thing. I didn't think that it actually applied in practice."

"Well, given that there're tests and those tests are graded, there'll be some students that fail."

"That's what's so confusing."

"Hmm?" Halter tilted his head.

To make sure, Marie asked, "They're taking lessons at school, aren't they? The contents of which show up on the exams? Final exams are basically a means of checking whether the students understood the lessons or not, right?"

"Well, yeah." Halter nodded, wondering why Marie was asking such obvious questions.

Marie looked utterly baffled, "Then...how can they fail?"

"Well..."

"I mean, that would mean that even though they took the lessons they still couldn't answer questions about the content.

Doesn't that contradict itself?! How truly profound. What kind of phenomenon is it, really..."

"Princess...you've just made every student in the world your enemy." Halter sighed. His shoulders drooped. The red cloth-draped bench creaked as the bear-like man shifted his posture.

They sat next to each other in a tea house in a tourist area of Kyoto Grid, Japan. The shop was located in the midst of a bamboo thicket, and the building itself was made of wood. There were even red paper umbrellas to provide shade for its outdoor seats—in other words, it was a total tourist trap.

In that regard, the teahouse was certainly successful. Sightseers seemed to enjoy its style, as the other foreign clientele around Marie and Halter would attest.

Kyoto Grid was a leading tourist city even for Japan. A thousand years ago, when the Earth was reconstructed with gears, nearly all of the cultural heritage sites in the world were preserved (as much as possible) in their former state. But among them, Kyoto was known for having preserved a particularly large number.

Biting into her second dumpling skewer, Marie tilted her head. "I could understand a little if things they didn't know appeared on the exams, but for stuff that they learned in the lecture? Why can't they answer that? I don't understand."

"I don't understand you either, princess." Halter sighed deeply. He was an average person who had experienced setbacks as much as anyone else in his life and found the girl genius's bluntly naive questions objectionable.

After paying the tab, the two of them left the teahouse behind and took a walk in the bamboo thicket.

Packed earth filled the gaps in the white stone paving of the promenade. The sunlight was gentle thanks to the shade of the bamboo leaves, which made the air nice and cool. When the wind rustled the leaves, an earthy scent tickled your nose.

This scenery wasn't man-made; it was real, authentic nature.

This super-ultra-finely-tuned Clockwork Planet. Because its mechanisms were simply too complex, maintenance of this hollow planet remained exceedingly difficult even now, a thousand years later. Maintaining natural greenery above the gears of this planet... just how much money and technology did the sight before them require?

"Really, the Japanese get hung up on the strangest things. Was it really necessary to be *this* thorough?" Marie blurted out in admiration.

Completely reproducing the scenery of a thousand years ago... you could feel the dedication, even unrelenting obsession, of the artists who had made this place.

"Well yeah, Kyoto isn't one of the world's leading sightseeing cities for nothing. It's precisely because of that consideration. For the last thousand years... a few thousand years if you include the period before the planet died... they've preserved 'this' amidst countless climate changes and calamities. Of course the tourists are impressed."

"Well, true, I would like to express my heartfelt respect for that great effort, but..." Marie smiled bitterly. "When I think that the government was ready to purge it, I'm forced to wonder if they have any regard for the will of the people at all."

"Humans all have some things that they won't yield, princess. For the artisans, thoroughly preserving nature is an obsession that they won't compromise on." Halter fiddled with a fallen leaf in one hand. His expression seemed to harbor some hidden meaning.

At the end of the ancient promenade were the grounds of a large temple. Kyoto's five-storied pagoda—one of the city's most famous tourist destinations.

"Humph, should I say I expected something like this? I can see why *he* would recommend it." With another bitter smile, Marie held up the hand-drawn sightseeing map unfolded in her hands.

In the corner of that large scrap of paper were the words "Naoto Miura" signed in awful handwriting. When Marie had pressed Naoto about what she and Halter should do during his remedial lessons, Naoto had retorted, "If you're so bored, go sightseeing like a normal exchange student, why don't you?!" and thrust this hand-drawn map at her.

The twelve tourist spots it listed were all ones that Kyoto was famous for. However, their outward appearance was just a facade. Inside, they were all clock towers. Despite the name, they weren't the kind of buildings that notified the public of the time. Rather, these twelve towers assisted Kyoto's core tower in maintaining the city's environment.

This five-storied pagoda was one of them. A wooden pagoda with a height of twenty meters. Since it was deeply involved in the city's functioning, its location was a secret held only by the military. Naoto only knew about it himself because of his superior hearing. As such, it maintained the outward appearance of a temple building and tourist attraction, even though its interior had been secretly replaced by clockwork.

Marie probably wouldn't have realized it if Naoto hadn't told her.

She made her way to an inconspicuous spot near the tower and gazed at its flawless disguise while she fetched a small device from her shoulder bag. It was a measuring instrument used by clocksmiths. A vibrational frequency measurement device—the kind of tool used to examine gear-based mechanisms in detail without taking them apart.

When Marie activated it, the device made a sound like a typewriter and displayed a number. She remained expressionless as she studied the readings, then clicked her tongue. "I suppose it's too hard to tell with a mere toy like this."

"You're calling equipment that you pilfered from the Meister Guild a toy?"

"I know that it's cutting-edge equipment, and it hasn't made it to market yet. It bills itself as a convenient and portable, but what good is that if *this* is the degree of accuracy I get when I'm so close to the tower? It's useless."

Three weeks ago, Marie had been involved in the attempted purge of Kyoto and had successfully stopped it.

It was a major and unprecedented incident where the government, military, and Meister Guild had conspired together to destroy a city and sacrifice its twenty million residents as collateral.

In order to prevent such a catastrophic tragedy, she and Naoto had worked together to temporarily seize control of all the gears that made up the city of Kyoto.

Marie had come to this clock tower to investigate the aftereffects of the climate interference they had caused at that time—as well as the many other irregular phenomena, such as their forced manipulation of gravity. However, now that Marie had lost her status as a Meister and was just a regular civilian, it went without saying that she no longer had the authority to enter the core tower or the clock towers, both of which were under the military's jurisdiction.

She had no choice but to examine the mechanisms from the outside using a portable measurement device, but...

"There's no helping it." Marie said with a dangerous expression.

"If you're thinking of illegally trespassing, then spare me, princess. You're just an ordinary person now," Halter reminded her sharply.

Marie pouted. "I know that. Do you think I'd cause trouble over each and every little thing?"

You'd better believe I do, Halter thought. He knew the girl's "criminal record" but chose not to say anything.

Marie, unaware of Halter's inner thoughts, continued, "I was thinking of using that *idiot*," Marie growled. She emphasized the word "idiot" with a peculiar intonation. Then, as if struck by a sudden inspiration, she took a deep breath, crossed her arms, and closed her eyes.

"..."

Marie strained her ears, just like Naoto Miura—the dunce who was in the middle of remedial lessons at this very moment—had done when demonstrating his superpower.

It was a miracle she'd witnessed in the middle of that nauseating conspiracy. Naoto Miura was able to perceive the operation of ten quadrillion gears. You could make the mistake of labeling his talent "irregular hearing" and call it a day. But Naoto possessed much more than a special talent...and Marie understood that instinctively.

No matter how hard you pushed the latest advanced measurement devices, they couldn't rival Naoto's level of ability. Not even close. Even when Marie strained her ears and focused her attention like this, she couldn't manage even a poor imitation of his ability. The most she could hear was the sound of the wind, the chirping of birds, chatter of the tourists, and a dull vibration coming from underground. That was it.

Sound was a series of vibrations, and when two waves of sound collided with each other, their shapes would change. Common sense dictated that you couldn't recognize the original shapes of two colliding waves, to say nothing of an unfathomable number of them.

Several hundred million, several trillion, several quadrillion... he had "understood" the sounds of an epic, immeasurable number of gears. Just what had he *heard*?

Either way, the miraculous talent no one could replicate was currently stranded elsewhere. And for the ridiculous reason of failing a high school test, no less.

"God! What is this bullshit?! For an imbecile who can't even digest basic high school to possess such an absurd power... am I being played for a fool?!" Marie turned the measurement device off violently and thrust it back into her bag.

"But he'd be less loveable if he were a flawless superman. Not that it'd mean his character made any more sense." Halter paused briefly before grumbling, "But given that his talent goes beyond all reason, what's the big deal if his grades are terrible?"

"For God's sake... if things had gone as planned, we'd be in Tokyo by now!"

"Personally, I'd like to have us stay under the radar for the time being. It's only been three weeks since the attempted purge, and we aren't sure that things have completely cooled down yet, you know?" Halter sighed.

The tumult that Marie had caused by anonymously exposing a great deal of top-secret information wasn't something that would fizzle out in a month or two. Although society was calming down on the surface, the revelations were so incriminating that people wouldn't just forget about them.

Marie pouted. "Humph. More importantly, what about Tokyo? Has there been contact since?"

The reason Marie was so irritated in the first place was because, despite receiving important information about an anomaly in Tokyo, she couldn't leave. She was stuck waiting on Naoto's *stupid* remedial lessons.

"Thankfully, no," Halter replied. "For starters, although you've been calling it an anomaly... in short, an Initial-Y Series automaton was sighted. The military is also behaving somewhat suspiciously. Those are the only things that have happened, right? So how about calming down a little, princess?"

"That Initial-Y Series automaton—was her name AnchoR? Just the confirmation that she's there is reason enough. You should know, having seen RyuZU in action."

"...Yeah, I guess."

Halter ran a hand over his buzzed head and shrugged. The miracle that they had witnessed three weeks ago... Naoto's superpower wasn't the only thing that was absurd.

The Initial-Y Series.

The automata that "Y", the designer of this Clockwork Planet, had left behind. RyuZU, the First of the Initial-Y Series, was yet another absurdity that smashed Marie's common sense to pieces.

One of RyuZU's abilities, Mute Scream, allowed her to move within a world frozen in imaginary time and annihilate an entire battalion of military automata in an instant. Her capabilities were, to say the least, alarming. And yet, according to the automaton herself, she was the weakest of her sisters.

Just the fact that one of the Initial-Y Series was in someone else's hands was dangerous in itself. However, it was also true that rushing off to Tokyo wouldn't accomplish anything. Not when there hadn't been any follow-up information.

"Going to school in Japan is a rare opportunity for you. How about relaxing and enjoying the life of a commoner?"

"The last two weeks have been more than enough for that." Marie pouted, sporting a stern expression. "The exchange student

Maribel Halter is just a cover. A facade for the girl who's secretly a terrorist that saves the world, understand, *dearest big brother*?" The sarcasm nailed home her point.

Being siblings was the provisional character background that Marie had created for them in order to attend high school after faking her own death, but...

"Even now, I find that...unbearable." Halter grimaced, looking annoyed.

Seeing him so uncomfortable, Marie managed a sadistic smile. "Oh, would 'big bro' have been better? Or perhaps something like 'elder brother'?"

"Stop it, princess, I'm begging you. I'm going to puke."

"My, my what a thing to say to such a cute girl! Are you *that* unhappy at being siblings? In that case..." Marie brought her lips to Halter's ear. "Should I call you '*daddy*'?"

"..."

Halter recoiled so hard that he nearly fell backwards.

"Dual role of bodyguard and secretary," Marie muttered. "Well, I'll let you off the hook for now. Staying here any longer would just be a waste of time. Let's head back home."

"Ahh, I guess you were beyond the life of a commoner the moment you could call a suite in a high-class hotel 'home,'" Halter groaned, standing up. "Especially after so casually booking it."

Marie knitted her eyebrows. "What choice did I have? A workspace and equipment is vital for a clocksmith. We wouldn't have been able to find a private place with enough space and security to cram in the necessary equipment in such a short amount of ti—"

"Hold up, princess."

Halter gestured for Marie, who had been rattling on, to stop with the palm of his hand.

"What?" Marie asked quizzically.

Halter furrowed his eyebrows and stroked his chin. "Ah... princess, I've just received a transmission that's a bit unusual."

"Is it a follow-up report regarding what's going on in Tokyo?"

"No, I'd told them to send that to our suite's access terminal. Ah... I wonder if it's okay to relay this to you."

Seeing Halter looking so conflicted only made Marie more curious.

"Just tell me already, what does it say?"

Halter sighed. "Well... I'll obey your order, princess, but... make sure to keep in mind that these aren't my words."

After emphasizing that point, Halter cleared his throat. He slowly opened his mouth and read the message aloud.

• • ● ⬤ ● • •

At that same time, in a manga café...

"...gh?"

Naoto looked up. RyuZU was nestled right up against him in the couple's seat. She had the textbook open and was grumbling with half-closed eyes.

"Master Naoto. If my private lessons are boring you, could you kindly just say so?"

"Eh? Ah, no, I'm not..."

RyuZU's voice was beautiful as always, calm and composed and full of elegance, but Naoto heard a minute change in her inflection. Her voice, slightly higher than usual, creaked faintly—in other words, she felt hurt. Realizing that, a flustered Naoto shook his head in a hurry.

RyuZU pressed him in a dispassionate voice. "Please provide me with a reasonable explanation as to why you were paying more attention to the stains on the ceiling than to me. Given what a great man Master Naoto is, I'm sure there must be an equally great reason for his distraction. Have you succeeded in some great feat? Establishing contact with alien lifeforms, perhaps?"

A peerless beauty who was jealous of ceiling stains. RyuZU's voice echoed throughout the café due to its beautiful, glassy, bell-like nature. It triggered many clicking tongues which struck Naoto's sensitive ears from every direction.

The regular patrons even spat under their breaths. "Those damn lovebirds again? God..."

Indeed, at this point, the couple's seat was their designated place. This was Naoto and RyuZU's "home" right now. They were manga café refugees, so to speak, but it wasn't like they were starving.

With the money that RyuZU had made from her "investments," they could have bought a new house—even an entire mansion if they so desired—and still have money left over to play. However, simply accepting such an enormous gift was too much for Naoto's meek heart. More than anything...

"Or...was it a lie when you said that you preferred this place because we can snuggle more easily here...?"

People punched the walls of their booths in unison. Naoto didn't need his superhuman hearing to understand what their neighbors were getting at: *just blow up and die.*

Finding the atmosphere of general unrest unbearable, Naoto looked at RyuZU's face. At a glance, she looked the same as usual: dignified and beautiful as a flower. She had bewitching, pure silver hair, pale skin, ripe peachy lips, and rosy cheeks. Her golden eyes sparkled like a crown. Her beauty was otherworldly—a living jewel.

But her beautiful countenance wavered ever so slightly in insecurity. Naoto, desperate to change the topic, took up RyuZU's sarcasm.

"Aha ha ha, er, so, umm, do aliens really exist?"

"I apologize... I tried a sarcastic turn of phrase that you weren't used to. Let me rephrase. I am asking if Master Naoto's great brain, simply too outstanding for a human, has finally awoken and transcended human limits and worldly sense. Have you, somehow, reached a place beyond even my level of understanding, Master?"

RyuZU scrutinized him even more coldly, and Naoto shook his head desperately.

"No, that's not it! It's because I heard a sound that made me think, 'If aliens really existed, their voices would probably sound like this.'"

"...Master Naoto, even if there is no room for doubt that you are the most outstanding human being on this planet, hearing sounds that don't exist would typically be considered..."

"I'm coming in!!"

Someone kicked the door of the manga café violently open, cutting RyuZU off.

The fury stormed closer, bowling over countless things and screeching, "Naoto Miura! Naoto Miura who is a pervert in many different ways! Answer me this instant!!"

Naoto stood up from the couple's seat in a hurry. Seeing the girl in the narrow aisle between the booths, he shouted, "Naoto Miura, at your service! Hey Frenchie, you do realize that 'I'm coming in' is meant to be polite, not a declaration of war, right?!"

Marie paid his words no mind. Glaring at Naoto, she leapt at him.

"There you are, pervert! Now's the time to put your ultra-pervertedness to use! Come now, show me this second, you pervert!!"

"Wai... sto... I can't bre—?!"

Marie reached past the partition between the booths and pulled Naoto up by his collar.

"Uh, umm, Miss? Please be quiet inside the sto—nothing, never mind! Please enjoy yourself." A brave employee tried to warn Marie, but ran away like a startled hare on being pierced by her glare.

RyuZU stood straight up. She stared down Marie with a menacing look that signaled she could explode at any time.

"Oh, Mistress Marie. They say to keep your eyes peeled if you haven't seen a boy for a while, as boys can mature into men in just three days. But I see that you are just as childish and boisterous as ever... how very disappointing."

"Wow! First of all, I'm not a boy, and second, sorry for being energetic!"

"Given your mental age, and your figure for that matter, I expressly determined that a boy's idiom would serve just as well."

"Today's the day I'll take you apart!"

RyuZU met Marie's threatening glare with her own. "If Mistress Marie refuses to free Master Naoto from those naughty hands, then I will have to free those naughty hands from *you*, yes? Who will really be the one that's taken apart, I wonder?"

RyuZU's skirt fluttered menacingly.

"Cool it, you brats!" Halter brought his fist down on the top of Marie's head.

"—gh!"

It must have hurt a great deal. Although Halter had held back, his fist *was* made of metal. Marie crouched down silently, holding her head. She glared at the large man behind her with tears in the corners of her eyes.

"You—"

"Got something to say?"

"...gh. Why did you only hit meee..."

"Setting aside the punishment for that rampage of yours, princess, and even if it's clear that RyuZU overreacted, it isn't physically possible for me to discipline her. Let's not forget that even if I *did* somehow manage to lay a hand on her, I'd die," Halter asserted flatly. He turned towards RyuZU, "I apologize for our shrewish princess causing a scene, and thank you for not getting physical with her."

Halter sincerely lowered his head. RyuZU sighed mildly and smiled.

"I never cease to be amazed by you, Mr. Junkbot. Though I am very much loathe to admit this...it appears that, excluding Master Naoto, you are—by process of elimination—the smartest person here."

"That's an honor. So Naoto, are you all right?"

"Ah...I guess? Well, if anything, I'd like an explanation for why I was suddenly given a shakedown, but..."

"That's understandable. There's something we'd like to ask you, knowing full well that it may be an unreasonable request. Well, princess? Have you calmed down now?"

Urged on by Halter, Marie slowly stood up. She was still a bit teary-eyed, probably because her head still hurt. Rubbing it, she said, "We'd like you to trace a transmission to its source."

As far as Naoto knew, all transmissions were either sent through a wired connection made by a chain of sound-conducting gears, or through a wireless connection of gears that could communicate across long distances via resonance. Put plainly, the underlying principle behind both methods was no different from a tin can telephone.

As such, if you reeled in the string connecting the cans, you should be able to find the party at the other end.

So why were they asking him?

"You see, the transmission didn't go through any relays. To tell you the truth, it was a short-wave transmission sent using electromagnetic waves."

Naoto squinted his eyes at Halter's smooth answer.

"It just so happens that I just learned all about those in my remedial lessons. They're illegal, yes?"

"Now now, sweating the small stuff will make you lose your hair, you know?" Halter laughed, slapping his receding hairline for emphasis.

Looking at him with eyes filled with compassion, RyuZU whispered discreetly, "Master Naoto, they say that experience speaks volumes. He must have lived his life worrying about small things. The state of his head makes his claim profoundly persuasive. I believe we should pay close attention to what he has to say."

Halter nodded, then made slight movements with his lips.

"*Protecting the law won't be worth anything if we're defeated because of it.*"

Ordinary people would have no chance of hearing his sarcastic whisper, but Naoto heard it clearly.

"There are certain jobs out there that don't play by the rules. It doesn't matter how dirty the job is, or how illegal, if there's a chance that the enemy will use it, you have to be able to deal with it. Even things that don't seem particularly useful, like radio communication, can count in a pinch. In any case, like I said, don't sweat the small stuff."

So he says, but...being an ordinary person with no affinity for the rough-and-tumble, Naoto stiffened.

"No way. Even if you say that, I don't want to be arrested at such a young a—"

"By the way, you do know that it's unquestionably illegal for you to own RyuZU, right? Her specs far exceed anything permitted for a civilian-use automaton."

"Law shmaw! Now, why don'tcha tell me what it is you had to say, Mr. Halter!" In a record reversal, Naoto shook Halter's hand firmly.

That's right, RyuZU said so as well didn't she? That crime is crime only upon coming to light.

"Well then," Marie interjected. "I'll cut to the chase. Naoto, didn't you hear a strange sound?"

"Sound? If we're talking about your angry voice, then I heard it nonstop, but—"

"That's not it! It's more like a very high frequency wave. If we were to call it a *sound*, then it would probably be abnormally shrill, but..."

"'Abnormally shrill', you say?" Naoto crossed his arms, thinking hard.

"I do think this is a bit too unreasonable to ask even of you," Halter muttered with a sigh.

RyuZU nodded as though she'd thought of something. "I see. So that was the source of Master Naoto's 'ceiling aliens.'"

"Th-that was an 'electromagnetic wave'? No wonder I thought it was a sound I hadn't heard much before."

"Hah?!" Halter widened his eyes. "Come on, Naoto, I know your ears are good, but you've gotta be kidding me."

The transmission that Halter had received was an electromagnetic wave with a frequency of thirty megahertz. Catching a wave with a frequency fifteen hundred times higher than the upper auditory limit of the human ear, and through 100% soundproof headphones at that?

Just what does this guy "hear"? A chill ran down Halter's spine. However, Marie just nodded, not showing even the least bit of surprise.

"Why are you so amazed? Compared to distinguishing the sounds of *all* the gears in this city's core tower, this isn't much, is it? More importantly, Naoto, can you tell roughly where the sound came from?"

"Umm, straight above... no, about eighty-eight degrees. From this direction, I think? Hey, wait, what are you doing?!"

Without waiting for his reply, Marie forced herself onto Naoto's lap and snatched up the pencil and notebook lying on the nearby table. Retracting her legs, Marie curled up into a ball and began to write something at an astonishing speed.

"Excuse me," said RyuZU. "Mistress Marie. Just whose permission did you receive to climb onto my Master Naoto's—"

"Ah, RyuZU, your expression right now is amazing!!" said Naoto. "If you'd like to sit on my lap, I'd be happy to oblige at any t—"

"Shut it, you lovebirds!" Marie yelled. She assumed the tone of a lecturer. "It was a short-wave transmission. Short waves are deflected by the Planet Governors at the North and South Pole, which deploy a magnetic field to protect the planet from solar radiation. If we know the direction and angle it came from, we can use trigonometry to pinpoint the source of the transmission. If the electromagnetic wave came from almost straight above, then the source has to be close... if we further calculate how far the gears have moved in the elapsed time, then..."

It seemed like Marie had already figured out the answer. She vigorously circled the coordinates that she had worked out. "The location is...Mie. It's a neighboring city. From the relative coordinates, it's in the industrial zone. We're going there right this instant."

"Uh, look here..." Naoto scratched his head. *I don't get it.*

He was clueless as to why this blonde-haired walking landmine was so angry. Naoto turned his gaze toward the furious girl on his lap and tilted his head.

"What did that transmission say?"

Marie froze.

"Y-you see, that's... huh? Ow?!"

As Marie began to mumble, RyuZU deployed the scythe from under her skirt. She deftly hooked Marie's collar with the blade and tossed her out of the couple's seat.

"Now then." RyuZU showed a smile so gentle it was fit for a saint. "Just what kind of emergency transmission would warrant this continuous violence against Master Naoto? You surely have an *appropriate answer* for this, yes?" Past her flowery smile, her gaze affirmed the chilling malice of her words.

"Ah... well, how should I put this..." Halter glanced at Marie and reluctantly opened his mouth. He cleared his throat and repeated the message...

"'Hey, harlot.'"

Marie started. She began to tremble all over again. Watching with a sidelong glance, Halter sighed and continued with as bland and emotionless of a voice as possible.

"'I see that you've been getting awfully cocky for the ghost of a bratty girl. What's wrong, is your pussy feeling lonely without the attention?'"

"..."

Silence.

Marie made tight fists with both her hands and smashed those trembling fists onto the floor. Taking his eyes off her, Halter read out the last paragraph.

"'No need to worry, there're a bunch of small guys with surprisingly big cocks here waiting impatiently. They can give you the bang you're lusting for. Shake your cute little ass and beg for it, and they just might do you the favor, bitch.'"

"So yeah," Halter muttered. "That was the message we received."

"...That was sent to Marie?"

"No," said Halter. "Short wave transmissions aren't precise enough for that. It was sent to this whole region, I just happened to pick it up."

Well, in that case. Naoto tilted his head, pointing at Marie, who was trembling on the ground.

"In that case, why is Marie blowing her top as if the message were directed at her?"

"Master Naoto," said RyuZU. "Thick-headedness is the prerogative of a main character, but asking such a thing is simply too cruel. People get angry when they are faced with the truth. It has been like that since time immemorial. Mistress Marie, if your hole is feeling lonely, there are shops that carry tools for that sort of thing nearby."

"That's absolutely not it!" Marie shouted, springing up. Her face was completely flushed red. "Ghost. Of. A. Bratty. Girl! Here! This is clearly referring to me, isn't it?!"

"Rather, why do you know about those stores, RyuZU?"

"That, of course, would be because your sexual fetishes have distorted so much that they're no longer recognizable, Master Naoto," RyuZU replied. "Satisfying her master's lust falls under the duties of a servant. Thus, in order to promptly meet your expectations whenever such a request might be made, I had—"

"Listen to me!" Marie shouted angrily. She held her head as if exhausted, "Ahh, I've had enough! Talking to you guys makes me nauseous! At any rate, you're coming with us right now."

"Eh, to buy toys?"

"I'm really gonna kill you, ya know?! We're going to tie up the idiot who sent this message and mount him on the wall! What else could it be? Or do you want me to try that out on you first?!"

"Please spare me from such advanced sexual play..." Naoto groaned, his eyes half-closed.

RyuZU nodded. "I am also unable to understand the meaning in our going together. While I could not be more opposed to them, Master Naoto *does* have remedial lessons. Not to mention the personal lessons that I'm giving him so that he is no longer looked down upon by the imbeciles of society, so please, you are welcome to go by yourself," she said curtly.

"Say, Naoto," Halter interjected in a calm voice. "Tomorrow's Sunday. You shouldn't have remedial lessons then, right?"

"Hm? Well, yeah, but..."

"If these coordinates are on the mark, it's somewhere in the industrial zone. And, if my memory serves, there's a seaside resort there."

Twitch.

Seaside resort. Those two words made Naoto freeze.

Curling his lips, Halter continued his barefaced act in monotone, "Oh my, I'd forgotten, it's February right now! The absolute perfect season for fun at the beach. It's truly the best season for appreciating swimsuits—"

"Ah, excuse me, we'll be checking out. Please ring me up!"

Even Halter turned around in shock at the fact that Naoto's voice came from behind him. More precisely, from the front desk.

"Well, it's fine if we return by Monday, right? Let's go everyone! Don't drag your feet, time won't wait for stragglers y'know!"

"As expected of Master Naoto," said RyuZU. "Could you not take the energy that you currently exhibit when you are filled with twisted, vulgar lust for a clockwork doll, and use it on other things? Perhaps, if I said that I would fulfill one request if you were to receive perfect scores on the makeup exams—"

"All right! Leave it to me! I'll memorize the entire textbook in one day when I come back!"

Naoto and RyuZU rushed out of the manga café in a commotion. Watching from behind, Marie sighed.

"You're good at dealing with those two."

"When you seek cooperation from others, show the other party what they have to gain. That's the basics of negotiation, you know, princess." Halter ran his hand over his smooth head.

"Well, let's get going as well. We're gonna be left behind at this rate!"

Halter urged Marie on, but suddenly felt a discomforting sensation.

Will things really turn out as expected? Was that message really just a mere provocation...?

Clockwork
Planet

• Chapter Two / 18 : 10 / Searcher

I'M GETTING SLEEPY, the girl thought, her mind covered in dense fog.

She just couldn't seem to grasp where she was or what she was doing. She'd been like this for so long, she could hardly remember when it began. However, recently her drifting had been especially troublesome.

Like a harsh winter landscape where everything was frozen, her heart sank into numbness.

Playing cards, solving puzzles, drawing... none of it seemed as interesting as it did before. There weren't even any cards, puzzles, or crayons here to begin with. And simply *cleaning things up* wasn't interesting at all...

Ahh, the girl thought. I see, that's why I'm dozing off.

There wasn't anything she had to do. She didn't even know what she *wanted* to do. As such, there was nothing left but to sleep and dream.

I want to go back.

The faint thought popped into her head. Recalling her memories lifted the fog of her mind just a little. A room filled with toys, gently warmed by the sun.

Word puzzles and code puzzles.

A clockwork bear.

A collapsible chess set.

A curiously distorted mirror.

A hand organ that sounded towards the player instead of outwards.

A spring-wound bat that flew in the sky.

She'd surely be scolded by her big sister if she left those toys scattered around her as she slept on that luxurious sofa, but it would feel very good.

But, she thought, as the fog came upon her once more. *Just where* was *that house I remember...?*

• • ● ● ● • •

The sun was about to set.

Above the ocean in the distance, the sky was turning scarlet, dyeing the steel planet red.

The Clockwork Planet.

On this planet of gears, the cities people lived in were built atop enormous cogwheels that ranged from several kilometers to several dozens of kilometers in diameter. Gears of neighboring cities meshed with each other—turning slowly as they circulated the enormous energy generated by the Equatorial Spring to every nook and corner of the planet.

One of those mechanisms, numbering several million gears in total, was Kyoto Grid. At this very moment, Kyoto Grid was about to mesh with the gear of a neighboring city, Mie Grid.

On one tooth of that absurdly enormous gear were countless holes, each about ten meters in diameter. The holes looked like a beehive, lined up next to each other in an orderly manner.

The gear moving in to mesh with this one was covered in similar-looking holes.

The enormous municipal gears slowly connected with each other, their gaps lining up perfectly with each other. In that instant, a deafening roar rang out from both gears. Screeching, thunderous sounds as if several thousand cannons were firing at once. The roar was so loud, it sounded like the gears would break.

The sounds eventually subsided when the perforated teeth detached from one another and the gears continued turning.

It was the sound of transfers happening on the cylindrical railway—a means of transportation that connected cities together.

At the connecting station where the municipal gears meshed, large numbers of massive cylinders holding passengers and cargo were simultaneously shot out and exchanged between the two cities. The cylinders gathered at the terminal, were sorted, and transferred to each grid's municipal transportation.

Although there were clockwork trains and buses and self-driving taxis, because every city was constantly rotating, there was no road that connected them together. This kind of special means of transportation was necessary, but...

"Hey Naoto, what's with you? You look like you're about to die." Marie said in annoyed disbelief as they disembarked the passenger cylinder and onto the platform. Naoto was walking like a zombie.

"Shut up... how are you guys all fine? It feels like my brain is still shaking." Naoto pressed down on his headphones and let out a pained groan.

The passengers' cylindrical railway was piled with many layers of sound insulating material, more than enough for the ears of any ordinary traveler. But for Naoto, even though his headphones also had a 100% noise-cancelling function, the roar of transferring had taken its toll.

"Well...being a normal person, I guess I have no idea what a pervert who can pick out electromagnetic waves heard just now. Those ears of yours must make everyday life a challenge."

RyuZU, looking after the staggering Naoto, opened her mouth to speak in his stead. Though she maintained her characteristic elegance, an undercurrent of hostility could be heard in her voice.

"What a truly barbaric method of travel. It may be fine to transport base lifeforms and cargo this way, but to force Master Naoto through such torment without even preparing a first-class seat... could it be that you do not even know of the word 'accommodation'?"

"Like there would be a special seat made for such a singular super-ultra-pervert," Marie muttered coldly.

Halter followed apologetically, "Sorry about this, we didn't think it'd be this bad for Naoto. We thought it'd be overkill to use air travel just to travel to a neighboring city."

Muttering curses, Naoto shook his head unsteadily. "Ah... no, it's not your fault, the shock just now made me remember. I rode this thing once when I was a kid, and the noise crippled me that time, too. Guess it was so traumatic I'd erased it from memory... damn it."

"Dang. I'm sorry about that," said Halter. "I'll arrange for us to travel by air for the return trip."

The four of them walked, RyuZU supporting an unsteady Naoto with her hands.

The cylindrical railway system instantaneously moved a great number of things and people several times throughout the day, so the terminal was jam-packed. The four of them wove their way through the crowd, climbing up the stairs to ground level and exiting through the ticket gate.

They were already in Mie Grid.

At the entrance of the above-ground connecting station were the cornerstones of urban transport: a circular shuttle and a pool of unmanned taxis lined up and waiting for customers.

To get out of the way of human traffic, the four moved to a rest area in a corner of the entrance. Settling in, Marie locked her fingers together and placed her chin in her hands.

"Anyhow, let's not forget that there's a masochistic punk in this city who's been patiently waiting for me to slap him. Mwa ha ha..."

Halter looked askance at Marie. "Ah, princess, I think this goes without saying, but we still only know the general location that the message came from, right? It's not like we've pinpointed the specific location of the sender."

Marie smiled, brimming with confidence. "Are you making fun of me, Halter? Since then, I've already narrowed the sender's location down to an area with a radius of five hundred meters by making various approximations from the weather data and rotational speed of the municipal gear at the conjectured time of transmission. I couldn't narrow it down further than that since the original data had some uncertainty, but if we just match it to local information, the rest should work out one way or another. Pleasure time is just a step away, mwa ha ha ha..."

"Just how serious is this girl gonna get 'cause of a prank message?" Naoto muttered in annoyed disbelief, watching Marie's evil countenance.

"To be unable to dismiss disparaging and slanderous remarks shows not just a simple lack of composure, but of self-confidence." RyuZU kept a smile on her face as she spoke those cold words, but Marie only sneered.

She closed her eyes and sardonically shook an index finger. "Tsk tsk tsk. It appears you misunderstand, RyuZU. I'm used to hearing words of envy, jealousy, and abuse from the masses."

"In that case...why are you so pissed?" Naoto asked, squinting at her. He had straightened his posture and seemed to be feeling a bit better.

"Pissed? Me? Ha ha ha, you're a joker... angering me would be an astounding feat, you know? Yep, no kidding. I'm not pissed. No siree, not at all." Marie stared at Naoto with glazed eyes. She curled her lips into a smile. "'If a lady is slighted, she shall snap at each and every insult with a smile, and slap the offender silly after chasing him to the ends of the Earth.' I'm simply honoring the words of my elder sister."

Naoto sighed, looking incredulous. "Wow... I hope I never meet your sister."

It was a sincere wish from the bottom of his heart.

· • ● ● ● • ·

Mie Grid.

Although it was next to the city where Naoto was born and raised, this was his first time actually visiting it. To begin with, traveling to a different city wasn't easy. Many people never left their native city for their entire lives.

But leaving that aside, Naoto thought as he looked around...

"It's...hot. Why is it so hot?"

The sun was setting. It would be night any moment. But despite that, the heat and humidity were so high that even standing in the shade was enough to make you sweat.

"It's because the neighboring Shiga Grid was purged in the past, isn't it?" Marie said.

She headed towards the end of the terminal, where you could board the clockwork trains that revolved around the city. The ring-line.

Following behind, Naoto asked, "Was it a conspiracy? Like the recent incident at Kyoto...?"

"Just...what are you learning at school? I can see why you failed your tests." Marie shook her head. "Dropping a city into the earth... it's true that doing so will inflict fatal damage to the planet in the long run, yes. But even so, if cities with irreparable malfunctions were left alone, the entire planet would be affected. Choosing to sacrifice the afflicted city to contain the damage before that happens. That's what a purge is for.

"It's normally only done after going through the formal procedures, which include many thorough calculations and discussions. And generous aid is set aside for the people who are displaced..." Rattling all that off in one breath, Marie seemed unable to bear the heat. She fanned herself with her right hand. "It...really is hot, isn't it? For the air to be simmering like this after the sun has set..."

"Well, even so, it's better than Siberia," Halter said. As a cyborg, he seemed perfectly cool.

RyuZU tilted her head slightly. "As far as I remember, Siberia should be a frozen tundra, no?"

"During the time you've been sleeping... on the eighth of June forty-two years ago...Neryungri Grid was purged," Marie said.

"The grid to the south of Siberia had malfunctioned, you see," Halter continued, elaborating for Naoto and RyuZU from behind them. "Since the grid had been largely uninhabited to begin with, it took an especially long time to organize and conduct the purge. So nearly all that region became a scorching desert. The tundra melted and Lake Baikal flooded, submerging everything around it... the effects even reached Northeast Asia.

"Nowadays, the area's a greatly prosperous resort spot." Halter laughed cynically. "Humanity's indomitable spirit never ceases to amaze me."

Marie wiped away the sweat on her forehead. "It's the perfect example of what happens when a malfunctioning city is left alone and unpurged for too long. There are times when a purge is unavoidable. A last resort, of course, but..."

Even so, Marie thought.

It was the most frightening aspect of the Clockwork Planet—the absurd object that "Y" had molded into being.

In the first place, machines that could function properly with parts missing didn't exist. When it came to precise clockwork, losing just a single gear, cylinder, screw, spring, or wire was enough to cause everything to collapse. Even the smallest part was critical to the entire mechanism.

This planet smashed such common sense.

It was almost as if the purges had been taken into account from the very beginning. Even if an entire municipal gear was missing, the other cities would adapt and make up for its absence—like a living organism.

The astoundingly synergistic behavior of the gears was complicated and full of mysteries. There had even been cases where a single purge affected a city four thousand kilometers away.

As such, a purge required the approval of an international agency and the grid's neighboring countries, as well as the permission of the local government. It was a literal last resort that could cause harm to the entire world.

"Of course." Marie clenched her fists. "Stopping things before they get to that point is what we clocksmiths are here for... wait, what?" She sounded confused.

She tilted her head. Naoto and RyuZU were gone. All she saw when she turned around was Halter scratching his head, looking bored.

Marie furrowed her eyebrows. "What happened to those two?"

"Ah, how should I say this..."

Marie looked to where Halter was pointing.

There...

"Ooh?! A swimsuit that suits you? Gah, how difficult!" An idiot stared at the mannequins in the window of a store next to the station, groaning happily. "This one... wait, actually... the swimsuit pales in comparison to the fine specimen it's intended for! Shouldn't it be the other way around?! Am I supposed to pity it?!"

"It appears that is the case, Master. Swimsuits are designed with consideration for those with disappointing figures, so as to supplement them. When it comes to someone shaped as perfectly as myself, it is all the more difficult to find something worthy of adorning me."

"I couldn't agree more! In that case, should we go to a dedicated automaton clothing store? No wait! A swimsuit for someone on RyuZU's level has to be custom-made, right?!"

"Do you think we have the time for that, you idiot?" Marie said, her voice chilled to below freezing. She grabbed Naoto's collar and pulled him away from the window. "Tomorrow's Sunday. You can play all you want with your automaton—whether on the beach or in the mountains—*after* you help me finish my business here, so let's get going already."

"Ahhhh... RyuZU! I'll think about it while we're on the move. So take their pamphlet if nothing else!"

"Certainly, Master Naoto."

•••●•••

With the pleasant sound of steel clacking against steel, the train on the ring-line ran around the outskirts of a city that had already sunk into the darkness of night. Naoto peeked out through a window in the front car.

"What a dreary-looking city..." he muttered.

The closed-loop train ran on meshed gears. Its absolute speed was a mere eighty kilometers an hour. However, because it was moving in a direction opposite to the rotation of the city, its relative speed reached a hundred forty kilometers an hour.

The scenery passing the window consisted of buildings with their gears exposed, more buildings, and yet more buildings. A small park would pop up once in a while, but the gray landscape buried in light gears continued on and on.

"Well yeah, you can't compare this city to Kyoto," Marie replied indifferently. "Kyoto is a tourist city that possesses a large amount of cultural heritage from ancient times. Meanwhile, Mie is fundamentally an industrial city. This is as good as the scenery gets."

Naoto looked at Marie, blinking a couple of times. "Hey Marie, doesn't it seem weird that you know more about Japan than I do, given that I'm Japanese?"

"Have you forgotten that I'm an ex-Meister? World geography is basic education. What's shocking is that you don't know anything about the city right next to your own. You should really get on that," Marie said in disbelief. She recrossed her legs and glanced through the window. "This country supposedly had a little more nature in the past," she muttered. "It even had four seasons."

"Four seasons?"

"Spring, summer, fall, winter—in the past, summers used to be hot, and snow fell during winter in this country," Halter answered.

Naoto tilted his head with a blank look on his face. It was the first time he'd heard of such a thing. "What? Are you talking about how things were a thousand years ago?"

"No, Master Naoto," said RyuZU. "The vestiges of the four seasons were still there, even just before I fell asleep a little over two hundred years ago. The Clockwork Planet had its climate settings adjusted so as to fully replicate the original Earth, but... things appear to have completely changed." Curiously, there was none of her usual sarcasm in her words. She was looking through the window, but rather than watching the passing scenery, it felt like she was looking at something that wasn't there.

"Yeah. Some things are going to reach their limits any day now," Marie nodded, closing her eyes sadly.

Silence fell.

Naoto didn't know what Marie was implying, and he wasn't sure if he wanted to find out. He looked down silently at the swimsuit pamphlet in his hands.

Some twenty or thirty minutes later, they arrived on the opposite side of the city's core tower.

Getting off the swaying train at their destination, the only things above their heads were starlight, moonlight, and the silhouette of the Equatorial Spring cutting across the night sky.

"……"

Naoto looked up in silence.

Next to him, Marie gave a malicious smile. "Now then, in terms of coordinates, my punching bag should be somewhere around here, but…"

"Princess, you've gradually escalated from slapping to punching, you know?" Halter retorted.

Marie ignored him.

"All right, Mr. Walking Measurement Device, I'm going to calculate the sender's precise location, so help me with… huh?"

Naoto ignored both of them.

He walked towards the exit from the platform, silently staring at the empty sky. RyuZU followed behind him.

"H-hey Naoto, don't just go off by yourself! I can't calculate how to find the dummy I'm going to use for crash simulations without you!"

"I see that the punishment you intend to inflict on the guy has finally exceeded what you can do with your bare hands…"

Left behind, Marie and Halter chased after the two of them in a hurry.

They passed through the station's ticket gate and into the sprawling business district that was located in front of the industrial park. Although Naoto had a head start, he simply stood there, unmoving, and stared off into space.

"Hey Naoto, what's the big idea?" Marie called out.

"Quiet."

"Now you look here..." Marie opened her mouth reflexively at Naoto's brusque reply, but—

"Mistress Marie, could I ask you to be quiet for a while?" RyuZU stood off to Naoto's side, keeping a respectful distance from him.

Marie answered with a slight nod.

She cast her gaze back onto Naoto, but he simply continued staring off into space as if lost in a daze.

Marie had seen him like this before, during the miraculous performance when he'd revealed the precise number of the gears in Kyoto's core tower—so numerous that you might as well consider them infinite. His ashen eyes that were staring intensely into space, seeing something that Marie couldn't.

He's straining his ears.

Marie didn't know why.

She couldn't comprehend the world as Naoto perceived it, but if he was intentionally straining his ears, there had to be something.

A cold sweat dampened her forehead. The noise coming from the gears, which had been boisterous on the journey here, was quiet. Perhaps because this area was a shopping district. The streets themselves were nice and tidy and had the smell of hot, moist air. That was all that Marie could notice, but...

Naoto, who could surely hear more, finally opened his mouth. "I can't hear anything."

"Y-you punk, what were you acting all serious for?!"

Marie almost fell over from the letdown, but Naoto's eyes stayed on the distant and barely visible industrial zone at the end of the shopping district.

"Say, what time is it right now?" Halter asked suddenly.

"Eh?" said Marie.

Everyone's eyes focused onto Halter.

"The time. I'm asking for the time. I believe it should be about seven right now, but..."

"It is 18:58:23 right now," RyuZU answered. "According to Western Japan Standard Time. I see, this is strange."

"What do you mean..." Marie began before stalling mid-sentence.

She looked around the area in a fluster, but before she could speak, Halter said:

"Isn't it too quiet?"

It was seven o'clock, and they were at the entrance to the station. The sun had completely set and the glow of the light gears was illuminating their surroundings.

There was no wind blowing through the broad avenue. The damp, stagnant air felt heavy. The only thing brushing against their skin as they stood stock still was the hot air still simmering from the surface of the road. The residual heat of day.

Despite the sweltering heat, Marie shivered.

There were no crowds of people crossing the street. No life in any of the open stores.

Although the lined-up shops looked a little old on the outside, their exterior designs were still chic. Their shutters were up, but there were no customers to be seen.

What appeared to be a police box stood at the intersection of the main streets, but even that was unoccupied.

A deserted shopping district... why hadn't I realized the contradiction?

Now that I've noticed, this place couldn't be stranger.

It was almost as if...

"It's a ghost town..." Marie whispered, dumbfounded. Unnerved, she let out a quiet groan.

• • • ● • • •

There was an elevated platform in Mie Grid's heavy industrial zone. From there, you could see the entire area in one view. An observation deck in the middle of a promenade, on the top of a small hill. The sun had set, and four silhouettes stood atop the broad, deserted platform.

Naoto bent over the railing and narrowed his eyes as he concentrated. Below him, the night's view of factories was illuminated by countless light gears. A forest made of steel, intertwined in such a complicated way that it reminded you of an artificial organ. While it could be described as eerie, it was filled with pulsing energy. Beautiful enough to make you sigh in wonder.

However...

"As expected, nothing," Naoto said quietly. "I can't hear anything. The clock tower here has *stopped*. Actually, it's completely empty."

The air filled with a heavy silence.

"Do you understand what you're *saying*?" Marie choked. The words caught in her throat before she could get them out. Her voice was dry and quivering.

The clock tower had stopped.

It might sound simple when you put it like that, but the situation was more than abnormal.

It wasn't a matter of a simple degradation in the function of one clock tower, and the others making up for it. If the core tower was the brain of a city, then the clock towers were its internal organs. Together, they formed the city's lifeline. Every one of them was irreplaceable. If someone was missing an organ, his body wouldn't be able to function correctly.

As an ex-Meister who'd been involved in a great number of municipal repairs, Marie could see how grave the situation was. But as Naoto turned to face her, Marie saw that his face was filled with a greater terror—it had turned ghastly pale, as if all the blood had been pulled from it.

"I'm telling you, this isn't a mere abnormality. This city..." Naoto breathed in. "It's already dead. It's been dead for a long time."

Sweat dripped down from his cheeks, but it wasn't because of the heat. And the trembling of his hands and feet had nothing to do with his will.

Everyone was speechless. Only RyuZU narrowed her keen eyes.

"I see. So that is the reason this city has no wind," she muttered.

Marie and Halter widened their eyes.

Indeed, there was no wind at all.

The ocean should have been beyond the industrial area in front of them. There should at least be a breeze, but not even a wisp of the ocean blew past the elevated platform.

"Looks like this ain't peanuts," Halter said, groaning. He felt an unsettling sensation creep up his spine and sighed. That out-of-place feeling that he'd felt when they'd set off was becoming an ugly reality.

Halter glanced at Marie standing speechless beside him.

"Princess. About that transmission you received... wouldn't it be a good idea to investigate it again?"

"Eh?"

"I wasn't going to say anything if it would help you kill time, but when things start to smell this fishy, it's a different matter."

"What do you mean?"

Halter placed his hand to his forehead and sighed. "Firstly...a short-wave transmission can't be sent to a wide area."

"I know that much. So the sender knew where—" Marie stopped.

Seeing the realization spread over her face, Halter nodded. The provocative message had been deliberately sent using archaic technology. If she considered things calmly, there were several points that made no sense in this interpretation.

Marie licked her lips. "If that transmission really was addressed to my location, then there are...conditions for someone to be able to send it."

"Right. The first is obviously that he would have had to know that the princess was still alive and in Kyoto. And second—"

"He'd also have to know there was someone with me who had the capabilities to receive that message." Marie nodded, taking over. "In other words, Halter."

"Ah, I see," said Naoto, seemingly remembering something. "You said earlier that those who work 'certain jobs' still use wireless transmission even now, right, old man?"

"It's not like it's standard equipment, but yeah." Halter nodded with a wry smile. "It isn't an uncommon function for cyborgs who dedicate themselves to special—illegal—activities. I have it. Any cyborg who's a covert operative or part of an infiltration unit probably has it."

Moreover, Halter thought, *someone with access to such an artificial body would easily be able to get a hold of information on us.*

Marie Bell Breguet had died, and the terrorist behind the information leak was unknown. But that was nothing more than P.R.

For a respectable agency—the intelligence department of one of the Five Great Corporations, for example—Marie and Halter's current whereabouts and identities were open secrets.

"Of course, there's still possibility that it really *is* a prank. The sender might have sent the message in every direction over the course of many transmissions. Or the intended addressee might not be Marie at all. But, given the situation here, let's forget about that for now and reassess things."

Marie nodded. "So the question is: why did the sender choose to use an electromagnetic wave?"

Let's ignore the possibility that Halter had merely received the transmission by chance. Unauthorized use of electromagnetic waves is a felony. The risk was too high for a simple prank message that, for all he knew, might never be received.

Marie crossed her arms and pinched her narrow chin.

In that case, the first possibility that comes to mind is...

"*...A trap?*"

"If that's the case, it's awfully sloppy," Halter said, rejecting that interpretation. He glanced at Naoto. "Which is precisely why I determined that it was more likely it *was* a prank. After all, even if we took the bait, it would have been impossible to trace the transmission back to its source if it weren't for Naoto."

"I see," said Marie. "So from the culprit's perspective, we would have lacked the necessary information for him to lure me out."

"There's also the fact that you're the only one who'd work yourself up over a message like this, prin—excuse my impertinence, let's continue." Halter noticed Marie's prickly gaze and held his tongue.

"In that case...perhaps it's a warning. Or maybe—"

"Are you thinking it might be a tip-off?" asked Halter. "Even if that's the case, it's not a good enough reason to deliberately use short-wave transmission."

He shrugged his shoulders. No matter what kind of message it was, it would only matter if it reached its intended reader. Even if it *was* a tip-off, there'd be no reason to take the unnecessary risk of using an electromagnetic wave.

"In that case," Marie raised her head. "What if using an electromagnetic wave was itself some kind of message?"

"Wouldn't that be too roundabout? Why not just write things

clearly? Or encrypt it in code, if he wanted to hide the message."

"Then...maybe he had no choice?"

"What kind of situation could you be in these days where you could use an electromagnetic transmission but not a gear transmission?" Halter groaned.

Naoto, who had been silent up to now, raised his hand.

"I see... all the riddles have been solved!" he said in one breath, smiling.

"......" Marie and Halter looked at Naoto with suspicious gazes.

"What's with the cold reaction..." Naoto muttered, turning serious.

"Well, I mean, you know..." Troubled by what to say, Halter turned his eyes away.

Marie sighed. "Say what you're thinking. Just in case. We'll listen." She sounded like she didn't have even a shred of faith in him.

Naoto nodded. "In other words: all this means is there might be an Initial-Y Series automaton here, right?!" he declared, full of confidence.

"..." Marie closed her eyes and thought about it, thoroughly mulling over his words. "So, Naoto..."

"Yeah?" Naoto proudly puffed up his chest.

Marie smiled gently, as if she were looking at a kindergartener. "Your conclusion doesn't follow what we were just saying in the slightest. I thought that your head was funny since the first time we met, but have the screws of your brain finally popped off? Don't worry, I'm sure you'll get better if you take your medicine... maybe just a little."

"No, listen to me, seriously. Doesn't it make sense when you think about it?" Naoto grumbled with his eyes half-closed.

Marie sighed, "How? I have no idea why you brought that up..."

"I see, so that was it," RyuZU said suddenly. "The sender was trying to extract information for his employer but was in a situation where he couldn't do so. As for the possible reason for such a situation... I see, that is a possibility."

Marie furrowed her eyebrows suspiciously. *What is this automaton even saying? Naoto spews nonsense out of left field all the time, but at least RyuZU normally has a proper head on her shoulders... other than her abusive verbal filter and her absurd functionality. In any case...*

Halter said what Marie was thinking: "Hey RyuZU...maybe I'm stupid, but I don't get what you're saying at all."

"Yes, that is certainly the case. But there is no need to be depressed about it. The very fact that you are aware of your own stupidity shows that you are superior to the typical flea in some respects, Mr. Junkbot," RyuZU said, not even cracking a smile. She narrowed her eyes. "It seems likely to me that this sender encountered my younger sister."

"Huh?"

Everyone's gaze was focused onto RyuZU.

"You were just saying so yourselves, were you not? That electromagnetic transmission is not an uncommon function among cyborgs who pursue illegal activities. And that the sender deliberately used short-wave transmission out of necessity. If we accept those assumptions, we can infer that he wasn't *in* a normal situation—in other words, he was in the middle of a mission," RyuZU said, weaving her words dispassionately.

"Most likely the sender had acquired some sort of classified information, but had become unable to escape due to an unforeseen circumstance. As a last resort, he sent an encrypted message to Mistress Marie. Doesn't that sound possible? So something must have forced him into such a predicament."

"Exactly, RyuZU! Right, right, that's just what I wanted to say!" Naoto nodded merrily.

Halter stroked his chin, looking unconvinced. "And you're saying that that 'something' is an Initial-Y Series automaton?"

"Do you have an objection of some sort?"

"I've got nothing but objections! There are a myriad of situations that could arise during a mission and make escape impossible. And what reason would a covert operative have to send information to our princess in the middle of an operation? The sender isn't someone affiliated with the Breguets, you know? I'm willing to bet on that."

"I do not know that much," said RyuZU. "Nor do I think it is a particularly important detail."

"But isn't that the biggest mystery?" Halter groaned.

But next to him, Marie nodded. "If the sender was a covert operative in the middle of an operation, that would explain why he used short-wave transmission instead of a more standard transmission by resonant gears."

"Oy, princess."

"Their reasoning might have skipped a few steps, but it does check out. If we also leave the question of why he addressed the message to me aside for now, the only question that would remain is: what's the true intent behind the message?"

The transmission that was the reason for Marie coming here in the first place.

RyuZU stated the message smoothly, as if playing back Halter's recorded voice.

Hey, harlot.

I see that you've been getting awfully cocky for the ghost of a bratty girl. What's wrong, is your pussy feeling lonely without the attention?

No need to worry, there're a bunch of small guys with surprisingly big cocks here waiting impatiently. They can give you the bang you're lusting for.

Shake your cute little ass and beg for it, and they just might do you the favor, bitch.

The vein in Marie's temple swelled conspicuously. She gave a menacing laugh.

"Even if there really is beneficial information encrypted in this, I'm still going to hang this guy."

"However, Master Naoto, with all due respect: Is there really a secret message in this?" RyuZU continued with a serious face. "Although he may have poor character, are his eyes not truly keen? No matter how I think about it, it seems to me that this letter contains nothing but truth."

"Do you want to be smashed into pieces?! I'm a virgin!"

"Wow..."

"Guh..."

It was an outdoor proclamation of virginity in a very loud voice. Marie turned her face away, flushing bright red from anger and shame. Her tightly clenched fist trembled. Placing his hands on her shoulders to hold her back if necessary, Halter carried on.

"Well...let's assume your theory is correct and try thinking about it from there? First, that section—what was it? 'Small guys with big cocks waiting to bang you'? It's clearly strange."

Naoto crossed his arms and opened his mouth. "If you think about it normally... well, it's gotta be that. Small guys with big... dicks."

"It can also mean 'rooster' or 'stopcock,' but yeah." Halter smiled wryly. "It can also mean 'nonsense' or 'weather vane'... or it could mean 'whim' as a secondary meaning, based on those two primary definitions. Also, though I don't really want to think about it, when I was in the army..." Halter broke off there.

Marie still looked agitated. She glared up at him obliquely. *"What?"*

"It...was used to refer to firing hammers."

"......"

Silence fell.

Marie narrowed her eyes, looked downward, and placed her right hand onto her chest. "In other words...a gun that's small but has gigantic firepower?"

"Yeah. But let me just say that you won't find many guns that use firing hammers these d—"

"I know. As in 'cocking' an antique gun, right? A small but high-caliber, antique firearm. Armament..." Marie muttered as if she were singing a rhyme, then suddenly turned her gaze towards RyuZU.

RyuZU tilted her head. "Yes?"

Marie licked her lips.

The First of the Initial-Y Series.

An antique automaton that could destroy modern arms with extraordinary ease.

Don't tell me...that what this secret message really means is: "A small body with a big cock... a small but powerful weapon...?"

The instant RyuZU heard Marie's mutter, she smiled sweetly and pinched up the sides of her skirt. The sinister sound of gears rang out from underneath the hem.

"Mistress Marie, to claim that I am equipped with a male reproductive organ... I am deeply sorry for not having noticed how tired you were of life. I shall humbly grant you your wish at once."

A black scythe that could easily cut through even a heavily armored automaton flew out from under her skirt. Marie raised both hands and shrieked.

"Wait, sto—?! Th-th-THAT'S NOT IT!!!"

Don't tell me... she thought. She turned her gaze towards Naoto. He was wearing a somewhat blank expression, but you could also interpret it as nonchalant. Even arrogant.

Did this guy end up with the same idea as me purely on instinct?

Marie squinted her eyes in suspicion. *There are holes to this. I can think of any number of objections, and the logic behind it is definitely a little loose. Even so, I can't deny that it's possible. It's just that it's both incredibly absurd and highly unlikely.*

The possibility of it being true was above zero. And Naoto's odd, even unnatural, thinking had led him to reach this conclusion in an instant. Marie had seen something similar before.

Her older sister, and a few of the Meisters that she had worked with, were like this. People who came to conclusions based on intuition. Who, rather than arriving at the answer through a process of logical deduction and verification, found the right answer with one big leap. People who possessed extraordinary judgment...

Their assertions always came more or less out of nowhere. Even so, if you inspected one of their ideas closely, you'd find that it was almost entirely correct. If Naoto Miura (who possessed a sense that was in the realm of the supernatural) was that type of person, wouldn't his intuition be extremely close to the truth?

Marie groaned internally and opened her mouth, admitting: "Although it's absurd, there really may be an Initial-Y Series here."

"Oy princess, are you serious?" said Halter.

Returning his exasperated gaze with her own, Marie held up her hands. "It's not like I know where all the Initial-Y Series automata are. I just can't deny the possibility of one being here."

"I mean," said Halter. "It's not like this *has* to be referring to an Initial-Y Series. There are many other possible interpretations... don't you think you're assuming a bit much?"

"I'm aware of that. I'm just saying that I can't completely deny the possibility. In practice," Marie said, turning towards the city below her. According to Naoto, all of this was already dead. It was a papier-mâché city, and all of its gears had already been pulled out. "We have no choice but to infiltrate those factories and check, if we really want to know for sure."

"Oohh! We're going to search for an Initial-Y Series! Marie, I'll be participating in the sandbag-punching as well, got it?" Naoto's inner fire was blazing, his desire at full throttle. "Encountering RyuZU's cute little sister, how outrageous! We're going, RyuZU!"

Marie swayed her shoulders. "You never break from character do you?"

Beside her, Halter lowered his head slightly. "I can't recommend taking action while we're uncertain of the information."

Marie accepted Halter's respectful warning, but shook her head. "Whatever the case may be...it doesn't change the fact that someone who knows about our situation sent a transmission from this abnormal place. A transmission that would normally be untraceable."

"Yes, that's true, but..."

"It might not be an Initial-Y Series. But the chance that the message was meant as a trap... or a warning... is low. That message could have been an offering of information from someone at his wit's end."

"You're...surprisingly cool and collected, aren't you, princess?" said Halter.

Marie nimbly lifted an eyebrow. "Don't tell me you thought a provocation like that could *actually* piss me off."

"I did, actually. Was I wrong?"

"Do you even need to ask? Of *course*, I'm going to kill whoever sent the message..."

Halter rolled his eyes.

Marie snorted and turned away. "But it's not like I'm acting on emotion. We're talking about your experience and my finesse, along with Naoto's senses and RyuZU's combat potential. With all of us, infiltrating an industrial facility should be a piece of cake, no? We'll probe around gently, and if nothing turns up, we can just turn back."

"Hmm..." Halter nodded, crossing his arms and stroking his chin.

It was as Marie said. It wasn't like she was talking about infiltrating a military base. If they put all of their abilities to use, infiltrating a common factory should be easy.

If they acquired more information, they'd be able to plan out their next move. And, even if their hypothesis was wrong, they wouldn't lose anything. *However,* Halter thought, *while I can't argue with that...I can't consent to it, either.*

It wasn't because the idea was preposterous. Regardless of what he thought, if Marie thought there was a possibility that it was true, he was certain that her line of reasoning was correct.

He couldn't articulate the reason for his reluctance. The back of his neck felt intolerably tingly.

I have a bad feeling about this.

It wasn't the same as the intuition that Naoto had displayed, or the analytical logic that Marie had used. If he had to put it into words, it was the sum of his life experience.

As someone who'd run through a field showered with bullets... an otherwise normal person who'd marched through scenes of carnage where life meant nothing, and lived to tell the tale… he possessed a vague sixth sense for danger that belonged only to cowards. You could just as easily, however, dismiss it as simple paranoia.

In truth, Marie's assessment of their capabilities wasn't incorrect. She was a genius-level ex-Meister. She was well versed in martial arts and, if she used her Coil Spear, would be able to deal with a typical combat automaton without a problem.

Halter himself was a full-body cyborg whose configuration made good use of the Breguet Corporation's cutting-edge technology. Most problems could easily be solved by the two of them alone.

On top of that, they had Naoto's detection skills, which saw through even "Goliath"—the state-of-the-art stealth weapon of the Acherons.

And finally, they had RyuZU. Placed against the overwhelming power of an Initial-Y Series automaton, any weapon would surely be powerless.

As Marie said, there wasn't a single problem. However…no matter how many times he told himself that, Halter's unease just wouldn't go away.

•••●•••

It was a giant factory in the center of the heavy industrial zone on the outskirts of the city. Though nearly everything in the district had come to a halt—this was the only factory that was still operating, albeit just barely. From outside, not even Marie could tell what kind of factory it was. Having identified its location with Naoto's hearing, the four of them observed the factory from atop a steel pylon a short distance away.

Security guards in military uniforms constantly patrolled the factory's perimeters. Marie was lying prone, peeking at them from their vantage point.

"I guess I shouldn't be surprised to see some human personnel here, even if the rest of the city is deserted."

"Well, all things considered, they can't just leave the security completely to automata," Halter replied.

He turned around to see Naoto facing the ground with his eyes closed. He wasn't wearing his trademark headphones. Naoto was mapping out the facility below them with his super-powered hearing—that allowed him to converse with others through 100% noise-cancelling headphones.

Naoto spoke without opening his eyes. "It's...definitely a big facility. It looks normal on the outside, but the walls are pretty thick, the workspace is abundant, too. The factory's connected underground to various other places. Its lowest floor is unnaturally spacious and... huh? There's 'something' down there, but it's non-operational."

Marie turned towards Naoto, furrowing her brows. "What do you mean 'something'?"

"Well, it's not operating so I can't tell... but it's seriously huge, whatever it is. This...*building*...is practically the size of an entire neighborhood."

"I see... sounds suspicious. Can you find a path for us to enter?"

"Well, I can tell you where the walls are, and the positions of the surveillance devices and security guards."

"That's plenty, please do."

Nodding lightly, Marie unfolded a blank map in her mind. Based on Naoto's report, she filled out that blank map and identified an infiltration route. After acquiring the necessary information, Marie stood up slowly. Halter picked her small body up with just one arm. Marie didn't mind, her eyes remained focused on the watch she wore on her wrist. She took a breath...

"Now."

Halter jumped. It was about a hundred meters from their position to the rooftop of the target factory. Halter covered the distance in a single leap. A small thud rang out as Halter landed on the concrete rooftop. A moment later, RyuZU soundlessly caught up to them, with Naoto in her arms.

• • ● ● ● • •

Inside, the factory was made with reinforced concrete, and the passageways were broad enough to allow the easy moving of equipment. Light gears, installed at regular distances, brightly illuminated the entire network of passageways.

A young man in a white lab coat, who appeared to be a researcher, walked through one of the passageways alongside a small, four-legged automaton. The man, who'd been looking down at the bundle of papers in his hands, suddenly stopped. The automaton by his feet matched him. He turned around. There was nothing there.

The man tilted his head, then sighed. *It felt like someone was watching me, but it was just my imagination, huh?* Smiling bitterly, he turned back around before hearing the word "Bonsoir," in fluent French. Surprised, the man swung around to see a beautiful blonde-haired girl smiling at him.

The man's eyes opened wide. He was unable to say anything in response. However, the defense automaton beside him had been built to deal with this situation. It unsheathed a gun from inside itself and announced a warning in a robotic voice.

"In-tru-ders. De-tec-ted."

The man was struck on the nape of his neck from behind and fainted. At the same time, the automaton was reduced to scrap iron.

"Bonne nuit," Marie whispered, looking at the man and the robot sprawled out on the floor.

Halter stroked his head, looking at the young man he'd knocked out. "Oy, isn't this too easy?"

It'd already been ten minutes since they'd infiltrated the factory, though you could also say that it'd *only* been ten minutes... in any case, the four of them easily made their way to the elevator that led to the deepest parts of the facility. It wasn't that security up to this point had been lax. Quite the opposite, it had been much too tight for an ordinary factory. But despite that, Marie shrugged her shoulders at Halter with a face that said "obviously."

"Why are you surprised? Naoto not only pinpointed the positions of the guards and the surveillance devices, but even informed us of the building's floorplan. There might as well be no security at all." Marie spoke over her shoulder. "Those ears of yours really are convenient, aren't they? If the world found out about your ability, I think you'd be dissected for research."

Actually, I wouldn't mind doing it myself. Marie glanced at Naoto, who was straddling RyuZU's back, but he didn't reply.

It was RyuZU who'd torn the security automaton to pieces. Because Naoto was the only one among them whose physical ability was below average, they had decided to have RyuZU carry him. Then he could focus purely on his hearing, without them having to worry about him becoming tired or out of position, but...

"........."

At the moment, he was ogling something just below RyuZU's shoulders. Considering how outstretched his neck was, it was obvious what he was looking at.

Marie addressed him with a smile that took all her effort. "*Mister Naoto*?"

"Huh? Ah, no, I wasn't thinking about it." Naoto spun off an obvious lie. "Wasn't wondering at all whether RyuZU would let me touch her boobs, you know, seriously, I mean it!"

"If Master Naoto wishes to indulge his carnal passions, which resemble those of a beast, then by all means, grope them to your heart's content," RyuZU replied with a composed face. "I have no objection to it."

"Eh, really?! But if you say it like that, my desire weakens somehow. Ahh, my boyish heart feels so conflicted..."

"No one cares, so could you two put that off for later?" Marie muttered, throwing them a freezing stare, her eyes half-closed in disgust. She pointed at the double door at the end of the passageway. There was a panel of buttons on the wall next to the doors, which were firmly shut. This was a high-security elevator that couldn't be used unless you entered the correct password.

"Well?"

"Its structure is the same as the one that was on the previous floor. If you unfasten the thirty-sixth hook from the right of the fourth inner layer, it'll open."

"Got it," Marie replied briefly before flashing her hands about. The panel next to the doors was removed in an instant, and screws began to float in the air as if there were no gravity.

On the inside of the wall was a multi-layered clockwork padlock. Normally, this kind of lock would take even an experienced clocksmith several hours of cautious work to unlock. However, Marie stuck her hands in indifferently. She unfastened the thirty-sixth hook from the right of the fourth inner layer—a part the size of one's pinky nail—with surgical precision, and closed the panel as if nothing had happened. With a sweep of her hands, the doors opened like a magic trick. It had only taken an instant.

"All right, let's go. It's under where we're standing, right?"

"Yeah." Naoto nodded without hesitation.

Marie boarded the elevator exultantly. Observing everything from the rear, Halter sighed and boarded the elevator last.

Naoto, the detection device that could expose the facility's security more perfectly than any sonar, no matter how advanced.

Marie, the clocksmith who disarmed the security at a godly speed based on that information.

RyuZU, the force that destroyed even heavily armored automata without allowing a single counterattack.

With this group, any level of security and vigilance was completely meaningless. Even if this were the headquarters of one of the Five Great Corporations, they could probably infiltrate it easily.

No security system could last longer than ten seconds with Naoto and Marie as its opponents. And physical barriers without a disabling password were sundered in less than a second by RyuZU's scythe. The latest traps and surveillance devices were meaningless as well. They were immediately detected, dismantled, and destroyed. As for the patrolling guards, researchers, and automata, they were either avoided or incapacitated.

They were infiltrating a facility with a tight web of security, but these three were behaving like they were on an educational field trip.

If this isn't cheating...then what is?

If I saw this back when I was in the army, I'm sure I would have retired immediately.

However...that feeling still won't go away.

If anything, the prickly unease that coiled around his neck was tightening. The elevator descended deep underground, to the lowest floor of the facility. Inside, Marie studied Halter's expression.

"What's wrong, Halter? Your face looks gloomy."

"It's...nothing." Halter shook his head, his eyebrows furrowed.

The infiltration is going well, true. Actually, it's going so well that I'm taken aback. Yet, what is this sensation? No, I should stop pretending. Halter let out a deep quiet sigh. *I know what this is. I've felt this sensation before. This is... that's right...*

The deja vu of this thoroughly equipped unit advancing forward, everyone made complacent by the enemy's weak resistance...

This is exactly the kind of time when something unexpected happens. For example, yes... it was just like this when, before we knew it, we plunged into the enemy's kill zone. Halter had a feeling that a terrible situation was waiting for them. Correction, he had the *conviction.*

"Ah, wait... I hear something," Naoto said suddenly, cupping his ears with his hands.

"What do you mean by 'something'?" Marie asked.

"The sounds are difficult to discern, they're pretty soft, but... the aggregate sound of missing parts? No, there are way more sounds than that."

"From where?"

"Roughly around 74,850 meters below, maybe."

"Around seventy-five kilometers underground? That's impossible," Marie said.

Naoto pouted, "Why?"

"Because there's nothing down there. That's below even the base of the core tower. When the Clockwork Planet was created, the crust and mantle of the Earth were used to make the enormous municipal gears, you know?

"This planet is hollow. If there *was* something down there, it would be the cooled core of the planet at best..." Marie paused, seeming to realize something. "If that's the case," she muttered.

"I can only think that a floor was *added on* after the Clockwork Planet had been created."

After about an hour and a half, the elevator arrived at the lowest level. The four of them exited the opening double doors and saw a plate on the wall that read, "The 25th Floor". As far as Marie knew, this was the deepest point in Mie Grid.

Beginning right outside the elevator, this floor was a spacious atrium. Exposed gears operated systematically over the ceiling and walls. It was as bright as noon thanks to the radiance of the light gears embedded in the walls. Naoto slowly shuffled his feet, walking towards the center. He turned around, and kicked the floor lightly.

"It's under here. As expected, there's a hollow space...and 'something' underneath."

Marie looked down at the floor where Naoto was standing. There was a metal panel affixed to the ground. Below that, there should be a protective layer, then the outer shell of the building. Any floor beyond those layers would be a very deep underground level. In other words, it would be a floor below the municipal gear.

And Naoto was saying that there was something there.

"To confirm...you're certain that there's one more floor below?"

"Yeah, there's no doubt about it. I don't know where the entrance is though." Naoto nodded.

Nodding back, Marie squinted. "That floor is probably connected to the core tower. Where we are is simply the base of the city, so there wouldn't be an entrance to anything below here to begin with."

"Then, what are we gonna do?"

"Let's rip the floor here to shreds and descend," Marie said nonchalantly. "If it's just this, even my Coil Spear should be enough to dig a hole. Stand back."

"No, wait, the depth of the floor below is –327.3 meters, you know?"

"Just how big is it? Jeez, I assume that RyuZU can carry you down, but...it'd be too much for Halter's legs, no matter how strong they are. Let's use an anchor wire."

"...Roger," Halter answered briefly and narrowed his eyes. His expression was stiff. He was still on guard. "Stay focused, princess. I've been smelling danger for some time now."

"I know. This isn't normal no matter how you look at it." Marie nodded, then flashed her Coil Spear.

They dove into the hole she'd created. It was a free fall of over three hundred meters, but despite that, RyuZU, carrying Naoto, elegantly adjusted her stance in midair and landed silently as if it were nothing. A few seconds later, Halter landed with Marie in his arms, having rappelled by wire. Jumping out of Halter's arms, Marie blinked again and again.

"It's so dark."

It was pitch black, without a single light. Forget Halter's face beside her, she couldn't even make out her own arms and legs. Looking back up at the ceiling, the large, glowing hole looked like a full moon in the midst of all this darkness.

"Hey, Marie, this is..." Naoto began, seeming timid.

"Wait a second. I'm not a pervert like you who can tell everything just through sound. Let me put up some light first, all right?" Marie whispered.

She transformed her Coil Spear with a swing of her hand. Pointing the muzzle up high, she fired a flare. In an instant, the vast space was flooded in bright light as the device violently turned its flash gears.

Something emerged from the darkness.

"What kind of a joke is this?" Halter groaned, seeing what was before him. *Why can't my bad premonitions ever end up being wrong?*

"What, is this..." Marie's eyes widened, flabbergasted.

Halter clicked his tongue. "It's obvious isn't it?"

He took a deep breath.

"It's something nefarious that's going to be used for another fucked-up scheme. Sons of bitches!" Halter glared at it through his heavily shaded glasses.

Mountains of steel. That was the only way to describe it.

It was enormous. Simply *too* enormous, no matter how you looked at it. Anyone who saw it would only be able to comprehend it as that. Try as you might, it simply wasn't possible to capture the entirety of it in your field of vision.

As Marie took it in, somehow keeping perspective in her mind despite its massiveness, she thought it looked like a spider.

A terrifyingly enormous, multi-legged...automaton, probably.

The idea of *this thing* moving was so implausible that it was insane to believe it ever could. However, as far as Marie could tell, its exterior structure was made to do so. Even so, its mammoth size exceeded the realm of sanity.

Even the joints of its folded legs were each the size of a skyscraper. Those legs were covered entirely in black plating that looked like the scales of a fish, equipped with an absurd number of cannons sticking out through countless gunports.

The trunk of its body was as big as a full-sized aircraft carrier. Like its legs, the exterior was also clad with countless protruding cannons that covered every inch of it like the spines of a hedgehog.

Marie didn't need to rely on Naoto's hearing. There was no room for doubt: this was a preposterous weapon.

She opened her mouth, and managed: "Halter, you know the Military Force Limitations Agreement that was established by the International Grid Management Organization? I wonder if you remember what its first article says?"

"'All research, manufacture, and possession of weapons of mass destruction that could inflict fatal damage to the municipal gears (and consequently the planet's mechanisms, therein threatening humanity's habitat) are permanently banned,' right?"

"So, why am I seeing this thing that looks like a superdreadnought WMD? There wasn't something in my coffee, was there? Is this just my imagination?" Marie's voice was dry and cracking.

"Yeah, unless it's papier-mâché, you're right on the money," Halter replied shakily.

As the two of them stood frozen, Naoto threw something at the gigantic weapon. Something the size of his palm, maybe an iron scrap. It spun in the air before hitting the plating. *Clack.* The noise resounded through the air.

After the small echoes had completely faded away, Naoto said: "Miss Marie, Mr. Halter, I probably don't need to tell you this considering you two are professionals, but can I say it anyway?"

"What?"

"We're in a staggeringly dangerous situation right now."

"Yup, we know," Marie replied, gazing at the ceiling in a daze. "Now then, Mr. Naoto. Could we hear your expert opinion on the situation? As someone with your ability, what kind of danger are we in?"

"First, I can assure you that this was where the missing parts of the hollow clock tower went."

Marie swallowed her breath. *So the parts of an entire clock tower were diverted to make a weapon.*

"I see... so this is the city's cause of death."

"I thought the Japanese fondness for giant robots ended a thousand years ago," Halter groaned, stroking his bald head.

Naoto shook his head and went on. "Even that's not enough. I can't clearly tell because this thing isn't operational, but at the very least, it's using six times the number of parts needed to make up the missing parts."

Marie raised a hand above her eyes, still silent. Narrowing her eyes and shading them from the flare, she glared at the gigantic weapon, trying to gauge its depth.

"Naoto, I can't get an overview of this thing, it's just too big. Can you tell how big it is?"

"Look here, do you think I'm a sensor or someth—"

"Just answer me!"

"It's not in operation so I can't tell exactly, but judging from the respective sounds I hear from the gear closest to us and the one furthest away, I would estimate its height to be about 320 meters and its depth to be 932 meters... damn! On top of that, it seems like it's fully ready to start up at any time!! *Shit*!" Naoto panicked, pointing diagonally to his left. "There are forty-two sets of human footsteps and eighteen sets of unnaturally heavy footsteps filled with killing intent coming right at us!!"

Found us, huh? Marie ground her teeth. *It doesn't matter. Whatever this weapon is, we can't just leave it as it is.*

"RyuZU."

"You are acting unduly familiar toward me, but yes, what is it?"

"Can you destroy the exterior of this thing with your scythe?"

RyuZU silently tilted her head and looked towards the gigantic weapon. With a flutter of her skirt, a scythe shot forward too fast to be seen by the eye.

A sharp, clear sound rang out. Sparks flew.

"...?!" RyuZU's eyes widened in surprise.

Scrutinizing the mere scratch on the plating and her black scythe, she curled her lips. "This is...most surprising. It appears that even with humanity's mosquito-sized brains, something unexpected can be accomplished if they train their minds toward the singular purpose of making something 'very hard' and nothing else. This is a new discovery."

"So can you destroy it or not?" Marie asked with a suspicious squint.

"Mistress Marie, to think that your intellect was so deplorable that you would have to ask whether a kitchen knife can cut through tungsten alloy—"

"Start with a yes or no!!" Marie cut RyuZU off as she began to scramble. "Hurry up and snatch something, documents, schematics, anything that's proof of its existence! We're getting out of here!"

"Wai—wha? Are we just going to leave this thing?!" Naoto yelled.

"What do you expect me to do against something that piece of junk can barely even scratch?!" Marie shouted back without turning around.

"But isn't this thing absurdly dangerous?!"

"I'm a clocksmith, not a mercenary!"

This isn't a joke, you know? Marie thought. *That's right, this absolutely isn't a joke. Just how exactly are we supposed to be able to deal with a monster like this?*

In modern municipal warfare, the strongest deployable weapons were, undoubtedly, heavily armored automata. When considering the main model in current use, it shouldn't come as a surprise that they would be unable to match the offensive capabilities of the behemoth. The construct's unmatched defensive capabilities were truly alarming.

The fact that RyuZU's scythe could easily cut through the armor of heavy automata was already absurd, but...

You're telling me that a swing of her scythe did absolutely nothing to this monster? In other words, by process of elimination, there are no existing weapons that can do anything to it.

Well, even if this conclusion is a bit hasty, at the very least weapons made for intra-city warfare have no chance of damaging that plating.

However, weapons that were made for extra-city warfare—for wars conducted on uninhabited lands—were a different story. The weapons at the upper limit of permissible military force, established by the International Grid Management Organization, might be able to destroy it. Resonant cannons or heavy artillery that fired ultrahigh frequency shells. One of the limited massive projectile weapons would surely be able to destroy any type of plating.

The problem was this thing's size.

If the large-scale weapons of extra-city warfare were used to destroy something as enormous as this...

"If it comes to that, there's no way the city would escape unscathed... tch!" Marie spat and clenched her fists tightly.

What was this thing even made for?

It was surely intended for some military goal. However, weapons could have different natures but be otherwise the same. Weapons were tools that cost a tremendous amount of money and labor, so they were generally made with a concrete concept in mind. For example, to invade others, to defend the homeland, or to deter enemies by simply existing, and so on.

I feel like this gigantic weapon doesn't fit any of those categories...

If an automaton of that size started up, it was clear what would happen. Whether it be invasion or defense, if something like that moved around, the city would be battered to pieces. Even as a deterrent, its size was unnecessarily large. Feeling as if she had been plunged into total darkness, Marie groaned. *Disregarding the weapon's intended use...*

If that thing moves, the city will be destroyed.

It's possible to destroy it before that happens.

However, if we do that, the city will be destroyed along with it just the same.

In that case, that would mean that's just the kind of weapon it is.

"*Tch*... what a joke..."

A weapon made to destroy cities? No, this is a weapon made to destroy the world.

What kind of idiot would make such a thing, and for what purpose? We need to gather information to figure that out.

The enemies and their goal, the weapon's structure, its weak points, and its capabilities... there was a mountain of things that Marie needed to investigate. *I have to find the blueprint documents and communication records someh—*

"Hm...?"

"Stop, princess," Halter said with a sharp, still voice.

Only the two of them had noticed *her* presence.

• • ● ● ● • •

A little girl was standing there.

It took a second before Marie could respond. "A child?"

No. She's an automaton.

A little doll girl, smaller and daintier than even Marie, who was petite herself. She was wearing a formal dress dyed red and white, and her arms and legs were encased in silver armor. A pendant in the shape of a cube dangled by her chest, and a ring made of two half-gears rested above her head like the halo of an angel.

The girl's face was the avatar of innocence and purity, but covered by a black, uncouth mask.

That black mask was singularly ominous somehow.

Sweat traced Marie's forehead, and a chill ran up her spine. Halter quietly stepped in front of her and held up his fists, ready to protect her. Out of context, it might have looked like a bizarre spectacle. A large, cyborg man was on the highest possible alert, taking a measured fighting stance against a little automaton girl.

However, Marie didn't find Halter's reaction strange or unnatural. Facing an automaton who looked like nothing but an adorable child, Marie was so scared that she couldn't breathe.

RyuZU stepped in front of both of them with a smile on her face. "My...you are AnchoR, after all. It's been a while, hasn't it?"

"Huh? This girl...is AnchoR-chan?" Naoto asked with widened eyes. "Based on what Marie said, isn't AnchoR-chan supposed to be in Tokyo?"

"I interpreted what she said that way as well. However, in the end it seems it was a mistake to take information from someone like Mistress Marie at face value. In any case, what is with that mask, AnchoR? I must say, it is a bit much."

The girl didn't react. She girl simply looked at RyuZU through her mask with a mineral gaze.

Naoto tilted his head. *This is her?*

The Fourth of the Initial-Y Series. AnchoR, "The One Who Destroys."

Considering RyuZU was saying so, there should be no doubt that this girl was indeed AnchoR. RyuZU could never mistake another automaton for one of her sisters.

Even so, Naoto thought. *Something is off.*

The girl was standing silently still. Her operational sounds were practically nonexistent. So quiet that even Naoto, not wearing his headphones, couldn't be certain that she was operating.

There was no friction, no inconsistency, no redundancy in her mechanisms. Nothing was grating and nothing was bending. Like trickling water, everything was running in absolute harmony.

Naoto had never heard such a quiet operational sound. Considering that, there was no doubt that this girl was an automaton made with aberrant, transcendent technology.

Still, Naoto thought. *Something's definitely off.*

He took a step back. Clenching his jaw, he glared at the girl in front of him. He was sure of it. She was quiet. Too quiet. Her mask distorted her beautifully serene operating sound, ruining it.

It was like an elegant violin solo played on a single string: something delightful twisted and distorted into a vehement, violent scream. Such a ferocious, aberrant noise enveloped the girl.

RyuZU called out her name again. "AnchoR?"

"Enemy threat level, Category Two. Requesting a boost from the Power Reservoir. Approved."

The girl opened her mouth. What came out of her mouth wasn't a reply, but something much more dangerous and dreadful.

"Initiating shift to the Third Balance Wheel of Differences."

The girl transformed.

Her hair grew longer and her limbs bigger. The red of her clothes turned scarlet, and the white turned black. The ring of half-gears above her head split into two, each standing upright on one side of her head, and the cube at her chest transformed into a solid gear.

The girl who was as pure as an angel transformed into the figure as tainted as a demon.

"Chrono Hook. Initiating output of imaginary power by means of the Perpetual Gear. Materializing."

Naoto heard grating noises coming from the girl as the aberrant sound warped. It sounded like a cry of anguish as the girl uttered words of imminent doom:

"...'Bloody Murder'..."

The next instant...

"Get out of the way!" Halter and Naoto yelled at the same time, Halter from premonition and Naoto from instinct.

Without questioning Naoto's words, RyuZU automatically obeyed. She picked Naoto up and leapt backwards faster than the blink of an eye.

The girl, AnchoR, raised her hands. The solid gear floating above her head changed and, immediately after...

The air exploded.

Whatever it was, it was completely overwhelming. Things

that shouldn't be breakable broke, and things that shouldn't be tearable tore. The noise pierced Naoto's eardrums.

The spot where he and RyuZU had been standing until just a moment ago was annihilated. The floor, made of a complex alloy which most things couldn't even scratch, had disappeared without a trace.

"Wha..."

No way.

Marie was left speechless.

The floor sank into a crater. RyuZU narrowed her topaz eyes, and a dark cloud came over them.

"AnchoR?" RyuZU called out again.

Her tone and gaze were no longer that of one addressing someone close to her.

"I shall give you just one chance. Explain yourself wisely. What are your intentions in baring your fangs at Master Naoto? Even if you are my sweet little sister..." RyuZU's emotions froze. All signs of human warmth receded, and she became a machine that cared only for fulfilling its purpose. "I'll shatter you. Thoroughly. Beyond repair," she threatened AnchoR in a flat, frigid voice.

RyuZU's eyes turned red. The sign that she was initiating the native functionality that belonged only to her.

"Wait a second, RyuZU!" Naoto yelled. "That girl, she isn't functioning!"

"Even though we were just attacked?" RyuZU replied without diverting her gaze.

"That's not it. Even though she's operating, she isn't

functioning! She's broken—no, that's not exactly it, either. In any case, she isn't in a normal state!"

He could hear it even now. The sound of gears twisting, bending, grating. Naoto knew what kind of sound this was: the "cry" of gears desperately trying to defy an overwhelming power.

It's almost as if...

Naoto turned his eyes towards AnchoR.

"—gh" His eyes met with hers through her mask.

It's not my imagination. He felt it. He was sure now. The eyes behind the mask were saying:

No, I don't want this! Despairing because she was unable to convey that to anyone. Lamenting because she was unable to be heard. She yelled hoarsely over and over again with her inner voice. *Big sister, please, destroy me.*

"Damn it." Naoto ground his teeth and clenched his fists. *Don't say something so sad.*

"Just to be sure, miss... can you win against that thing?" Halter whispered. His gaze didn't leave the girl in front of him for a single moment. Every little movement could lead directly to their deaths.

"Under 'Mute Scream', I would say that my chances are around twenty percent," RyuZU replied without turning around.

Silence fell. RyuZU, who had single-handedly destroyed an entire battalion of cutting-edge, heavily armored automata in an instant by manipulating imaginary time, was asserting that she had almost no chance. The other three paled.

Each of them recalled what RyuZU had once said: The Fourth of the Initial-Y Series. AnchoR, "The One Who Destroys."

She was the one who boasted the strongest combat abilities of all automata.

Notwithstanding, RyuZU took a step forward.

"There is no problem. In the worst case, I can at least hold her back long enough for Master Naoto to esc—"

"Rejected! Halter, turn right!" Naoto yelled, cutting RyuZU off.

At the same time, the cube floating above AnchoR's head twisted again. Responding to Naoto's words, Halter immediately picked Marie up and jumped to the right. In an instant, the space where Halter had been standing was hollowed out.

The cube twisted.

"RyuZU, behind you! Halter, it's from the left!!"

Relying on Naoto's instructions to evade the silent, invisible attacks, Halter groaned internally. *He's reading her attacks? Just what can he possibly hear that would let him do that?!* He couldn't comprehend it, but it was their only lifeline. He had to entrust his life to something he couldn't understand. Halter tasted something bitter. The thought was unbearably frightening.

After several rounds of attacks, AnchoR seemed to judge this method to be fruitless. Changing strategy, the cube rotated at a fierce speed, then stopped. An enormous sword appeared in AnchoR's hands.

"You've gotta be kidding me!" Marie cried. "She's capable of spatial manipulation?!"

The enormous sword looked terribly mismatched against her small body. It hadn't been stored through compression with clockwork technology—it had materialized from nothing in

AnchoR's hands. That was technology that couldn't be mimicked by current clockwork science.

This is AnchoR's native ability? Marie's eyes opened wide. The frozen gears in her head began to turn again, accelerating.

RyuZU can't use Mute Scream. There's no way this opponent would let RyuZU activate it. No, even if she managed to activate it somehow and defeat AnchoR, her spring would come fully unwound in doing so. It would be game over.

Even Marie could hear the enemies that Naoto had detected earlier. Forty-two soldiers and eighteen military automata. If they engaged in direct combat while RyuZU was asleep, there would be no way for them to win, no matter how hard they struggled. *In that case, what do we do?!*

"RyuZU! Halter! Target the floor!" Naoto yelled.

"Halter! Throw me up!" Marie shouted.

With the enormous sword in her hands, AnchoR closed in on RyuZU at the speed of an artillery shell while spinning like a top. RyuZU evaded her attack by a paper-thin margin. Her black scythe ripped the floor open below her.

Meanwhile Marie, catapulted into the air by Halter, whipped her Coil Spear around and shot out a high-explosive shell. The shell scored a direct hit on AnchoR, just after she had swung down her sword. A thunderous roar rang out and flames burst forth.

Despite this, Marie thought, *AnchoR is uninjured. I'm sure of it.* She hadn't counted on injuring AnchoR in the first place. Buried in flames and smoke, AnchoR couldn't be seen, and couldn't see them, either.

Halter charged, going on the offensive. From his ankles to his knees, thighs, waist, torso, shoulders, and arms... Halter shifted his entire body into double gear and instantly accelerated. He drove his fist forward with the maximum output a cyborg was capable of, a punch that exceeded the speed of sound. However...

Slap.

AnchoR caught his fist with one hand.

Halter groaned, his lips stiffening.

"Oy oy, what kind of shock absorption mechanism are you equipped with, friend? You're gonna hurt my feelings." He smiled and opened up his fist, casting the gunpowder in his hands towards AnchoR's feet.

His target was not AnchoR, but the floor itself.

It exploded.

First RyuZU's scythe, then Marie's explosive shell, and finally his directional detonation with the help of a metal jet. Even the complex alloy floor with a thickness of more than twenty meters couldn't withstand these successive attacks. A giant crack ran through the ground, and AnchoR lost her footing.

Broken pieces of metal fell through the jagged hole and into the abyss. Marie clenched the grip of her Coil Spear tightly, making sure that AnchoR really was gone.

This is what you meant, right Naoto?! She asked with her eyes, dangling from the anchor wire she'd shot into the ceiling.

This was a "dock" that had been created below even the city's lowest level. Beyond it was the hollow interior of the planet. A vacuum where only the thoroughly cooled core of the Earth awaited.

RyuZU was more than capable of escaping with Naoto, and Halter could escape the explosion by firing his own anchor wire.

Only AnchoR would fall into the abyss!

However, as the floor collapsed, AnchoR became visible again. She adjusted her posture. Halter reeled in his wire and moved himself to where Marie was. AnchoR chased him with her gaze. Once again the cube rotated, and the gigantic sword in AnchoR's hands disappeared. A warped pillar replaced it, the tip twisted into the shape of three drills. They began rotating fiercely.

Hearing their sound, Naoto gasped. "Holy crap, this sounds super bad."

I've never heard this sound before, but I do remember reading about something that operates with three drills like this. If I remember correctly, the textbook said that...

Naoto turned his face upward and yelled, "Marie! What's the phenomenon that occurs when three linked drills turn in resonance with each other?!"

Marie swallowed her breath. "A resonance cannon?! At that size?! Don't mess with me!"

It should be a massive, destructive weapon installed on a heavily plated helicopter, or perhaps a destroyer. Both its firepower, and the energy it required, limited how compact it could be. There was no such thing as a portable version.

A resonance cannon had enough firepower to cause a building to collapse with one shot, and the barrel of such a weapon was currently pointed towards Halter and Marie.

There was no time to evade it.

If AnchoR pulled the trigger, the two of them would evaporate without a trace. Feeling the premonition of inescapable death, a chill ran through her stomach.

I've gotta... I've gotta come up with something...

Her mind spun without direction. She couldn't collect her thoughts. Couldn't come up with an answer. Her genius faltered. With the end before her eyes, she became aware of her own helplessness.

I won't make it. There isn't enough time. But...can this at least buy enough time for RyuZU and Naoto to escape? Marie considered their chances in the corner of her mind...

"RyuZU!" Naoto yelled. "Stop that *thinggggg*!!"

"Wha?!"

Marie and Halter doubted what they'd just heard, but RyuZU faithfully dispatched her black scythe.

It pierced the barrel of the cannon AnchoR held in her hands. With a screech, the barrel exploded. The scythe, caught up in the explosion, was blown to pieces. Halter embraced Marie, shielding her from the blast.

AnchoR discarded the broken cannon and turned her gaze towards RyuZU and Naoto. Her cube twisted, but before it could finish, RyuZU turned in midair and threw her remaining scythe. It struck AnchoR's blind spot, and RyuZU swiped powerfully at her feet, making AnchoR lose her footing.

However, RyuZU lost her balance in midair.

"Naoto?! RyuZU?!" Marie yelled through all the debris.

RyuZU tried to adjust her posture while carrying Naoto, but

her bearings were still a mess and debris pelted her in the face. AnchoR drew a new cannon from the void, pointed it towards RyuZU and Naoto...and fired.

Watch out!

Before Marie could verbalize her warning, Naoto yelled: "RyuZU! Fall!"

RyuZU gave up on trying to find her balance. She swung her scythe through the debris floating above them, accelerating their fall through the principle of equal and opposite reactions.

They were able to avoid a fatal hit, but AnchoR's shot grazed them. Unable to fully withstand the impact, RyuZU fell into a tailspin, disappearing into the falling debris. What lay beyond was...

"Halter! The anchor wire!"

"It's no good, princess, it won't reach them!"

RyuZU fell into the abyss with Naoto in her arms. Marie and Halter quickly lost sight of them amongst the falling debris.

Beyond was the core of the planet. No one returned from there. Even RyuZU was helpless. Even if she was a legendary automaton who could manipulate imaginary time (a force which remained beyond the grasp of modern technology a thousand years later) she didn't have the ability to fly.

Narrowly managing to grab the edge of the hole, AnchoR hung on. Her eyes were pointed down. She watched RyuZU and Naoto fall into the abyss. Her face, concealed by her mask, betrayed no sign of emotion. However, the cube twisting above her head swayed ever so slightly.

• Chapter Three / 23 : 20 / Avenger

NAOTO FELL.

Before Marie could swallow that, Halter turned the gears of his artificial body to full throttle and carried his mistress away from the hole they had made in the floor.

"Wait! Stop! Halter!" Marie yelled as the distance between her and the abyss grew at a ferocious pace.

Halter didn't wait.

He didn't stop.

He was a cutting-edge cyborg operating at full throttle. Even as she struggled to breathe from the violent speed at which they were moving, Marie swung both her fists, bashing Halter's back.

"Turn back, you idiot! We have to save those two!!"

"It's useless," Halter replied with stony dispassion. Marie was speechless. "They fell into the great abyss. You know that. It might be one thing if it were just me or RyuZU, but a human with flesh and blood can't survive in that environment. You understand, don't you?"

Of course I know that!

Falling into the great abyss was the equivalent of falling into outer space. It was a hollow void down there. As the mantle of the Earth was fully mined, it became a vacuum containing only the Earth's cooled core. It wasn't an environment that humans could survive in.

"Are you telling me to abandon them?!" Marie yelled, clenching her fists. "I was the one who got Naoto involved. I was the one who brought him along, you know?!"

"I'm saying it's futile, princess." In contrast to Marie's voice, Halter's was absolutely calm, cold, and dry. "Naoto Miura is dead," he asserted decisively.

"..."

"There's no way he's alive after falling into the great abyss. Are you going to commit suicide to confirm that? What would be the point in that?"

"—ugh!" Marie ground her teeth. Her passions were raging. Her fists clenched. She wanted to smash something into pieces. At the same time, her guts wrenched. "Ah... Ahh..."

The corners of her eyes heated up.

How great would it be if I could just scream and bawl my eyes out?

But...that isn't acceptable. I can't do that.

She brought Naoto along. She got him involved. She couldn't do something as shameless as pity herself over the consequences of her actions. That wasn't allowed. Marie Bell Breguet didn't have that right.

She should have been prepared to face this the moment she took a boy who'd never had any training to such a dangerous place just because he had a somewhat unique talent. This was nothing but the obvious conclusion to things. An end that would have come someday, sooner or later.

"Still...!"

Even so, it should have come *someday*. For it to happen now, so suddenly...

"..."

Halter adjusted his hold on the convulsively sobbing girl, and jumped. Jumped with so much force that the floor beneath him cracked. He rose twenty to thirty meters above the ground. As he reached the height of his jump, he kicked off against a pillar and jumped again, just before he began to fall. By repeatedly springing off of the pillars, he dashed up through the empty space.

"Look at that... lucky us."

Finding a small tunnel in the walls, Halter clung to that stroke of luck. Taking care not to let Marie bump into anything, he slipped into the opening. Halter advanced through the passage and ducked his head. Reaching the end, he kicked open the shutter blocking the exit and stuck his head out. There, he found a large shaft that extended vertically.

Its diameter was around thirty meters. It wasn't clear how far it went downwards or upwards, but along its walls was a spiral staircase. At that point, Halter stopped and lowered Marie onto the ground.

They couldn't get out the way that they'd come in. Their

infiltration had already been discovered. A tight security web should already have been deployed throughout the facility. Even so, they couldn't just stay here dilly-dallying, either. Even at this very moment, their pursuers were likely on their way.

Without RyuZU, combat wasn't feasible. If they were assaulted by AnchoR, they wouldn't even have the means to resist.

"Have you calmed down yet, princess?" Halter asked.

Marie was sitting silently on the spiral staircase, unmoving.

"You can understand the situation we're in without me having to tell you, right?" he said. "With those two gone, our current combat strength is nothing like it was before. We're in a real pickle."

Marie didn't answer.

Sighing, Halter continued. "Even if we bet on a slim ray of hope and try to fight back, it'll be impossible if we stop here. First and foremost, we have to escape to the surface."

"..."

"I've memorized the full layout of the factory that Naoto revealed for us, but we can't go back the way we entered. So, we have no choice but to look for other exits, right? As such, from here on out, we have to slip past the enemy's security web without cheating. Sounds fun doesn't it, oy!"

"..."

"Should I be frank with you?" Halter rubbed his smooth, bald head and narrowed his eyes sharply, "We have to evade the military's security without prior information now. If we're not careful, we'll be assaulted by heavily armored M.A.'s and the Initial-Y

Series. It makes things harder for me if you keep being dead weight, you know."

"Don't make light of me!"

Marie raised her face and glared at Halter. Her eyes were wet and swollen, but Halter didn't mention that. Marie raised her shoulders a great deal as she took in a deep breath and lowered them as she breathed out.

"This is probably where they transported the parts." Marie looked at the altimeter wound around her wrist. "Considering they managed to create such a thing in secret, they couldn't have been bringing the parts in through the warehouse entrance on the surface. They likely made the parts in the factory on the surface then transported them underground for assembly on that hidden floor."

"In that case... does that mean that this shaft is connected to some of the factories on the surface?"

"No, it'd simply be too inefficient to bring in parts all the way from the surface every time they needed something. There should be a storage place somewhere midway ... which should be connected to multiple factories."

"Hmm... we might be able to escape somehow if that's the case," Halter said. He looked up through the shaft and stroked his chin. "It'd probably take the people pursuing us around...an hour to give up and another hour to contact their allies on the surface and suspend the lifts and elevators. If we climb quickly up this shaft and slip into that storage place before then... well, we should be able to escape one way or another."

The problem is, Halter thought as he looked at the girl sitting by his feet, *Marie's stamina.*

The shaft was more than seventy kilometers tall, even by the most modest estimate. They would have to dash their way up that height in about two hours. It wasn't impossible for Halter's cyborg body, but it was questionable whether Marie would be able to handle such a grueling climb. She had more stamina than typical girls her age, thanks to her training, but she was only human.

"Don't mind me," Marie said, returning Halter's gaze.

"Can you handle it?" Halter asked doubtfully.

"Are you saying that there's another way? If I can't make it, then just leave me behind."

"I can't very well do that, now can I?" Daunted by Marie's surrender, Halter furrowed his brows.

She stood up slowly. Halter could see that her arms and legs were trembling. It wasn't from fatigue, it was psychological. Naoto Miura's death had crushed Marie Bell Breguet's heart.

I guess it's to be expected. Halter sighed to himself, masking his thoughts from his face and voice. *Even an idealist girl genius whose assertiveness bordered on arrogance was ultimately, still, just a girl.*

This girl wasn't perfect enough to be able to swallow the death of someone close to her. However, the current situation wouldn't forgive such weakness.

"Listen up, Marie. Get this through your head," Halter said sternly.

"..."

"We don't have time to rest. I'm going to dash up as fast as I can, starting now, so cling onto me and expect to die if you stop. If you really can't bear it any further, no matter what, then say so. Otherwise, keep your mouth closed."

Marie gulped for a moment and nodded silently.

"Good," Halter nodded back. "Well then, let's go."

• • ● ⬤ ● • •

"...Ah!"

Marie fell from Halter's back onto the staircase. She couldn't move a single finger... correction, they were moving, but the twitching of her arms and legs had nothing to do with her will. Her muscles had completely stiffened, like a dead body.

In an hour, fifty-eight minutes, and thirty-four seconds, Halter scaled the roughly seventy-two kilometer high shaft. Marie had clung on as Halter ran up the spiral staircase in a leaping dash. Facing the instant acceleration and deceleration made possible by his extraordinary cyborg functionality, Marie narrowly managed to endure a level of G-force that would knock an average person unconscious.

But now she was at her limits.

I...can't stand. Marie groveled on the floor, gasping violently. Her lungs squeaked, her heart was crying as if it would sunder at any moment. Her entire body was drenched in nasty sweat, and tears welled in her eyes from the pain. Her vision flickered and she gagged. Her bones were aching dully as if they had been broken, but...

So what?

"Ah...gh—"

So what if that's the case?

"Are you unable to stand, princess?" Halter whispered stoically, crouching down beside her.

Who do you think you're saying that to, bastard?

Marie tried to curse, but failed. Only the moan of a stomped-on frog came out. She saw Halter's cool face, blurry through her tears. A human versus a full-body cyborg. Comparing the two would be unreasonable, but even so, Marie couldn't help but be angry. *How is he completely fine when I'm in such a sorry state from just clinging on?*

Thanks to that, her willpower returned. She flexed her trembling hands, folded her fingers inward one by one, starting with her pinky, and made a fist. Still on the ground, she punched the floor and, pushing up against it, flipped her body over. She pulled her knees in under herself and lifted her waist. She breathed deeply. Clenched her jaw.

I can still move. She was still alive, unlike that boy...

"Don't push yourself," Halter said.

He picked her up, and Marie choked. Her face flushed from the anger and humiliation of being treated like a child. She wanted to complain, but she kept her mouth shut. She was in no shape to walk right now, even if she could stand.

"Let's get away from here for the time being. Continue being luggage just a bit longer."

Nodding lightly in return, Marie closed her eyes. She thought about what they should do. In other words, she reflected on what had happened up to now.

...Naoto Miura died...

She bit her lip. She didn't have intuition as good as his. She could only assemble the pieces of information she had in a way that made sense.

Just what was that massive weapon that we saw on the ghost floor? It definitely wasn't something made with noble intentions. Even if you ignore the fact that it violates the treaty, what legitimate use could it have? How could that monster possibly be used effectively? It's something that can only be used to ruin and destroy, nothing else. As far as a group that would need such a thing... terrorists?

...I got him involved...

Her heart jarred.

As if something so silly could be true. There was no way some terrorist organization could make something on this scale using a hidden floor of the city in secret. There was no way they would have enough funds or materials or manpower. In the first place, who could be so incompetent not to realize that all this is happening right under their noses?

...Incompetent? Like I'm one to talk...

Her eyes were hot.

The enemy is the military, or perhaps someone who is capable of controlling the military. Furthermore, they were capable of recycling an entire clock tower into that monster. If that's the case, then it's not just the military. Even Mie's parliament is surely a fellow conspirator.

...This information is something you were only able to obtain thanks to the boy who died because of you...

Her head hurt.

And one more thing. Why was AnchoR here? Although RyuZU ridiculed the trustworthiness of my sources, that report should have been accurate. So, AnchoR was taken to Tokyo first, then moved to Mie? If that's the case, why Mie? She was originally in the possession of Kyoto's military, so wouldn't it make more sense for her to have returned there? This strangeness has to be related to that massive weapon somehow. Is this detail the key to this entire mystery?

...At this point, no matter what I do, I can't bring him back...

Marie tumbled from Halter's arms. Groveling on the floor, she assumed a fetal position. Unable to suppress the bile that rose in her throat, she threw up.

"Ugh, gueeeeeeeeeeegh!"

She vomited onto the floor of the staircase, over and over again. Despite the intensity, there was no blood mixed in.

Ah, my internal organs aren't injured, Marie thought. She despised herself for noticing such a detail.

"I must look pretty pathetic..."

"Yeah, you look quite awful," Halter agreed.

"I failed... they beat us to a pulp."

"Yeah. We screwed up big time. It's a crushing defeat," Halter said quietly.

Right now, Marie was thankful for his bluntness. She was glad that he didn't offer her cheap condolences.

"Naoto is really dead, isn't he?" she asked.

"Yeah. There's no way he'd survive down there," Halter nodded coldly.

...Everything is your fault...

"I'm sure you're right!!" Giving in to emotion, Marie punched the floor with both hands. Pain reached her bones, but she didn't care. Compared to the discomfort of feeling like her organs had been entirely flipped inside out, this was nothing. Sharpening her gaze, her emerald eyes filled with a dark flame. "I'm going to make the payback extravagant."

"Of course. You're going to pull out all their hair, including that on their asses, right?"

Nodding at Halter's words, Marie stood. There was something she had to do immediately, even a second sooner if possible.

Ahh, that's right. She had gotten Naoto involved. She had poked the bushes just to amuse herself, and a tiger had appeared. He had lost his life because of that, so she had to take responsibility for his death. She didn't have the time to bask in regret or be crushed by guilt. *I can enjoy that luxury after everything's been dealt with.*

"The fact that AnchoR is here in Mie, when she was supposed to be in Tokyo, has something to do with that massive weapon," she said, wiping her soiled lips on the sleeve of her coat.

"Yeah, it would be natural to think that."

"That would mean that Mie and Tokyo are connected. At the

very least, it would mean that someone in Tokyo, who is capable of dispatching the Initial-Y Series, is backing Mie."

"Don't overlook the fact that this person also has the technological prowess to manipulate that AnchoR or whatever."

Marie nodded. When AnchoR had assaulted them, RyuZU was extremely shocked. AnchoR's actions had been something RyuZU had not thought possible. She should have been certain of that. Besides which, AnchoR should have been asleep under Kyoto until now.

"Someone either internally modified her or hijacked her will through an external device."

"And that mask is suspicious. Well, in any case, if the one responsible has the technology to accomplish something like that, one of the Five Great Corporations has to be involved." Halter stroked his chin. "The Vacherons, the Pateks... you can't discount the Langes, either. Though I hear the Audemars keep their hands relatively clean, I can't say for sure that they're innocent, either."

"Whoever it may be... that's a question to answer *after* we return to the surface." Marie sighed. "We'll have to ask our people in Tokyo first."

• • ● ⬤ ● • •

By the time they returned to the surface, it was near daybreak. Their exit turned out to be an abandoned factory in otherwise good condition. After leaving the property and walking for a short while, they arrived at the station on the ring-line.

They boarded and sat on the train as the streets of Ise came into view. It had a cylindrical train station like the one that the four of them had used last night. However, they couldn't return to Kyoto just yet.

Marie and Halter patted the dirt off their clothes as they exited Ise station and walked onto a nearby side street by the shopping district. It was dawn, and the shutters of the stores along the road were lowered, but there were people traveling to and fro. Unlike the shopping district around the industrial complex, the streets here were alive.

After turning several corners, the two of them ran into an old, derelict hotel. It was the kind of establishment that someone who had had too much to drink might rent to pass the night. It had an exterior that made one question whether it was really operating or not, but on entering, its interior was surprisingly in order.

Marie booked a room, entered it, and headed straight for the communications device installed there. Picking up the receiver, she dialed the Breguets' encrypted line. Shortly after, she heard the robotic voice of the operator and declared her authentication code, along with the number she wished to reach. Using the line, she could contact her people in Tokyo.

After a few seconds of ringing, a voice came on the other end.

"Hey, Dr. Marie. It's been a while, hasn't it?" he said in an intimate tone.

"It's been a while," Marie replied in a curt, tense voice.

"Did...something happen?"

"Something, huh… indeed. A whole lot has happened. Truly," Marie cast her eyes downward and muttered, trying to spit out the words. If she faced the events of the last twenty-four hours head-on, she might break.

Stifling her emotions, she continued in as even a voice as possible. "I apologize. I don't have time for pleasantries today so… cutting to the chase, do you know the location of the Initial-Y Series that I had you investigate the other day?"

"No, what's this about?"

"Several hours ago… I encountered it here."

"What did you say?!" The other party raised his voice, sounding shocked. "By here, do you mean Kyoto?!"

"No, I'm in Mie Grid."

"Mie?"

"I was infiltrating the bottom floors of the city due to a certain…anonymous report I received, and I discovered something dreadful."

She told him about the massive weapon she had seen on the floor that shouldn't exist. She did her best to cover its appearance and functionalities based on what her eyes had seen.

She also mentioned AnchoR, who had appeared to guard it, and her insane combat strength.

There was also the fact that the culprit was likely Mie's city council and the military, and by conjecture, that one of the Five Great Corporations was behind them.

When Marie had finished explaining everything, the man on the other end of the line groaned.

"To think...that there's a conspiracy that can exist on that level."

"That's why I want to confirm: Are you certain that the Initial-Y Series was transported to Tokyo?"

"The military sent it to Tokyo... at least temporarily. We have the records of the transfer *and* eyewitness accounts. We confirmed it ourselves, so we're certain."

"That would mean that it was then sent to Mie from Tokyo."

"As you say... I can't imagine that it doesn't have anything to do with that weapon you mentioned."

"I think so too. Mie and Tokyo are connected by this incident somehow. Can you find out who's the current handler of the Initial-Y Series in question?"

"I see. So you suspect that the one managing the Initial-Y Series is cooperating with the brass of Mie."

"Yes."

"If you could give me a little time, I should be able to discover something."

"Thanks. I'm counting on you."

Marie was about to hang up when he stopped her.

"On a separate note, or probably not, there's been something strange going on in Tokyo as well."

"..."

"Tokyo's military is rallying all of its forces in one place. Considering that Tokyo is a federation made up of multiple grids, and almost all of its military force has been stationed in one area, right now the core tower and the clock towers of many other grids have been left defenseless."

That's...

Marie groaned. The suspicious actions of the military... the core tower and clock towers that were currently defenseless. She couldn't help but be reminded of the incident that had just recently taken place in Kyoto. The incident where Kyoto's military had tried to purge the city along with its twenty million residents...

The man on the other end of the line proceeded cautiously, trying to reassure her. "Leaving history aside, in the end, Kyoto is nothing but a regional tourist city. On the other hand, if the entire domain of Tokyo were to fall, it would surely affect all of Asia."

"Are you suggesting that there's no way the military would purge Tokyo? That's..." For a moment, she lost hope. Marie tightened her grip on the receiver, lowering her voice. "But by that logic, Kyoto wouldn't have been purged, either."

Ultimately, it was a question of ethics.

How could you be sure that the people, organizations, and schools of thought that had determined it was "right" to slaughter twenty million people, would care about the effects that their actions would have on all of Asia? Even with drawbacks, it still wouldn't be out of the question. It would just mean that they would need *a greater reason to do it*.

"It's as you say. Indeed...you're right," the other party replied in a cheerless voice.

"At any rate," said Marie. "Please look into the matter we discussed earlier. I'm going to stay here a little longer and continue my investigation. There are many places that might yield clues if I just dig a little."

"Understood," he affirmed, before warning: "Please be careful, Dr. Marie. The enemy is a fearful one."

"I will. Thank you."

Marie hung up for real this time and let out a bitter sigh. Unable to contain her irritation, she kicked the bed by her side with all her might.

"Really! Every last one of them!"

"You sure are throwing quite a fit, princess," Halter teased.

Marie looked back over her shoulder, glaring at the large man, who was leaning against a chair.

"Yes, that's right, I'm throwing a fit! What, are you volunteering to be my punching bag?"

"If that would satisfy you, then sure, punch me." Halter curled his lips provokingly.

Marie's eyebrows knotted together, and she flipped her hair like a dog shaking water from its coat.

"How stupid," she spat. "Forget it. Let's get going, since we've already decided on the next step."

"Oy oy... we just barely managed to escape intact, you know? Can't say I'm feeling eager," Halter chided.

Marie snorted in displeasure. "Very well then. I'm going, even if I have to do it alone."

"That's exactly what I'm talking about, princess. Try to calm down a bit. Well, I suppose you're calm, but your methods are needlessly reckless."

"So what? What's the problem?" Marie continued flatly. "I'm only alive because Naoto died, you know? Considering RyuZU's functionality, she might be able to return from that great abyss. If that happens, she'll probably kill me." Marie hugged herself, shivering. "If my time is limited, then I might as well use it effectively. I want to fulfill my duties before I'm killed."

Halter frowned, as if he wanted to say something, but decided against it. He sighed instead, and nodded.

"I get it, princess. Do as you wish. But let me warn you sincerely, as a pro: rest right now. If you want to fully dedicate yourself to this cause, then you should be in your best condition for the greatest possible result, right?"

"..."

"Take a shower and drink some sweet cocoa or something. Then get some sleep. Recover your stamina and clear your head. You can flatten anyone you don't like afterwards to your heart's content."

"..."

"That would be more rational, right?"

"Yeah. It's...just as you say."

Perhaps she liked the ring of the word "rational," because Marie nodded obediently. Halter waited until she entered the shower, and left.

Buying a sandwich and hot cocoa from a small shop nearby, he quickly returned to their room. He could still hear the sound of running water coming from the bathroom. He sat down on a chair. Waiting for Marie to come out, Halter wondered...

There's no way she'd go and slit her wrists in the shower, right? But he immediately laughed it off. *Nah. Impossible. I know Marie. She would never do that, no matter what.*

Shortly after, Marie stepped into the room, blow-drying her hair. He was right about her. She was only wearing a bath robe, walking around with wet feet. Seeing her dejected look, Halter silently handed her the cocoa and the sandwich.

"Thanks," she muttered weakly before stuffing the sandwich into her mouth. She finished her cocoa silently, then crawled into bed.

Halter moved his chair next to the door and settled there. Seeing the girl with her back to him in a fetal position, he had a sudden thought. He opened his mouth hesitantly.

"Say, Marie. I think that as an adult, I'm obligated to say this, just in case."

"What?"

"You're just a kid. A brat. You said that yourself before, right?"

"Yes... and?"

"No one's going to complain if a brat cries."

Marie didn't answer. She kept silent for a long time, but just when he thought she'd fallen asleep, she finally gave him a grave answer.

"Someone will complain. Even if no one else does, I will. I absolutely wouldn't be able to forgive myself. If I break down and cry here, I'd... *I'd be ruined.*"

She didn't stir at all. She didn't tremble, either. Her voice was flat and calm. Halter decided to leave it at that.

Marie Bell Breguet is not omnipotent, he thought silently. *I know that.*

A girl genius who became the youngest Meister in history. If you hear that, you'd be sure to have a certain kind of image of her... that she's smart and can do anything...but that's definitely not the case.

The real reason she's a "genius" is this: Marie Breguet's overwhelmingly strict level of self-discipline is simply baffling. That's why her supreme talent for hard work has been simplified to a single word: "genius."

She tries her best to be wise.

She tries her best to be strong.

She tries her best to be virtuous.

In other words, she strove to manifest her ideals with her entire being. In Halter's eyes, the strength of her faith was equivalent to madness at this point. The point where a normal human would have had his heart crushed and given up was Marie's starting point. She had this destructive will to endlessly improve herself, even when her internal engine was already scorched. She was strict to others and even stricter with herself due to her indomitable self-restraint.

That is the core of Marie Bell Breguet.

That's why this girl wouldn't break. She knew that if she broke down just once, she'd sink into being just another ordinary person. She was afraid of that more than anything. She wouldn't pamper herself. She had decided that she would live this way. She understood that that was what made her Marie Bell Breguet.

To compromise would mean death.

"All right. So, what should we raid when you wake up? I think I know what you're thinking, but I can't say I recommend it."

"Then you should also know that I have no intention of backing down."

"I figured as much," Halter nodded.

Marie continued in a soft, yet menacing voice, "You know what they say, 'if you want to take down the enemy general, begin by ripping off his head.'"

• • ● ● ● • •

"Damn it!"

Morikatsu Muroi, the governor of Mie Grid, agitatedly turned the communication device's dial. After finishing his work for the night and eating a hurried dinner with his family, he had holed himself up in his study. He would usually enjoy drinking with his remarkably fat wife after dinner, but he didn't have the time tonight.

Ever since he'd assumed the office of the governor, his days had felt tepid. His job consisted of simply performing set routines. It was plain, boring, and meaningless.

However, he had been satisfied with that. There was a time when he had burned with the ideals of his youth, but upon reaching middle age, and now nearing his golden years, he could only laugh bitterly at how naive he used to be.

After all, he was ultimately nothing but a replaceable cog in society. But that was just how he liked it. He wanted to live out his days simply working his job and receiving his pay, buying his daughter's contempt with his fault-finding and being scolded by his wife.

It's fine like that, he thought. He didn't need change. No one wanted change in the end. Which was all the more reason why today's incident was unacceptable. It appeared there had been infiltrators on the bottommost floor of the city. Together, they had somehow breached an exceedingly classified area, and what's more, the guards had failed to capture the perpetrators.

When he had received that report in the morning, he let loose his anger, something he rarely ever did. He stayed in a bad mood through dinner, and offended his wife and daughter with his conduct.

I'll have to apologize to them later. Thinking about how best to please his wife and daughter in the corner of his mind, he turned the dial. Shortly after, the line was connected.

"It's me."

"......"

"Yes, about the incident this morning. Just what is the situation now? I believe you assured me that preservation of secrecy is guaranteed."

"......"

"That was the deal, you know? If we close our eyes and shut our mouths, you won't jeopardize our lives. Are you breaching our agreement at the eleventh hour?"

"......"

"Threatening you? Please don't jest. I'm making a request: just don't betray me when the chips are down. Yes... yes, I believe I understand your situation. But hate and ideals alone won't put food on the table."

"......"

"That's fine. Well then, please hurry up with the results. It's been thirty years. It can't be helped that things are a bit looser now than before, but we can't let it end like this—for both our sakes."

With those last words, the line cut out. Muroi sighed deeply and returned the receiver to its holder. Just noticing the sweat on his forehead, he dabbed it with his handkerchief and sat down in his chair.

Thirty years...

Thinking back on how much time had flown by, Muroi sighed bitterly.

Up until now, his job had been to keep Mie turning without a hitch. Sure, there had been troubles along the way, some bigger than others, but even so, he had done his job. It wasn't really anything to be proud of. His job was simply to feign ignorance of the bomb that could explode at any time and take all of Mie with it.

But to have this arrangement spoiled at this late hour was unbearable. He couldn't contain his rage, whether it be for the infiltrators who expressly came to prod his sore spot, or the people who had let that happen.

Why is it that every last one of them can't keep their mouths shut?

"Damn it," Muroi cursed bitterly.

He wanted strong liquor. *That's it for tonight. Let me go to bed after a shot of whiskey. I can apologize to the wife tomorrow.* He stood up, massaging his temples.

Suddenly, he was pulled back into his chair with a forceful jerk of his collar. His heart jumped.

A soft piece of cloth was stuffed into his mouth just as he was about to scream. Something was wound around his wriggling body... duct tape. They finished binding Muroi to his chair in no time. The one who had bound him remained silent, but their intention was clear.

Be quiet.

Or else.

Sensing the threat, a cold sweat covered his face. This wasn't a prank. Someone with malicious intent had snuck into his study. He couldn't believe it. This was the official residence of the governor.

Though the security might not be on the same level as the top-secret facility in town, there were guards permanently stationed here. Muroi had been completely unaware of anyone hiding in the room, from the time he entered to the end of his call.

And he had just been bound to his chair. With his body wrapped from feet to shoulders, the one who'd pinned him stood right in front of him. He was a tall, broad man wearing a black rubber suit and exuded an intimidating air that spoke of his experience with this kind of work.

"I'm going to remove your gag now," the man whispered in a low voice. "If you want to keep all of your limbs, then don't say anything unnecessary."

Muroi nodded, his shoulders shaking. The man removed the cloth from his mouth, and Muroi exhaled roughly. Just when he thought the interrogation would begin, the man grabbed the back of the chair, turning it around.

"—!" Muroi's eyes widened in astonishment.

A young girl was behind him. She was also wearing a black rubber suit. Muroi could distinctly make out her slender body, but she didn't give off the impression of frailty. Her brilliant blonde hair and her emerald eyes made sure of that. They shone like a cat's in the darkness. She was like boiling magma. That was the feeling she gave off.

Morikatsu Muroi recognized her face.

"Ma-Marie Bell Breguet... you're alive?!"

The younger Breguet girl should have died three weeks ago—yet, here was someone with the exact same face. The girl pulled out a baton and swung it casually.

It swept through the air and connected with a crack.

Muroi's right temple ached with what he imagined was a fractured skull. He groaned, because he couldn't scream. For the first time in his life, Muroi discovered that screaming actually required a certain level of composure.

The girl ground the tip of her baton against his throat, and he gasped desperately for air.

"Who said you could speak?" the girl said in a light, indifferent voice.

Hearing the bored ring to her voice, Muroi flared up. "Y-you bastards, d-don't think you'll get away with something like t—"

His reply came in the form of another blow from the baton. It was a merciless strike. His vision flickered. Muroi writhed in agony, unable to even let out a cry.

"I'll say it in a way that even a feeble mind like yours can understand," the girl said in stone-cold voice. "I'm not making a request. I'm giving you an order. You and I aren't equals."

"D-don't mess with me!" Muroi's face turned grotesque with rage. "I-I'm the governor of Mie! You won't get away with a stunt like this!"

"Is that so?" the girl said with a mocking nod, then shifted her gaze to the large man. "Go downstairs and bring his wife up here. It seems like it'd be a good idea to show him just how serious I am. His daughter, too."

"Stop, please!" Muroi cried out, "I beg you! Don't hurt my family! I'll answer your questions."

"That's what I was hoping for from the beginning."

Muroi was terrified by her dry tone. Her unreadable emerald eyes stared at him. *Just like a praying mantis,* he thought. Although her sharp eyes seemed almost inhuman, they harbored a fierce will that he couldn't comprehend.

"Always begin by saying, 'Yes.' Answer the questions frankly. Do not trouble my hand with the chore of beating a worthless creature like yourself."

Muroi nodded, trembling. The girl didn't think anything of him. If he hesitated even a little... she would do just as she'd threatened.

"Let's begin with an easy question, shall we?" The girl sat on his desk and crossed her legs. "Given your words just now, I assume that you didn't know I was alive?"

"R-right... I thought you'd died."

"Halter, hang him up."

Lifted up by his collar with staggering force, Muroi couldn't breathe. Suspended in midair and strangled with the weight of his body, he squirmed.

"Your speech is lacking due respect," the girl announced coldly. "Also, begin your answers with 'Yes.'"

The man let go of his collar. Muroi dropped back down and coughed violently. His shoulders trembled in fear, and he uttered an apology through tears.

"Y-y-yes, I-I'm terribly sorry..."

"This is why I hate training ignorant dogs. It's such a hassle." Curling her lips, the girl asked, "Next question. You know of the massive weapon that was constructed in secret on the bottom-most floor of the city, yes?"

"Y-yes. I do."

"And that it's a weapon of mass destruction that violates the international treaty on military force."

"Yes... I-I don't know the details, but I hear that that is the case."

"My my, how convenient," the girl scoffed, raising an eyebrow. "You say that you don't know the details, and yet you allowed such a dangerous thing to be built underneath your own city? Just how incompetent are you? Do you think that anyone would be stupid enough to believe that?"

"I-I'm telling the truth! It was decided that we'd leave such things to them."

"It was decided? You're the person with the greatest authority in Mie Grid, aren't you? It follows that you have to be the ring-leader of any conspiracy taking place here."

"I-I'm but a mere representative...! All of Mie's council is like this. We perform only routine work on the city's mechanisms. We came to an agreement with them not to interfere with each other."

"What kind of gibberish are you spouting? Are you suggesting that the military created that weapon by themselves and you simply turned a blind eye to it?"

"Y-yes... that is correct."

"Why should I believe you?"

"Th-that's... you see, the council members were threatened by the military..."

"Don't," the girl said, looking down on Muroi with a gaze below freezing. "There's no way that the military would be able to take over an entire city just by threatening military force. Mie—at the very least, Mie's city council, including you—must have proactively assisted them."

"Th-that's..."

"What I don't understand is the reason. At first, I thought something like financial gain through bribery, but there wasn't any trace in the city council's financial accounts. Just the opposite—you were the ones *sending* the money. I couldn't piece together what you might have received in return. What a truly unnatural relationship, right?"

"......"

"Explain yourself."

Muroi stayed silent.

The girl sighed and signaled Halter with a jerk of her chin. "It's penalty time. Go kill one of them."

"Don't! Stop!!" Muroi yelled.

The man slowly pulled out a knife from his waistband and turned towards the girl. "Which one should we kill?"

"Good question...?" The girl tilted her head cutely, then smiled at Muroi. "I'll let you choose. Your wife or your daughter, which would you prefer?"

"Please. Stop, I'm begging you...!" Muroi yelled in agony, his face ruined by dripping tears and snot.

The girl looked down on him coldly. "Shouldn't you be saying something else? You're gravely mistaken if you think that I'm going to continue gently disciplining you forever."

"We share the same lot...!" Losing his resolve, he hung his head. "Not because there's a massive weapon. If it came to light that they are in Mie, we would be in danger as well. That's the reason we cover for them and aid them..."

"I...can't follow what you're saying." The girl furrowed her brows, irritated. "Do you intend to explain clearly? Yes or no?"

"Th-they...are not Mie's military..."

"What'd you just say?" The girl frowned.

Muroi's breathing was in disarray from fear and shock. "They're the military of Shiga Grid, the city that was purged thirty years ago!" he spat.

•••●•••

It happened before Marie was born.

Following a sudden and fatal malfunction in the city

mechanisms, the federal government speedily approved disaster management measures. They followed up with the compulsory purge without even waiting for the Meister Guild to arrive.

It led to quite a ruckus, and the cabinet was pressured to resign. However, a later investigation established that, if they'd delayed their decision, the effects of the malfunction would have reached all the grids in western Japan, and public opinion changed.

Nowadays, it was seen as an unavoidable, but difficult decision. There were even those who praised the federal government for taking decisive measures and accepting the necessary sacrifices.

However...

"That's...nothing but a lie," Morikatsu Muroi said, denying history in a trembling voice. "Research on electromagnetic technology was being conducted in Shiga Grid. It was a grand-scale, national project. Close to ten thousand Technical Force officers were gathered there."

"Electromagnetic technology..." Marie muttered, eyes grim. It had been used ubiquitously in ancient times, but in the modern world, where everything operated on gears...

"That's right... it was a violation of the international treaty. A large electromagnetic field leaked from the research facility in the middle of an experiment, and the city mechanisms malfunctioned. 'Dispose of everything and cover it up before Meister Guild arrives and realizes the truth.' That was the true reason for Shiga Grid's purge."

Marie's face became expressionless. Only her emerald eyes were blazing as she stared at the governor.

"The paperwork needed to purge the city had been prepared beforehand in case of just such an event. It had been ready at any time, needing just the signature of the Chief Cabinet Secretary. According to the records, the vast majority of Shiga's residents were able to escape to the prearranged city of refuge. That city... is Mie."

"......"

"However, they... the clocksmiths who'd been discarded by the federal government... survived. They decided to permanently settle in Mie, using their refugee status as camouflage to hide from the authorities. Everything happened behind the scenes. Quietly, and rapidly."

He raised his head. Sweat had oozed over his old and wrinkled forehead. "Twelve years. That was how long it took for them to gain control of Mie."

"Why would that be necessary?" Marie asked in a low voice. "They were engaged in illegal research on the nation's orders. The project was almost exposed, so they were silenced. I get it up to that point. But if that's the case, then why didn't they simply expose the truth?"

"Then what? Have Mie, their only refuge, be the next city to sink into the earth?" Muroi let out a deep sigh and shook his head. "Shiga was sunk solely to cover this up. Are you certain that the federal government wouldn't sink Mie too if they realized that Shiga's clocksmiths were still alive, wiping the slate clean?"

"That's... there's no way they could have purged another city so hastily. The loss of Shiga alone must have been painful."

Cities were national territory. As long as modern technology remained incapable of reconstructing cities, to purge a city meant losing territory.

Sinking Shiga to conceal the illegal research there should already have been something that was only decided on with difficulty.

If Japan continued to purge its cities one after another, it would come under serious scrutiny from foreign countries.

However, Muroi curled his lips at her words. "That's some sound reasoning. However, if I may? Quit joking. We saw the feds sink Shiga firsthand. Shiga's Technical Force was actually left to die.

"Don't tell me you're saying we should believe the insane people working at the top of what we call our federal government? Are you really asking us to bet our lives on that? Or the lives of our families?"

"......"

Marie couldn't answer him.

A stiff, agitated smile appeared on Muroi's face. "At the time, I was merely an aide to a council member. I came into contact with 'their' leader by chance and understood the situation immediately. If 'their' existence were discovered, Mie would be sunk. I needed something I could use to negotiate with the federal government at any cost."

"Are you saying that something is the enormous underground weapon?"

Muroi nodded. "I haven't been told any of the specifics, but

I know that Shiga's Technical Force is pursuing tangible power. A deterrent so strong that even if the federal government were to dispatch the national army to purge Mie, it could repel them."

Marie scowled at Muroi, her expression still grim. "Is that worth cannibalizing even your own clock tower?"

"There weren't enough materials in Shiga's ruins... or so I'm told. We determined that it was unavoidable," Muroi said flatly, his face turning pale.

Marie narrowed her eyes. "For the sake of a deterrent?"

"That's right." Muroi forced the words out, practically gasping. "It's as effective as we anticipated. The existence of Shiga's Technical Force was discovered by the federal government a few years back. Possessing a powerful military deterrent, and being in de facto control of Mie, allowed them to somehow negotiate a pact of confidentiality with the government.

"Its monstrous power is one obvious factor, but the very existence of that enormous weapon is proof of the illegal purge that they had forced on Shiga. As such, we've never had to use it, even though we've had it all this time."

Muroi made a feverish appeal, but Marie looked down on him silently. She understood what he was saying. Even if they should have known that Mie couldn't be purged so easily, they couldn't believe in that logic. Driven by their fear, they had sought a more definite power.

However, that's...

"You're lying."

"It's the truth!" Muroi yelled, his expression desperate.

Marie peered at his face, then asked, articulating each syllable: "If that's the case, why has that weapon been left on standby?"

"What...did you say?" Muroi widened his eyes, dumbfounded.

"We've been underground and seen that weapon," Marie continued, surprised by his reaction. "It's set for deployment at any time. If you don't actually plan to use it, there shouldn't be a need for that."

"......"

Muroi sank into silence. It wasn't that he was keeping his lips sealed, nor was it the silence of a liar who'd just had his lie exposed. His eyes simply widened in shock as his broad shoulders trembled.

"I see... so that's how it is!" His shoulders drooped. Marie and Halter sent him quizzical gazes. Muroi took a long breath and shook his head lifelessly. "It's over. It's all over..."

"I'd appreciate it if you don't just decide things all by yourself, you know. Do you intend to explain?" Marie inquired.

Muroi laughed, and raised his head to stare right into Marie's eyes. Though the rest of his face was pale and trembling in fear, his mouth was distorted into a sneer.

"Ha ha ha... you really don't understand anything. Even though you made such a clamor of lecturing me, in the end you're nothing but a naive little princess, huh?"

"—!" Marie frowned.

Halter, who was standing behind Muroi, pulled him up by his collar. "Oy, don't get cocky. Watch your words."

"Shut your mouth!!" Muroi shouted. His expression was so threatening that Halter inadvertently let him go. He glared at them both. "You still don't get it?! That weapon was supposed to be a deterrent that would never be used. It was insurance to avoid being purged! Yet, it's ready to boot now? Even an idiot would know what happened!"

He paused for a breath.

"The deal is off! The feds plan to dispose of us. And they, Shiga's military, surely plan to resist. This is all your fault, Marie Bell Breguet!"

Marie furrowed her brows. She couldn't understand his rationale. However, Halter appeared to have gotten it. He gulped.

"Hah! It looks like the big thug gets it now. Can you even imagine how many losses the feds and the national army suffered, how much trust they lost from the international community?!"

"......"

"They need to find an enemy to justify their existence!!"

"—!"

Everything connected in Marie's head.

Tokyo was rallying its forces, while Mie's military—or rather, the former military of Shiga—was readying the enormous weapon for battle. The federal government had been turning a blind eye to their existence, but now they were trying to crush them. Why?

The only incident that could have led to this...was Kyoto's attempted, premeditated purge.

It was designed to sink Kyoto into the earth, along with all of its twenty million residents. After the plan had been thwarted, the full story was brought to light by an anonymous whistleblower.

Damage was done to the dignity of the nation. The citizens lost trust in both their government and the corporations. In such a situation, what should the government do to recover from these injuries?

The answer was simple: they needed to accomplish a feat that everyone would recognize as meritorious. For example, the annihilation of a rebel army that had secretly constructed a weapon in violation of an international treaty. That would be very convenient indeed...

"Get it now? It's all your fault!" Muroi cried out, shaking so violently that the chair he was tied to shook with him. "The whistleblower was you, right? What a shock! Do you fancy yourself some hero of justice? It's time to grow up, little girl! What you did caused mayhem, nothing else!"

"......"

"Thanks to your meddling, the feds were driven to the wall! That's why they plan to paint us as the villain while they play the hero! You were the one who forced them into this!!"

"......"

Marie didn't reply. Her face, fair to begin with, became even whiter. Like paper. Her lips were pressed stiffly together.

Seeing her like that, the governor snorted. "However, it appears that the feds don't get it, either. How Shiga's military... no, how *we've* felt living like this for the last thirty years."

He curled his lips. "This whole time... for the last thirty years... we've been afraid. When will the feds sniff out their existence and decide to purge us? We were tormented by despair. Our fear became an obsession: what if the trump card we created in desperation turned out to be just an empty threat...?"

Marie understood what he meant.

The enormous weapon I saw on Mie's deepest underground floor... just how much damage would be done if such a thing were unleashed? Even if Tokyo's military rallied together, there's no way they'd be able to annihilate Mie easily.

"..."

Marie bit her lips and stifled her breath. She'd started breathing heavily at some point. The man in front of her probably didn't know the details of the weapon. However, he did know something else very well: he was absolutely certain that the weapon, the culmination of the fear and obsession of Shiga's clocksmiths, could not be something half-baked.

Muroi smiled. "I imagine you understand what choice we must make to survive, Miss Self-Proclaimed Genius. History is written by the victor. Shiga's military will mercilessly pulverize our enemies in the name of 'justice.'

"Although..." He paused, adding in a dry voice: "Who knows how much damage will be done in the process. It could be that a grid or two somewhere might fall. Now then, once again, who's responsible for that?"

Marie didn't reply. She couldn't. Her eyes were stretched wide open from the shock, her limbs were trembling. An audible gulp sounded from her throat as she swallowed the saliva accumulating in her mouth.

"It's you!!" Muroi yelled, his voice seething with hatred. His face distorted from spite. "If you would have just shut your mouth and died quietly, it wouldn't have come to this, you stupid brat!!"

• • ● ● ● • •

Since when?

When Marie came to her senses, she was walking through an unknown street at night.

It was a place she had no recollection of, a narrow path formed by the gap between tall buildings. There was no sign of other people. An unlit path, an alleyway that the dim lights from the surrounding streets didn't reach. The hustle and bustle of the city sounded distant.

What am I doing here...?

Halter was following behind her, matching her pace.

Her shoulders felt cumbersome, and her gait dragged. Turning around, saying something, it felt like too much trouble. She spat out a long sigh.

My memory ends in the middle of the interrogation. I have no idea how we dealt with the governor or cleaned up the scene but, seeing as Halter isn't saying anything, he must have taken care of it.

"......"

Their strategy was a success.

Wringing information out of Mie's governor. That goal had been thoroughly accomplished. What was going on in this city, how things would proceed... she had more or less learned everything that she had wanted to know.

However, she couldn't feel happy about it. Her mood right now was that of someone who'd suffered a defeat.

"......"

Marie stopped.

When you tried to do something, your efforts could end up having the opposite effect. Like if you tried to turn a clock hand to synchronize the time and ended up breaking the clock instead.

Marie wasn't naive enough to think that striving for justice was enough to keep the world turning. Even so, she had tried her best to live a life she could be proud of.

And this is the result, huh?

She had become full of herself after saving Kyoto and exposing the misdeeds of the elite. Because of that, she'd suffered a crushing defeat and lost Naoto in the middle of it. And now, because of her, Tokyo and Mie were about to go to war.

I can't leave things like this.

Marie reached what was, to her, a very natural conclusion. However, a problematic question arose in her mind.

What should I do?

Everything that happened was a result of acting on her sense of justice. She couldn't make any excuses. Everything was her fault. She had to take responsibility. But how? What would enable her to take on this burden? Just what could she do to overturn the current situation?

"What exactly am I supposed to do about all of this?" she muttered in a moment of weakness.

Rain began to fall.

Just as she thought it was a tepid drizzle, it turned into a violent downpour. Marie didn't seek shelter from it, but stayed right where she was.

"You don't need to do anything."

Halter stopped behind her.

"This situation isn't something that should weigh on your conscience. The governor's words were just sophistry. 'The one responsible'? Who else could it be but the feds who sank Shiga in the first place?"

"Yeah…I know that much."

They were the ones who started it all by promoting illegal research in Shiga. They were the ones who purged Shiga to conceal that truth.

On the other hand, choosing not to deal with that through the proper channels is the fault of the refugees from Shiga. It doesn't justify the creation of a weapon that ignores the international treaty.

There's no way that saving Kyoto was the wrong thing to do, and the whistleblowing afterwards was just karma for those responsible, no?

As such, Marie Bell Breguet bears no responsibility whatsoever for this situation?

There's no way that's true.

"But, I can't leave it be."

Even if her actions harbored no ill intent, they were still a factor in bringing about the present situation. *How can you pretend that you don't see that, Halter?*

"That's not the problem." Halter coldly rejected her conclusion. "The situation is too huge. It's way past something that you, a clocksmith, could do something about."

"That's not...!"

"Then what are you going to do? Leak this information? I'd be willing to bet that won't accomplish anything besides expediting the government's plans. And what you have is just idle gossip without proper evidence. They could lie their way out of it with any number of excuses. While we're at it, they could just say something like: 'We had attempted to purge Kyoto for the same reason as Shiga.'

"You know them. They wouldn't have any qualms about lying through their teeth. The attempted purge of Kyoto was a bitter pill they had to swallow for that exact reason."

"In that case...!" Marie turned around and glared at him.

"In that case, what?" Halter said, withstanding her glare without flinching. "Are you going to put a stop to things behind the scenes? How? You'd be up against the government of both sides, their armies, and one of the Five Great Corporations. What could you do as you are now?"

His tone was calm, even gentle. "Did you forget that you're supposed to be dead? You should be quietly living the life of a student in Kyoto until things settle down. That holds true even now."

"Then what are you saying I should do?!" Marie yelled indignantly. "Are you telling me to quietly watch from the sidelines?!"

"That's an option, yes." Halter nodded, letting out a sigh. "The feds are probably going to use Tokyo's army to crush that massive weapon. If they do that, they would probably recover a level of trust with the public.

"A bunch of good-for-nothings and a bunch of incorrigibles are going to try to destroy each other of their own accord. There wouldn't be anything wrong with just observing."

"...Are you serious?"

Halter shrugged. "I'm not much of a joker, unfortunately."

"You saw it too, didn't you?" Marie scoffed. "That underground weapon? Do you seriously think that Tokyo's army could restrain that thing? Remember that Mie has AnchoR as well. If that weapon and an Initial-Y Series assault Tokyo together, do you still think the feds can win?"

"It might be too much for them, yeah." Halter nodded readily. "So, is there a problem? Is it important whether the feds win or lose? As the governor said, the feds' script might be turned against them, but so what? It's not like that's really a problem for us."

"Lots of people will die!"

"Yeah, true."

"There will be consequences if a weapon like that goes on the rampage. Regardless of who wins, some city somewhere is going to suffer fatal damage!"

"Yeah, probably."

"If that happens... *if that happens*, then the death toll would easily exceed the twenty million lives that were almost lost in Kyoto, you know?!"

"You're not wrong, princess. However, if I may repeat myself:

that would be the result of idiots doing stupid things. It's not something that a brat needs to feel responsible for."

Flabbergasted, Marie stepped back. She couldn't understand what Halter was saying. No, she could understand it. At the very least, she recognized his logic was sound. Whatever happened now, even if she couldn't do anything, it wouldn't really be her responsibility—that's what he was saying.

"Quit joking!!" Marie shouted angrily, clenching her teeth.

Her pride had been wounded. *Are you seriously going to strip me of accountability when things have already come to this?*

Halter took a breath, loosening his expression and shaking his head. "I'm not really joking. I'm simply stating the truth, princess. If you're saying that you don't like that, then... very well. I'll abide by your decision. So, what are you going to do?"

Marie couldn't answer. There was nothing she could do. She knew that. She understood both her abilities and her limits. She had come this far by making the impossible possible. By pushing her abilities beyond those limits. It had become her way of life, but... she had no cards left to play.

"......"

Her knees buckled.

She dropped down on the spot. The dirty rain water that had pooled on the ground soaked into her underwear. It felt disgusting, but she didn't care.

She couldn't stand. Some precious part of her heart felt like it might snap at any moment.

Marie pursed her lips, fully aware of her powerlessness. There were things that she couldn't accomplish just by conducting herself in a way she could be proud of.

Even so... if Naoto was with her, she felt that she could overcome it, somehow. Now that she had gotten him killed, there was nothing left that a paltry girl like her could do.

"No..."

That was just an excuse. She smashed both her fists on the ground. Water and mud splattered, and a numbing pain shot through her arms.

Don't get the wrong idea.

What could be done, even if he were here? Just how convenient do you think he is?

Thinking of his talent as some kind of magic or miracle because she couldn't understand it was exactly what led to this situation. She couldn't give up. She couldn't do that, even if it meant that she would die. However, there was nothing she could do. She couldn't change anything.

She was spinning her wheels.

The downpour became stronger.

Pounded by the incessant rain, Marie felt her body getting heavier and heavier. She couldn't see anything in front of her in the darkness.

The only thing she could see was herself, unable to advance in any direction.

"Why..."

...did things turn out this way? If I had quietly died like the governor said, would things really have turned out better? The lives of

twenty million people were almost thrown away just to save face. I managed to save them through furious effort, and now even more people are about to be killed because of it?

"What's up with this..."

Marie couldn't understand it.

There was always someone pulling her down. It had been like this her whole life.

Even if you were right, from another's perspective, you might be wrong as well. Justice didn't exist. Fidelity and passion were easily corrupted by even the tiniest bit of malice. What was convenient was true; everything else was a lie.

She'd been troubled by it. She'd understood the way the world worked and resolved herself accordingly. Lamentations wouldn't change anything. She accepted that this was the world she lived in every time reality strove to remind her of it.

Even so, the truth was that, ever since she was a kid, she had been irritated by this disgusting world.

Marie wheezed slightly and looked up at the sky. What she could see from between the tall buildings was narrow and dark. The relentless rain hit her face, tracing a line from the outer corners of her eyes and down her cheeks.

Words that shouldn't be said, that she had always kept inside her heart, spilled out...

"*...What value is there in a world like this*?"

Such a thought was the height of insolence. A single person questioning the value of the world was laughable. The world was continually made better by countless people working to solve

problems, little by little, crying and laughing along the way. That was the answer to her question.

Fuck that.

I'm sick of it. I'm tired of pretty ideals.

The Clockwork Planet is littered with patches that extend its life, but isn't it already too late? Haven't the people living here long since set their own undoing in motion?

So what if this crappy world is overhauled?

It's been roughly a thousand years since we humans managed to force this dead planet to continue to function. The end result of all that is the situation we have now. To just what extent has the nature of man improved in that time, if at all?

Marie lost her strength. Her fists unraveled.

It was then...

Clank!

A nearby manhole popped open. The narrow hole was just large enough for a human to barely squeeze through.

A boy with a rather dull face poked his head out. "Wow, what the hell, it's raining? Seriously?! We escape the water below and it comes falling down from above! Damn it!"

"If you consider that the filth will be washed away, it should quell your anger to some degree, Master. Then again, if this rain is the result of poor maintenance, then I would like the supervisor of the weather system to take responsibility and allow me to bury him in the earth for sullying my clothes."

"......................"

This isn't real, Marie concluded. *My reason has blown so far off course that I'm hallucinating. The great Marie Bell Breguet has finally hit rock bottom.*

From the corner of her eye, she watched a boy and a girl she knew too well crawling out of the nearby manhole. It was nothing but a mirage. A nonexistent delusion. Maybe it was the rain.

I mean... this definitely can't be real.

"Christ, it's freakin' steaming! If you're going to have it rain, at least lower the damn temperature! God, what's up with this city?!"

"Master Naoto, is it so upsetting that you will be unable to see me in my swimsuit due to this rain, even though it is finally Sunday?"

"Ah! That too! Gah, dammit! Talk about kicking a man while he's down! Ahh, but that person just now... hm? Ah, it's Marie. Crap, let's avoid her."

"Master Naoto? Could it be that you have finally acquired the high-level skill of 'learning'?!"

As real as they seem, it's a hallucination. This is too much, even for a breakdown. Immersing yourself in a convenient delusion and ending up an invalid would be disgraceful beyond belief. Even if you discarded your name, you mustn't discard your pride. Even if life is sad and painful, keep facing forward. Be gracious even in defeat... wait.

She stopped breathing.

Marie placed her hands on the ground and pushed all of her strength down into her legs. As she relaxed her joints, all the muscles in her body coiled like a spring.

Pouncing, Marie bounced up in spite of her wet clothes and, like an acrobat, flew spinning through the air...

And drove a flying roundhouse kick right into the phantom who couldn't possibly exist.

"Gehwaha?!"

"Master Naoto?! Such inhumane violence! I see that you care little for the value of your life, Mistress Marie. Very well, if you wish to be turned into mincemeat so badly, I shall oblige y—"

"Wait, wait! Both of you calm down, especially you, princess, come to your senses already!"

"Gwahhhhhhhhhhhhhh!!" Naoto cried in agony.

Marie grabbed him, and let out a gasp in shock.

Choking, she surrendered herself to a torrent of emotion. All her mental anguish over his death had been for nothing. Still, the physical sensation of restraining the idiot was definitely real, so, with great pain, she was forced to accept the situation.

"If you were alive then why didn't you say so?!"

"Gu... gueh... a-are you freaking kidding me?! We just got back to the surface moments a—"

"Shut up! Don't talk back to me!"

"Master Naoto, please wait a moment. I will immediately tear this mad dog to shreds."

"I'm telling you two to calm the hell down already!"

Somehow, it appears that this isn't a convenient delusion, Marie thought.

•••●••

Twenty hours ago...

Naoto woke and wondered where he was.

It's a dimly lit and pretty spacious area. The distance to the ceiling is more than several hundred meters. It's almost like I'm outside... Wait, outside? He suddenly remembered. *We were fighting AnchoR when we fell, me in RyuZU's arms.*

As Naoto recalled the chain of events, a voice came from above his head. "Are you awake, Master Naoto?"

Glancing up slightly, he saw RyuZU's face. She was looking down at him. He finally understood the situation.

RyuZU is providing me with a lap pillow. Once he understood that, he felt like getting up would not only be troublesome but wasteful, so he simply nodded slightly and closed his eyes again. Underneath his head was the softness of RyuZU's thighs. He focused all the nerves in his brain on that sensation.

"You appear to be tired, Master, so please listen as you continue to rest. We are currently beneath Mie, stuck deep in an underground floor. Normally, Master Naoto would have died within about ten seconds in a place like this, which should be equivalent to outer space—"

"GahhhhhhhHHHHHHHH?!"

Naoto leapt up in a fluster. As precious as RyuZU's lap pillow was, what she had just said was too important to ignore.

"C-crap, if we don't get back soon I'll die... wait, h-huh...? We've already been here for way longer than ten seconds, haven't we?" Naoto asked, using his hands to feel himself over.

RyuZU nodded. "Yes. That should have been the case but,

strangely enough, it appears that an environment suitable for human life is maintained in this area. Actually... hm? Did you not give me such an order because you sensed this, Master Naoto?"

"Eh? No, I just said that because it seemed like there was footing for you further below. I thought that, if there's another floor below, then falling wouldn't really be that big a deal..." *That was all.* Naoto shut up.

RyuZU was staring at him, all expression gone from her face.

"Master Naoto," she said, looking as dreary as a Noh mask.

"Yes?"

"As you stand above all other humans, you are, relatively speaking, quite sapient. However, I have determined that, from an absolute point of view, you are hopelessly foolish."

"Uh, umm..."

"Allow me to explain. These are the remains of the scaffolding from a mining project more than a thousand years ago."

"Scaffolding?" Naoto repeated in a daze as he surveyed his surroundings.

Straining his eyes, he saw a dark space around him, and countless aisles intersecting like a web. They looked old, but sturdy. They were being maintained. For some reason, it reminded Naoto of a construction site. That, or a stupidly massive, complex jungle gym.

Seeing Naoto catch on, RyuZU continued: "The Clockwork Planet was made by using the Earth's mantle as building material. As an obvious consequence, scaffolding was necessary to extract the mantle. After the mining was finished, it was put to another use, serving as the foundational framework for the Clockwork Planet itself. Similar frameworks exist underground throughout the entire planet."

"Uhh, that's..."

"Now that the planet's construction is complete and every city is operating normally, these floors are not being maintained by the Clockwork Planet's environmental management system."

"Which means..."

While there was scaffolding, and as such, footing everywhere in the deepest underground floors, Naoto had been mistaken in assuming it would be a place where humans could survive.

"Yes." RyuZU nodded, guessing Naoto's thoughts. "To put it bluntly, you should have died. Thank goodness we have been lucky. It must be a reward for the good deeds I do, day in and day out, that would put even an angel to shame."

"Gyahhhhhhhhhhhhhh?!"

Understanding what a dangerous gamble he had made, Naoto let out a cry. Even though it had passed, he broke out in a cold sweat, and his heart pounded furiously.

RyuZU stared coldly at Naoto, so flustered he was practically foaming at the mouth.

"Master Naoto, once we return home I will be lecturing you on matters outside of your school subjects, so prepare yourself. You have a rare and exceptional talent, but even so, I have determined that continuing to live your life without the bare minimum of common sense would be extremely dangerous."

"Yes... I am terribly sorry for my actions."

Naoto prostrated himself before RyuZU. *Still,* Naoto thought, tilting his head. Another question popped up in his mind. *Why is this place an exception?*

He asked RyuZU.

"There is only one possible answer for that, Master. Someone has been maintaining this place."

"Who do you mean by 'someone'?"

"I do not know. However, I suspect that it has something to do with that enormous and unsightly weapon."

"Hmm." Naoto nodded.

It's true that an irregularity, right under that ridiculous thing, is probably not a coincidence. This place is new, no matter how you look at it.

It's worn down, yes, but not as much as it should be if it were made a thousand years ago. On top of that, it's dim here, so there must be some kind of light source, when there should be absolute darkness.

The light is unreliably faint, but nonetheless, there are light gears installed here.

"In other words," Naoto muttered. "Someone is taking care of this place, right? As a transport route for that enormous weapon, or... well, I'm not sure, but in any case," Naoto strained his ears. "We have to get back to the surface."

If this area was being maintained, then there should be an entrance and an elevator somewhere as well. Naoto discerned which direction they should head in with his hearing.

"Over there," he said, turning around. "Although it feels pretty far, there's the sound of mechanical operation... not to mention people as well."

RyuZU nodded. "In that case, let us proceed. Please hold on to my hand, Master Naoto."

The two of them began cautiously testing the worn-down aisles. With Naoto's super-hearing and RyuZU's high-tech sensors, they wouldn't be inconvenienced by the darkness. But if they missed their footing, they really would fall into the abyss this time.

They moved on gingerly. The paths intersected each other in a complex web. And they were irregular: after a downward slope steep enough to slide down, was a gentle ascending slope, and so on.

Despite what a labyrinth the place was, Naoto's ears unfailingly guided them in the right direction. Continuing like this for a little under an hour, the path became wider—as if they had been walking on the branches and had now reached the trunk of a very large tree. The aisles became sturdier as well, the maintenance here seemingly more thorough.

Let's take a short break. Just as Naoto was about to say that aloud, he saw light. It came from a slightly different direction than where they were heading. Lots of light scattered from the ceiling, all the way down to the bottom of this abyss.

"What's...going on here?"

Naoto tilted his head. Somehow, he felt like it was a gigantic building, and one that wasn't originally built that way, at that. It felt almost as if it had collapsed and gotten caught in a spider web of scaffolding, somehow.

Though puzzled at the surreal sight, he strained his ears and quickly found the answer.

"The city... no, the core tower?"

To be more precise, it was the ruins of a core tower. Unsurprisingly, it wasn't operating. Its interior had been extensively excavated. Naoto could hear just how hollow the structure was.

Next to him, RyuZU tilted her head slightly. "Considering the direction the light is coming from, this tower likely belonged to the purged Shiga Grid. To think that it stopped at this depth... it must have been awfully light. Well, it was a city with holes everywhere to begin with, I suppose."

"Holes?"

"In ancient times, it was the region that held Japan's largest lake. Indeed, a sixth of its surface was occupied by the lake, and most of the remainder was backwater. It was said to have been a plain, gawky, provincial city."

Naoto stared at RyuZU sidelong. "Hey... do you have a grudge against Shiga or something?"

"No? Not at all. It is simply described as such in my records," RyuZU said with a composed face. "When Shiga was mechanized, it was turned into the water source for the whole of western Japan. Mie's climate is probably so sultry because Shiga was purged."

"Ah, now that you mention it, I think Marie said something like that before." Naoto gazed at RyuZU, who had finished giving her smooth explanation. "Even so, aren't you oddly well informed about it, RyuZU?"

"In case you have forgotten, allow me to regretfully introduce myself for the umpteenth time: the one who created me is the person who designed this planet."

"Ah, I see. That's why you're so knowledgeable about this. That makes sense." Naoto nodded.

"..."

"Hm? Is something the matter, RyuZU?" He noticed that she'd sunk into silence and was watching him intently.

"Yes. It is about AnchoR," RyuZU said. Facing Naoto she lowered herself, feet touching, in a proper bow. "I know this is late, but I deeply apologize for what I did."

"Eh...? Wait, RyuZU, what's this about?"

"Due to my negligence, I exposed Master Naoto to grave danger. The disrespect that my failure of a little sister showed to you could never be atoned for in any way, but... please forgive her. I beg you."

Naoto was dumbfounded, his mouth agape. RyuZU was still bowing and he couldn't see her face, but seeing the way she wrung her skirt... her quivering shoulders, Naoto said in a hurry:

"Please stop. Lift your head up, RyuZU."

"..."

"You know I'm not mad about that. I'm not even annoyed by it."

"But..."

"Isn't calling AnchoR 'a failure' going too far? I feel bad for her. Although she tried to kill us, she did say that she wanted us to stop her, after all," Naoto said, bright and nonchalant.

RyuZU raised her head, her beautiful golden eyes opened wide. "You heard AnchoR's voice?"

"Hm? Ahh, well, probably? If I wasn't mistaken." Naoto nodded.

RyuZU relaxed her expression ever so slightly. "To be frank, I am surprised. She was always the worst at expressing her emotions, but..."

"Hmmm? It didn't seem that way to me..."

"No, what surprises me is that someone like Master Naoto—a social reject whose communication skills are exceedingly questionable—was capable of deciphering what AnchoR was feeling. It is a miraculous feat, to say the least. I do not think anyone can dispute this."

"Please stop, you're going to make me cry." *I'm sorry for being a loner*, Naoto thought, trembling.

Paying him no mind, RyuZU knit her brows together. "Still, if it wasn't AnchoR's will to attack us, then it has to be...?"

"Ah... yeah. That suspicious mask is probably the culprit. It was the only thing that was making that awful sound, too. The mask seemed like it was suppressing AnchoR-chan's sound."

RyuZU cast her eyes downward. She made a fist with one hand and covered it with the other, as if holding herself back.

"How unforgivable..." she spat.

"Yeah. AnchoR-chan isn't at fault at all. When we find the ones responsible, we'll extract reparations until they cry."

"Of course," RyuZU said with a sweet smile like that of a saint. "I'll slice them up, bit by bit, starting with their toenails. I'll drill the revelation of their mistaken births into their very *bones*. And when they beg for death at last, I shall offer them a cruel public execution. On such a level of despairing agony that it will leave a mark in history, a warning for anyone who ever dares to try such a thing again."

"Try your best to restrain yourself from making too grotesque a scene, okay?" Naoto added fearfully.

RyuZU smiled and nodded. It was an equivocal smile that could mean either yes or no.

"Well... whatever. Let's keep going, shall we?"

They continued walking for some time, with several breaks in between, until they finally arrived at their destination. It appeared to be the ruins of a town. Above the scaffolding were heaps of scrap material in the form of crude but satisfactory dwellings. The tower in the center somehow soared all the way to the ceiling and appeared to be connected to the base of the city of Mie.

However, there were no signs of people anywhere. There were signs that several thousand people had once lived here, but every decaying house was now filled with dust.

"If we consider things logically, this is probably where the survivors from Shiga Grid used to live," RyuZU said, after taking a look at several of the houses.

"Surviving a purge... uh, is that possible?"

"They must have been very fortunate. Or perhaps one could say that they were very unfortunate, but..." RyuZU breathed out in admiration. "Still, to think that they would build a town in a place like this to survive. I see that humans are much more tenacious than I thought."

"Well, they say that home is where the heart is, but I wouldn't want to live here if I had a choice..." Agreeing with RyuZU's sentiment, Naoto pricked up his ears.

This town was a deserted ruin that had been abandoned by its inhabitants. However, Naoto could definitely hear the sound of just one person living here.

"What should we do, RyuZU?" Naoto asked, after sounding out the rough location.

"How about we ask him what he knows? He's living alone in a place like this. That makes him reek terribly of a loser who's leading a worthless life, but we might be able to acquire some clues on the people who manipulated AnchoR. In any case, I could deal with a single human in *any number of ways*, so..."

Naoto felt a chill run down his spine. "Well... let's keep it friendly for now, okay?"

They walked through the ruins towards the central tower and stumbled upon a small cabin before long. It was made of scrap material just like the other dwellings, but there was no dust around its entrance. The dull sound of a small power tool could be heard from the back of the cabin. Someone was here.

Naoto knocked casually on the door two or three times, then called out loudly:

"Umm... excuse me! We'd like to ask you about a few things if possible..."

"Who are you? What did you come here for?" A voice answered from beyond the door. It was the raspy voice of an old man.

"We're lost and just happened to be passing by. We'd like to know how to return to the surface if possible."

"........."

After a long silence, the old man said: "The door's not locked. Come in if you'd like."

Naoto exchanged glances with RyuZU, then resolved himself and slowly opened the door.

The room beyond was as suffocating as it looked. The ceiling was low and the lighting dim. There was a bookcase along one wall, and old books and bundles of papers had been stuffed into it messily. If you shifted your gaze a little to the side, you could see a simple kitchen and a small bed. The cabin had everything necessary for a single human to live.

A large old man was sitting in a rocker in the center of the room, illuminated by a light gear lamp. He was stout and broad-shouldered. Tempered muscles covered his entire body beneath his aged skin. His crumpled hair, and the beard that laced his chin, were gray like ash, but they exuded the gravity of a lifetime's experience rather than the feebleness of old age.

The old man propped his head up with one hand, resting his elbow against the arm of the rocker. He watched his two guests with radiant, moss-green eyes.

"Who are you guys? Where did you come from?"

"Ah, well, you see, we accidentally... that is..." Naoto stumbled, his words vague.

"We fell 34,258 meters from the base of the city," RyuZU explained.

"Right, right," said Naoto. "Well, something like that, I guess? So, how can we return? Dammit. All this is all Marie's fault. That walking landmine is a goddess of pestilence, I tell you."

The old man gazed suspiciously at the two of them, then shook his head.

"You...can't return to the surface," he sighed gloomily.

"Ah... could you please do something about that? You see, I have a duty to return to the surface so I can rescue a girl called AnchoR-chan."

"Everything in this town was thrown out and abandoned. The only things that remain are myself and a modest manufacturing plant. The elevator to the surface has long been out of order."

"In that case, why don't you just start it up again? Hey, would you get a move on, grandpa! AnchoR-chan is suffering even as we sp—"

Suddenly, Naoto felt suffocated. His vision dimmed, and he swayed unsteadily. He was about to fall over when RyuZU caught him.

"Master Naoto, while it is true that there is air here, its oxygen content is extremely low. Even if you have almost ascended to godhood, at present you are still human and have not become a higher dimensional lifeform capable of surviving without oxygen. As such, I would suggest that you calm down so as not to die."

"What, I'm going to die?!" Naoto widened his eyes in shock.

RyuZU patted his pale forehead. "First... your remedial lessons, then being dragged all the way here to Mie on Mistress Marie's exceedingly selfish whim, followed by infiltrating a military facility, suddenly entering into battle with AnchoR, falling down a distance of more than thirty thousand meters, and finally a long and continuing march in thin air…

"I am already plenty impressed with how proactive you have been when it comes to pursuing your perverted desire for automata," she went on. "So please, rest for a little while, Master."

"If he needs to rest, have him sleep on my bed over there," the old man said.

RyuZU turned her gaze towards the bed and nodded. Naoto had lost his strength. She picked him up and carried him to the bed in the corner of the room. She waited until Naoto fell asleep, then turned to face the old man.

"Now then, I will be asking the questions in Master Naoto's place."

"…"

"I have absolutely no interest in who you are, where you are from, or what you are doing here. However, Master Naoto has something he must do, and I have a duty to assist him with all the abilities I have at my disposal. Not to mention that this place is not good for his health…" RyuZU said dispassionately as a black scythe popped out from underneath her skirt. Like a snake targeting its prey, she lifted the pointy end of the blade.

"I request that you give me, as quickly as possible, information on how to return to the surface. Be aware that I am prepared to utilize the full measure of my knowledge and abilities to inflict all sorts of agony upon your person should you refuse."

"I see now, you're an Initial-Y Series, huh?"

The scythe flew out. It caressed the old man's neck as he propped his head up with one hand.

"You sure are devoted to your master." The old man smiled bitterly. There was no sign of fear in his eyes, despite the danger of being decapitated.

"What do you know?" RyuZU inquired.

"It isn't really unusual for me to deduce that you're an Initial-Y. You survived a bout with that 'thing' and fell all the way down here, right? Yet, you're unscathed. Only you and your sisters would be capable of such a feat."

"…"

"I heard that, just the other day, the Breguet daughter was caught up in a scuffle to save Kyoto from being purged. My guess is that you are the First of the Initial-Y Series, the one that she owned, am I right?"

RyuZU's eyes narrowing sharply. "To know of such a recent event… it appears you're not just a shut-in who fancies himself a hermit."

"You're not really wrong. It's true. I am someone who was defeated," the old man continued. "I wasn't lying when I said that the elevator to the surface is out of order. It'll move if you can power it though."

"Then do so," RyuZU ordered.

"Sure," the old man replied, a gentle smile still on his face. "If you would be so kind as to first humor an old man in sharing a story."

• • ● ● ● • •

"And that's how we got back to the surface," Naoto said, tying things up. The four of them had returned to Marie and Halter's hotel room and were exchanging information.

"So, you didn't expect to die from pulling a stunt like that?" Marie said, in a daze.

"Hah? Me? Die? Why?"

"I thought that you had sacrificed yourself to protect me and Halter..."

"The heck are you saying?" Naoto said, shooting her down. "I just wanted to stop AnchoR-chan. Who would die to save a walking landmine like you? It would make RyuZU sad if I died. Plus, I wouldn't be able to help AnchoR-chan. Marie, could it be that... you're actually an idiot? How would me dying help anyone? Use some common sense."

"......"

Marie trembled all over under Naoto's pitying gaze.

"Well... that figures, I guess," Halter muttered quietly.

Marie turned around to face him. "Halter... *surely*, you're not telling me that you knew?" she asked, with a growl that sounded like it rang from the bottom of hell.

"I mean, I wasn't sure," Halter shook his head under Marie's glare. "After all, we were mistaken to think he would die from falling into the deepest underground layers. That said, it is true that I couldn't quite buy the narrative that he'd risked his life to save you, princess."

"If that's the case, then why...!"

"If I had said something, would you have believed me? If

you couldn't actually confirm that Naoto was alive, my words wouldn't have comforted you in the slightest, right? I kept quiet, thinking that I shouldn't add oil to the fire, but..."

"......"

Marie fell into silence. *There were some details that didn't seem to fit, that much is true. For instance, Halter was unusually composed about Naoto and RyuZU's fall, but I thought that that was just his soldier's spirit. The grit forged through years of training and actual combat experience...*

But it all makes sense now.

I've been dancing around like a clown, huh? The despair and the anguish, the tears and the vomit, my determination to face what had happened head-on and figure out how best to atone, despite my heart feeling like it was being ground to pulp... it was all... all just my misunderstanding, a comical one-man show.

I'm gonna kill him, Marie quietly determined. *If I don't sink everyone involved with this to the bottom of the earth and purge all proof that this ever happened, I'll never be able to regain my thoroughly smashed dignity!*

"You three..." Swaying, Marie stood up.

Naoto was laying out a map on the ground, completely ignoring her. "Well, leaving that aside, shall we head to Tokyo?"

"Huh?" Marie stopped moving.

She hadn't told him about the information they had gathered yet. The truth behind why Shiga Grid was purged, or that they were heading closer to a headlong clash between Mie and Tokyo. *And yet, how do you know?*

"Hm? Did I say something strange?" Naoto answered, seeing her baffled gaze. "AnchoR-chan is here protecting that enormous weapon, but she was originally in Tokyo, right? In that case, that weapon should be heading towards Tokyo, now that it's moving… or so I thought, am I wrong?"

"You're not…wrong, but…" Giving up, Marie sighed.

I've slowly gotten more used to it, but his thought patterns completely ignore the need for proof and the circumstances behind a situation. Such things are trivial to him.

"So," she said. "What do you want to accomplish by going to Tokyo?"

"Huh? I'm going to save AnchoR-chan, duh. How could anyone say no to a plea for help from such an adorable automaton? Unthinkable. He'd have to be a real brute."

This guy's an idiot after all…isn't he? Marie massaged her temples, warding off a vengeful headache.

"You probably don't know this, considering you just got to the surface, but that weapon intends to attack Tokyo."

"Well, yeah, I mean, it's a weapon. That's what they do, what's your point?"

"'What's my point'? Now, look here, you—"

"I've been trying to tell you that AnchoR-chan asked me to help her," Naoto said, cutting her off. "Rescue AnchoR-chan and wreck that enormous weapon. Wouldn't that clean everything up nicely? Incidentally, the mastermind behind this… or the last boss… whatever you want to call him, he's gotta be in Tokyo too, no? Why not just round them all up and resolve this?"

"......" Marie sighed deeply and grimaced.

"See... the thing is, Naoto," Halter interjected. "It's easy to say that, but the question is what to actually *do* about it. Are the four of us enough to stop that weapon, now that it's started up?"

"Isn't that exactly what we're going to work on?" Naoto snorted.

"Tokyo has rallied its army, and Mie has booted up its enormous weapon," Halter continued dispassionately, stroking his chin. "By my assessment, Mie is the one with the initiative. So it's not a bad idea to go to Tokyo and lie in wait. But if they start fighting in Tokyo, Tokyo won't get away scot-free, you know?"

"In that case, let's think of a method that would keep Tokyo safe," Naoto answered without a shred of hesitation.

"Doing that," said Halter. "Would mean making an enemy of Tokyo's army, as well as that enormous weapon."

"They weren't our allies in the first place. It'll be fine. We can just manipulate them for our purposes with some clever trick."

"Well then, that would mean that—"

"Arrrggh, you're soooooo annoying! We'll just cross that bridge when we come to it, you idiots!!" Naoto shouted, exasperated.

He faced Halter and Marie, and continued to slam them. "No matter how many 'buts' you come up with, what we have to do doesn't change! I don't have even the slightest intention of giving up on AnchoR-chan. I don't care who prattles at me, or how sound their argument is. If they're gonna get in my way I'll cut them to pieces, whoever they are, even if they're the president!"

"......"

Marie was unable to respond. Seeing that, Naoto went even further.

"So? When all's said and done, what do you two want?! If it's just to escape responsibility by making excuses and talking about why we can't do anything, even an idiot could do that! Huh?!"

"Don't underestimate me!!" Marie shouted back angrily, seething at his tone.

Her emerald eyes blazed as she shot off the words. Naoto and Marie faced each other down, foreheads nearly touching, eyes glaring.

"Who do you think you're talking to? Just who do you think I am?!"

"I don't care, stupid! With all those complaints stuck in your throat, you're nothing but a landmine crybaby!"

Neither of them would back down. Sparks flew between their ashen and emerald eyes.

"It's not like you even have a concrete plan, so quit drooling in your selfish delusions, idiot!"

"If your idea of a concrete plan is to just give up because it's too much trouble, then who needs it?!"

"Hah! Who said we can't do anything?! Don't just shove words into my mouth!"

"Huh, really?! 'Cuz it looks to me like you guys have been making one excuse after another for a while now!"

Marie grabbed Naoto by the collar in a fit of rage.

"......"

She was about to shout some curses, but seeing Naoto's

expression, she swallowed her words. Marie regarded his ashen eyes, sensing the clear disappointment in them. She felt her body flaring up. The humiliation made her shoulders tremble. Fury smoldered in her heart.

She was fine with him thinking she was cheeky. Having someone to argue with was a fresh experience, too. She didn't need his respect. As far as spewing vitriol went, they were both at fault. However…

Being pitied by this guy is the one thing I won't stand for!!

That moment. Like a flash of lightning suddenly cutting through a dark night, she remembered…

"I'm—!!"

This had happened before. Her and Naoto glaring at each other. At that time, she had said something… words which she had believed unwaveringly. Words which she had somehow, to her shame, forgotten somewhere along the way. A few words of pride that defined who she was.

"I will never believe that something's impossible!!" Marie yelled, her emerald eyes shining fiercely.

"Yeah." Naoto nodded, relaxing. "That's right. If you weren't that, you'd 'just' be a walking landmine, right?"

Marie laughed aloud.

"Haha aha ha ha ha ha!"

Naoto, Halter, and RyuZU merely watched her, taken aback. That didn't bother Marie much, either.

Good Lord.

To think that I had forgotten such an obvious thing.

"Let's confirm something," she sighed. "You're an outrageous idiot."

"Oy."

"And at the same time, you're an idiot who's a much better person than I am," she added, shaking her head.

"It certainly is unusual for you to say something that I can wholeheartedly agree with," RyuZU said, her voice betraying a sense of astonishment. "Did you hit your head or something, Mistress Marie?"

"Yeah, I feel like my head's been smashed in with a hammer. Being an idiot feels good, doesn't it?" Her tension crumbled. She looked happy and carefree, her posture loose. She shrugged her shoulders.

It's true, she thought. *The whole of humanity may be nothing but a big group of idiots, just like RyuZU said.*

Like the words I uttered in my moment of weakness. Maybe there is no value in this world.

But if that's the case, so what?

"There's nothing but idiots in this world," she said. "Every last one of us is irrational, obstinate, and selfish. And yet we all still expect to be loved. Maybe there's no value in this tattered world, but there is meaning in it: even if your worth is acknowledged by others, the meaning of your life is something you determine by yourself."

That's why everyone lives out their lives trying to find their own meaning.

At the very least Naoto Miura understands that, unlike me.

"Okay," Marie declared. "As you said, going to Tokyo isn't a bad idea. Very well. Let's pick a fight with Mie and Tokyo and flip the world upside down, shall we?"

"I'm not really sure what you're saying, but I won't budge on the matter of saving AnchoR-chan, got that?"

"I know. Our goals haven't changed. You save AnchoR, and I'll save the world. We'll do it because we want to. We'll do whatever it takes to fulfill our duties."

"Oy oy, princess," Halter interjected. "I'm glad that your spirits are back, but what are you planning to do?"

"Isn't it obvious? *Whatever it takes.*"

That's right. I have no obligation to choose an honorable method. Whether or not there is leeway to do so doesn't change the facts.

"My goodness, what a terrible delusion I've been working under. We're not allies of justice. We're terrorists, right?"

The cogs in Marie's brain turned at a fierce speed. As she plotted, a restless aura emanated from her.

"I regret how I've been acting. I understand that I've lacked resolve up to now." Marie squeezed her fists tight.

Seeing her like that, Naoto was taken aback. "Uh... could it be that I just unknowingly spurred on a monster?" he muttered.

"Rest assured, Naoto. Thanks to you spurring me on, you'll be able to acquire AnchoR, I promise."

"Then I'll spur you on as much as you'd like! I'll push you forward with a truck, if that's what it takes! Leave it to me." Naoto said, changing his attitude at the speed of light.

Halter pursed his lips. "I don't know what you plan to do, but seeing how you're behaving, it can't be good."

"Isn't that obvious? We're going to do bad things." Marie nodded, grinning sweetly at Halter before turning to Naoto. "Now then, I'll have you answer two questions for me."

"Right… I have a really bad feeling about this, but what is it?"

Marie stuck up her index finger. "First, going by the way you've been talking, you seem to think that you can restrain AnchoR, but can you really?"

"We can," he answered immediately.

"With all due respect, Master Naoto," RyuZU objected. "No automaton can win against that girl in com—"

"That's not true. You can, RyuZU. It's possible. I don't even have to mention that I won't let either you or AnchoR-chan be destroyed. She begged us to save her, and we're going to save her. That's absolute."

"Is that so?" said Marie. "Then, I'll leave the details to you. I won't ask you why you are so confident, but in exchange…" She held up another finger. "How far are you willing to go to see both of them safe and sound?"

"That's obvious. *I'd do anything.*"

Marie smirked. "Halter, you heard him. Did you get that on tape?"

"Yeah, I guess…"

"You said you'd do anything, right? Yep, you said it. As such, I won't let you run away and make excuses, got it?" Marie pressed menacingly.

Naoto felt a bit of doubt. He was getting cold feet. "Uh... umm... if RyuZU and AnchoR are both safe at the end of it, yeah, I'll do anything, but... I'll pass on dying. RyuZU probably wouldn't accept that."

RyuZU stepped forward, her eyes grim. "If you are hoping for a situation that ends with Master Naoto dying, or being on the verge of death, then prepare yourself accordingly. I already have something to say concerning how carelessly you got Master Naoto involved with this incident, and nearly got him kill—"

"I won't let him die. Not him, not anyone." Marie smiled bitterly, relaxing her shoulders. "I'd just like to have him... hmm, right. Naoto, what subject was your next remedial lesson?"

"Huh? It's modern history, why?"

"Is that so? Perfect. That textbook will have been rewritten by the time we get back, so you won't need it anymore."

"Hm?"

"They'll write about us in that textbook. As the vilest terrorists in history, probably ♪."

"Say," Halter interjected. "You're putting on quite the airs, but in the end, what are you planning to stir up, princess?"

"It's simple," Marie answered, smiling.

She paused for a breath.

"We're going to attack Tokyo before Mie's weapon can get there."

Marie waited for the three of them to take in what she had just said.

"Adding the information we acquired to what you just told us in your report," she went on. "I have a pretty good idea of how that weapon operates. I didn't know how they were going to send such an enormous weapon to Tokyo, but now..."

Never mind how tough the plating on the grids was, if a gargantuan body like that walked on the ground, it would destroy everything in its path from Mie to Tokyo.

If that happened, forget just Tokyo. The military of every grid in its path would intercept it and, if they struggled to deal with it, armies from other countries would probably try to control the situation.

No matter how powerful of a weapon it was, there was no way it could move quickly with a body like that. If a city was purged while it was traveling through it, that weapon would be brought down along with the grid.

"In other words," Marie began. "That weapon moves underground. The reason it was made underground isn't just to conceal it. That hangar itself serves as the docking area that connects directly to the deepest underground layers."

And, that should be the greatest advantage for Mie's prospects of winning. There was no way an army could be deployed against them in the deepest underground layers. No one would even take a weapon that moves underground into consideration to begin with.

No matter how big an army they amassed on the surface, if they were ambushed from underground, it would be over. From there, the enormous weapon could destroy all of Tokyo, or perhaps even take its core towers hostage.

"That's why we're going to terrorize them before that weapon gets there."

"Terrorize, you say? But what are you thinking?" Naoto asked, puckering his face. "Are we gonna blow up the National Diet Building?"

Marie gazed at him, fed up with his stupidity. "What would that accomplish, dummy, even if we succeeded? What I'm thinking of is much more impressive... we're going to take over one of Tokyo's grids at the perfect moment."

"So... umm, just like what we did in Kyoto?"

Last month, Naoto and Marie had usurped control of all of Kyoto's core tower to save the city.

"You want to do that again?" Naoto asked.

Marie nodded. "That's right. If we pull it off, not only could we evacuate the residents, we could lead Tokyo's army to the city's underground actuator as well. Then their Technical Force would surely notice the enormous weapon advancing underground. If we leave the rest to both sides... Now *that* would be a real duel between men of honor, right?"

"I'd like to nitpick the details, but... well, I get what you want to do," Halter interjected. "But, princess, we're a bit short on the necessary manpower to execute that plan. And we don't have the time to thoroughly prepare for it. Even if we force our way through, no faction would be able to ignore us. In the worst-case scenario, we could even be assaulted by AnchoR."

"That's exactly what I'm hoping for... well, it's not a problem, in any case." Marie shrugged. "You might already know this, but I have lots of friends that I can count on, you know?"

"Is crushing the heart of an outcast fun to you?" Naoto muttered, his warped personality on full display.

• Chapter Four / 00 : 00 / Returner

10:34 AM on the sixth day of February, 1016th year of the Wheel.

About seventy-five kilometers below the surface of Mie Grid lay the base of the city's mechanisms. Something began to move that would never be seen by the people who lived on the surface.

It was an enormous steel spider.

All in all, it was 320 meters tall and 932 meters long. The fact that such a thing was moving at all was ridiculous. Nonetheless, it walked forward with an incredibly loud noise.

It slid under the bottom of the city into its deepest underground layer, where, free from the gravitational restraints of the facility's hangar, it headed eastward. The capital area of Japan lay in its path—the Tokyo Grids. It moved slowly. Most likely, it would take about a day and a half to reach its destination.

However, in spite of the noise and its lumbering pace, the thing crawling through the hollow space of the Clockwork Planet could sneak up on its prey and deal a lethal blow. It was a weapon that could destroy the very planet itself. There was no doubt that its existence alone was extremely dangerous.

The malevolent spider should have been crawling forward unseen by all, but someone secretly observed it from the shadows...

"It's finally begun moving, huh?" she muttered, her silver hair swaying. "It's an unbearably ugly, unsightly thing, but... it certainly is menacing." With those venomous words, RyuZU narrowed her eyes.

Confirming the monster's departure, its path, and its speed, she left quietly, and without being discovered.

• • ● ● ● • •

6:27 PM on the sixth day of February, 1016th year of the Wheel.

A building, referred to as the fourth clock tower, could be found on Yasukuni Street in Akihabara Grid, Tokyo, Japan.

As a rule of thumb, the clock towers were under military management, but for the purposes of technological research, this tower was among a handful of exceptions. Its maintenance was annexed to a university.

Multiple silhouettes walked through the campus of that university, the Akihabara Institute of Technology. They were wearing matching blue work clothes and pushed a cart with a large package in it, brazenly traversing the campus in the crimson light of the setting sun. Many students and faculty members were still out and about, but no one paid the workers any mind.

As a result, they arrived at the clock tower's warehouse without being questioned. There, they encountered an iron gate and a small accompanying room with a security guard. The guard, who looked to be in his late sixties, watched perplexed as the crew moved the large package.

"Hi there!" the man in front, large and bear-like, called out with a smile. "Thanks for your hard work as always."

"Y-yeah, you too... umm, what business do you have here today?" the guard asked.

The large man flashed him a grin as he took a single sheet of paper out of a satchel stuffed full with various documents. "We're from Seiko's shipping department. We came to deliver the new measurement devices."

"Eh, I haven't heard of such a purchase...?"

"Oh man. Another one, huh?" The large man gave an exaggerated scowl "This is the third time this year. It seems that university researchers are rather irresponsible when it comes to paperwork... ah, no, sorry, that was rude of me."

"No no, I know what you mean." The security guard smiled bitterly. "Let me guess, it's for Professor Kizaki, is it? The seminar students often complain about how strict he is, despite being pretty sloppy himself."

"I guess you could say that it's nothing new at this point, but..." The large man hunched his shoulders and pointed at a line on the document. "It seems like Dr. Kizaki went off on a sudden business trip today so he can't be reached at the moment. He told us to install the devices while he's out because he wanted to get to work immediately once he's back. But… maybe that would violate protocol?"

"Hmm… normally you would need a written form from the professor, but…" the security guard muttered, nodding sympathetically. "Well, your document looks official, so I guess it's fine. When the professor comes back, I'll give him a warning for next time."

"Thank you very much! Really, you saved us a lot of trouble."

"Not at all, thanks for your hard work. I'll open the gate."

With a smile, the kind guard flipped a switch on his desk. The gate opened, and the guard handed the stamped document back to the large man. He bowed and said his thanks.

The group in blue work clothes pushed the cart into the warehouse. Once the security stall was completely out of sight, the large man, Halter, burst out laughing.

"Well, that's university security for you, Dr. Hannes."

"My goodness. I can't believe you, Mr. Halter," the man pushing the cart replied. He had chiseled features and a long, rectangular face. He was the very picture of a straitlaced middle-aged man. "Is it really normal to let people into a clock tower with a single document when you aren't sure of their identities?"

"Normal people judge others by their clothes and their attitude. If you wear the uniform of a delivery man and throw in a joke, you really won't seem suspicious."

The other man, Hannes, didn't look convinced. "Still, it was a stroke of luck that the professor was conveniently away on a business trip, wasn't it?"

"Oh, that? No, we had the Breguets handle that."

"What...did you say?"

"We're dealing with a university, so we can't be too violent with our methods. That's why we made up some business for the professor to get him out of the way. Because of that, we're the only ones in this clock tower right now."

"My goodness," Hannes repeated, sighing deeply. "I can't believe you."

"You're rather straitlaced, despite having worked with that tomboy," Halter teased, grinning.

"Tomboy?" Hannes said, looking blank. "But she's the most serious, sincere, and outstanding woman I know."

"Well... words are an imperfect vehicle of expression, I suppose."

Although Halter couldn't dismiss Hannes's description of Marie as wrong, it didn't seem exactly right to him, either. Taking a breath, he shook his head and changed the subject.

"Well, if any problems arise, I'll handle them, so please take care of the work, professor. I estimate the installation of the devices should take about four hours. Is that enough time?"

"Of course. We're still Meisters, you know. Have a little faith, won't you?" Hannes, who had once served as an observation chief of the Meister Guild, puffed up his chest.

Halter smiled bitterly and lowered his head. "My, you'll have to pardon me for asking."

•••●•••

0:00 AM on the eighth day of February, 1016th year of the Wheel.

On the day that would be deeply carved into history, Marie Bell Breguet was in Akihabara Grid, Tokyo, Japan—inside its first clock tower.

In a mechanical room filled with gears, just like the inside of a core tower, several score technicians worked relentlessly to execute Marie's plan. Their first step was to synchronize the core and its supporting clock towers. They worked without rest to accomplish it.

They weren't the Technical Force who normally serviced this place. Their racial backgrounds, genders, and ages varied greatly. Their clothes and equipment weren't uniform, either. In fact, there was just one thing they had in common: a chrono compass on their wrists.

The proof of being a Meister.

A super finely detailed timepiece with nine clockfaces, large and small. The medal that showed they were at the peak of all the two hundred million clocksmiths in the world.

Hundreds of ordinary clocksmiths couldn't rival a single Meister. They were extraordinary clocksmiths who possessed both talent and a history of results. Among this gathering of Meisters, one of them yelled out:

"Dr. Marie!"

Marie lifted her head from her work desk. She had been focused on her calculations, a string of equations on the piece of scrap paper on her desk.

"Yes, go ahead. What is it?"

"We've confirmed the synchronization of the 3,340th to the 7,990th, as well as the linkage of all floors."

"Understood. Thank you for your hard work." Marie nodded.

Only a moment later, a different clocksmith who had been standing guard over the communications device yelled out, "Reporting! A transmission from the fourth clock tower says that the functions of all floors over there have been released. The administrative privilege over the atmospheric temperature system is being transferred to us."

"Understood, please send them this message in response: 'It's almost time for the operation. Once you finish the final confirmation, please escape immediately.' Also, please forward the administrative privilege to the rest of the clock towers."

Sorting through some more reports, confirmations, and requests one after the other, Marie sighed loudly. She stretched her back as far as she could in the chair, releasing the tension in her muscles.

A man in his late fifties came up behind her. "It looks like we made it somehow, eh?" He put a steaming cup onto the table with an elegant motion. "It's black tea. With plenty of milk and honey—you like your tea sweet, right?"

Marie relaxed and took the cup in one hand. "Thank you, Service Chief Konrad."

"I'm not the service chief anymore you know, Dr. Marie,"

"That's true... isn't it?" Putting her lips on the rim of the piping-hot cup, Marie cast her eyes down.

Konrad had been her advisor, serving as her service chief

when she was in Meister Guild. He was an old and experienced technician who'd lent a hand during the incident in Kyoto, staying in the core tower to the very end, despite the danger.

After the incident, he retired from Meister Guild and started working as a freelance clocksmith. He was also the one who had investigated the suspicious movements of Tokyo's military.

"I'm glad that the work was finished safely," said Marie. "I asked too much of everyone."

"Not at all. Everyone enjoys working with you. Plus, it was easier than expected, since most of the clock towers turned out to be empty."

"Yeah... it's like a parade of felonies."

She took a breath and sipped the sweet, black tea. She thought about the clocksmiths working here and at the other towers. Nearly all of them were like Konrad: Meisters who had once been her subordinates. They left Meister Guild after Kyoto's incident and became civilians.

Hijack the city mechanisms and defend against the approaching raid by that enormous weapon.

Anyone else who heard of such a plan would surely call it absurd, but they had readily gotten on board. They possessed a priceless level of technical skill that allowed them to work wherever they pleased, and they were helping her with a job that not only wouldn't pay much, but was illegal.

Just because Marie Bell Breguet had asked them to.

Marie blushed, filled with a deep gratitude that she could never fully express.

"Really, I'm so thankful for you all."

Just then, the correspondence device on the table started ringing. Marie flipped the switch to receive the call.

"Marie," a voice asked immediately. "Are the preparations done?" It was Naoto's voice. Perhaps he was nervous, because his voice was higher than usual.

Marie smiled. "Of course. Who do you think I am?"

"I'm counting on you, Meister."

"That's obvious as well. Just make sure to take care of things on your end."

"Roger," Naoto answered.

The transmission ended.

"Was that 'him' just now?" Konrad asked.

"Yeah, it was Naoto Miura." Marie nodded.

"It's still hard to believe, no matter how many times I see it," Konrad muttered with a sigh. "To be able to fully grasp the makeup of a core and twelve clock towers with just his ears and that level of equipment to aid him..."

"But it's real."

Naoto grasped the structure of Akihabara's grid by hearing alone, and Marie had drawn up its blueprint based on his description.

The plan was to analyze which functions were shared between the core tower and each of its supporting clock towers. From there, they would reverse-engineer a way to hijack the core tower from four of its clock towers, and seize control of the atmospheric temperature system and communications network. Then they'd construct their own system, which they could freely manipulate through the network.

Normally, it would take several hundred years just to get the overall picture of the tower network, but Naoto and Marie had managed to finish it in just three days.

"If the core tower is the brain of the city, then the clock towers are its internal organs. If I were to pick an analogy, what we're doing is something like interfering with the brain by stimulating the organs. While it's true that the core tower and the clock towers are connected, it isn't impossible in theory... my word..."

It was only made possible thanks to the cooperation of several dozen clocksmiths.

"As a clocksmith myself," Konrad whispered. "I find it somewhat terrifying."

He was a Meister, someone who stood at the pinnacle of all clocksmiths. He could safely say that he had mastered, even perfected, the latest clockwork technologies. It wouldn't be self-conceit—he had the resume to back it up. And yet there was a talent that even he couldn't understand.

"I wonder if he... or rather... if such an ability is really human."

"He's definitely human, Dr. Konrad," Marie replied, looking down. "He isn't a handy god nor a convenient magician. He's simply another idiot you could find anywhere, no different from any of us."

"......"

"He's an idiot, but at the very least, he's a better person than the ones responsible for Kyoto, or our current situation. However abnormal an ability he possesses, he at least feels human."

He wasn't absolutely good or the incarnation of justice. Not by any means. He wasn't truly omnipotent, either. If stumbling along, trying to find meaning in your life was how humans (born without inherent value) should live, then Naoto Miura was the most human person that Marie Bell Breguet knew.

Konrad stared at her for a while, and nodded quietly.

"Indeed, it's as you say." Then, as if it had just come to mind, he ventured: "By the way, I've actually thought this for a while now, but..."

"Huh?" Marie tilted her head.

"You're simply terrible at pretending to be a goody two shoes," Konrad whispered teasingly.

"Eh...?" Marie said, baffled.

"However," Konrad grinned. "Know that I think the real you is much more charming, Dr. Marie."

"P-please don't tease me!"

Konrad enjoyed the sulky look on the face of a girl who was like a granddaughter to him, then turned around. Marie hadn't realized it, but the other clocksmiths had stopped working to watch their exchange.

Konrad looked among their faces and clapped his hands twice.

"Now then," he declared with his smooth bass voice. "It's time, everyone. Shall we enjoy the moment when history changes its course?"

• • ● ● ● • •

On the threshold between the seventh of February and the eighth, what would come to be known as The Akihabara Terrorist Incident, which led to the Uprising of 2/8, began.

On the command of a certain boy, a severe earthquake with a radius of thirty kilometers shook Tokyo, centered in Akihabara Grid. All communication mechanisms ceased functioning as the city's internal resonance gears operated outside regulation.

And the group of gears that tuned the city functions in the core tower displayed unprecedented behavior.

It wasn't a malfunction, nor was the degradation in function due to age. The system was operating normally, it was simply that the administrator, a young girl, had networked them to a new system that she'd built herself.

Five minutes after it started, the hijacked communication mechanisms began operating again. And the helpless people watching the situation unfold received a rather enthusiastic claim of responsibility:

"Ladieees aaannnd gentlemen!! Along with the foolish and banal ordinary citizens who are neither gentlemanly nor ladylike, good evening! Pardon me for disturbing you while you're enjoying your weekend night!"

The processed voice sounded like a drunken master of ceremonies. It resounded at a high volume throughout the city from countless televisions and stereos.

Hearing those words, Konrad frowned, feeling conflicted.

"Good heavens, it appears I simply can't keep up with the sensibilities of you youngsters these days."

Beside him, Marie was also clutching her head. "No... could you please not treat that idiot as the representative of all young people?"

Marie and Konrad had devoted their time to building their own system and had left it to Naoto to make an adequate claim of criminal responsibility. This was what they ended up with.

For an unprecedented, unparalleled historical event like this... it is simply too crass. Marie regretted it, but it was already too late.

"Arghh, I need to have a word with him after this! How's the transmission of disinformation going?!"

"As planned!" answered the clocksmith standing watch over the control panel. "All 168 communication circuits are still under our control. There's no sign that they've noticed!"

"Understood. Observation squad, what's the current location of that enormous weapon?!"

"It's currently proceeding through the base of Shibuya Grid! Factoring in the projected movement of Tokyo's military, I estimate that the two sides will clash in about five or six minutes!"

"Understood, so it's going well. In that case, please prepare to boot up the atmospheric temperature system!" Marie said, tossing out the latest instructions in rapid succession.

"Dr. Marie," Konrad interjected. "We'll be fine by ourselves from here on in."

"Thanks. In that case, I'll meet up with them as planned and move on to the next stage. Everyone, please escape from here immediately after the operation ends."

"Understood!"

Hearing that chorus of voices behind her, Marie grabbed her coat and bag and dashed out of the room. She pushed her arms through the sleeves of her coat, rushing up the emergency staircase to the rooftop and throwing the door open.

Standing in the doorway, Marie felt the tepid air of the night brush her cheeks. The light gears of the city were all running, converting gravity into a florescent shine. The stars, overshadowed by their radiance, were invisible. The only things on the horizon were the silver moon and the Equatorial Spring, turning from its gravitational pull.

From a speaker somewhere, Marie could hear Naoto's joke of a terrorist threat.

"RyuuuuuuZU!!" she shouted.

"You do not need to shout, you know. I have been ready to pick you up for a while now, Mistress Marie," a cool voice called from behind her.

Marie turned to find an automaton before her, RyuZU's silver hair fluttering in the night's wind.

"It is you, Mistress Marie, who is about two seconds behind the projected time. In a situation like this, where even a slight delay could lead directly to crisis, your blunder is—"

"Then why don't you hurry up and make up for it!" Marie shouted, leaping at RyuZU.

RyuZU had the most glorious frown as she begrudgingly took Marie into her arms and jumped off of the building. She headed towards Naoto, currently delivering their claim of criminal responsibility from a rooftop beside the nearest train station.

The three of them were to meet up there for the next stage of the operation.

RyuZU raced through Akihabara, jumping from rooftop to rooftop with Marie in her arms. Perhaps because of their broadcast, the city flowing past below them exuded an air of alert stillness.

"It's starting!" Marie muttered, raising a finger.

She pointed towards a red building glowing in the night—the Tokyo Tower, a relic of the ancient times. It turned white as it froze over.

"It's nearly time for the final stage of the operation."

Freezing Tokyo Tower and then smashing it into pieces would be a threat that was visible throughout Tokyo. A show of strength, serving as definite proof that they had seized control of Akihabara Grid. Once it was done, they would end Naoto's broadcast and move on to the final stage.

"More importantly," RyuZU replied in a cold voice. "Something has been on my mind for a while now. It appears that the enemy's movements are approximately two minutes and thirty-seven seconds faster than anticipated."

Turning her head slightly to one side, RyuZU looked at something far in the distance.

Following RyuZU's eyes with her own, Marie recognized three large shadows flying silently through the night sky.

"Stealth helicopters...!"

They were military weapons, carrying assault automata. All three were heading straight towards the same destination—the rooftop where Naoto was waiting. His location had been purposely leaked from the beginning, so it was only natural that they would know where he was, but their response was quicker than anticipated.

Even now the stealth helicopters, the kings of the sky, were pulling ahead in the race to Naoto.

At this rate, Naoto will be shot at before RyuZU arrives.

"Furthermore, I can see security automata on the ground."

Looking down to confirm RyuZU's report, Marie found security automata rushing with flashing sirens towards Naoto. There was more than a dozen of them.

The security automata were several orders of magnitude less threatening than the stealth helicopters, but they still had to be dealt with. Although they looked awkward, like large steel cans with feet, even just one of them would be enough to restrain an unarmed human.

What should we do? Furrowing her brows, Marie was worrying about how to deal with the situation when RyuZU whispered:

"Mistress Marie, you are carrying a weapon, yes?"

"Huh? I'm carrying my Coil Spear, of course. What about it...?"

"In that case," RyuZU announced dispassionately. "I shall leave the riffraff below to you. I am currently in a rush."

"Huh? Kyaaaaaaaaaaaah?!" Without time to reply, Marie screamed as she was tossed in the air.

Seeing the sky and the ground in quick succession as her body spun in freefall, she hurriedly retrieved her anchor wire from her holster and fired it. Adjusting her posture in midair, Marie killed most of her momentum by pulling on the wire and managed to land roughly with a roll.

Meanwhile, having discarded her excess "baggage," RyuZU accelerated in a race against the helicopters.

"Ow ow ow ow... that shitty doll...!" Marie cursed, raising her head. She immediately swallowed her breath.

"Suspicious person detected."

The multiple voices of warning overlapped with each other. She had landed right in the middle of the automata rushing towards Naoto. They surrounded the suspicious, and armed, girl who had fallen from the sky.

"Wha...!"

Marie drew her Coil Spear from its holster. Confirming an increase in their target's threat level, riot guns emerged from the automata's torsos.

"Attempt to resist arrest confirmed. Commencing subjugation."

"If you're going to drop me, then drop me in a better spot, you piece of junk!!" Marie yelled, jumping backwards. It was an indiscernible cry of either anger or desperation.

Gunshots rang out immediately after.

• • ● ● ● • •

Having made it through several close calls, Marie somehow managed to defeat them.

Confirming that she had brought them all down, she hurried towards the rooftop where Naoto was.

She entered the building and ran up the emergency stairs. Through the windows, she saw the minced wreckage of several helicopters crashing down in a blaze.

Making it to the top floor, a scene of ruined assault automata awaited her, demolished into scrap metal. Halter had his back to her, Naoto was prostrate on the ground for some reason, and—

"……"

RyuZU had a composed look on her face.

Marie fired her Coil Spear without a second thought. Her aim was accurate, but RyuZU evaded it with a single step.

"That's dangerous, princess," Halter said, breaking out in a cold sweat.

"Halter," Marie called out, swiftly making her way to him. Her heart was at a boil, but her words were cold and businesslike. "Please restrain that piece of junk. Today's the day I dismantle her and fix that rotten personality for good."

Halter sighed and shrugged his shoulders. "Don't ask for the impossible, princess. Just what do you expect me to do?"

"When do you plan to capitalize on your experience if not now? Please use the Marine Corps'... uhh, hand-to-hand combat techniques to seize that piece of junk. I don't mind if you break her in the process, okay?"

"I was in the Army, not the Marine Corps. What's this commotion all about?"

Without answering, Marie swung the Coil Spear in her right hand, causing it to transform into a blade.

"This shitty piece of junk deserted me and ran away by herself!

Despite the fact that I was surrounded by security automata!" she yelled gruffly, slashing at RyuZU.

The swing was sharp and carried the momentum of Marie's upper body, but once again RyuZU evaded with a light step.

"Oh my, your facade is peeling off, you know."

"Shut it!"

"Mistress Marie, you are always calling yourself a multifaceted prodigy, so there is no way you'd have any difficulty with a small threat like ten or twenty generic security automata, right?"

"How could that possibly be true?! I thought I was going to die!"

"What?" RyuZU opened her eyes wide in astonishment. "I... apologize. I thought my opinion of you was already as low as it could be, but to think that you're such a complete wimp... you have my sincerest apologies."

"I'm gonna destroy you! I'm definitely, seriously gonna destroy you...!"

"Be quiet!" Naoto muttered, as Marie tried to transform her Coil Spear to extend its blade.

He knelt with his head against the concrete. When he spoke, the three of them abruptly ended their farce and turned their eyes toward him.

"As expected," he continued, pressing one ear snugly against the ground. "They're heading toward the 'Actuator.'"

Naoto strained his ears for all his worth. Far in the distance... footsteps sounded underground, 5,387 meters away.

He heard each and every one of them.

"There are 3,021 automata and 1,765 soldiers on foot."

"It's safe to assume that's almost all of the garrisoned forces that could be immediately mobilized."

Rubbing his head, Halter laughed as if to say: *what an opportunity.*

Marie retracted her Coil Spear. "They should know where we are, too."

"There are seven sources heading straight toward us. They're not stealth helicopters this time. They aren't loaded with automata, even. They're authentic assault helicopters."

"Out of all the heavily armed helicopters that Japan owns, the ones that could be mobilized right now... they're PTK-A74s," Marie deduced.

"How much of a threat are they?" RyuZU inquired.

"They're heavily armed, unpiloted, autonomous fighters. They're equipped with two resonance cannons... with seven of them, they can scorch this entire grid without needing to resupply."

"All right, let's get the hell outta here. Hey Naoto, how much time do we have?" Halter asked.

Naoto got up quickly. "About 372 seconds until they arrive. Something like that."

"Well then, let us withdraw before we come into contact with them. I shall carry the luggage." RyuZU piled up the pieces of Naoto's equipment and lifted them easily.

Naoto unplugged the unnecessary lines from his favorite pair of headphones, put them back on, and turned on the noise-canceling function.

Ahh, he sighed. *It's finally quiet.*

"Hey Naoto, are you okay?" Marie asked quietly.

"Well... yeah, somehow."

"That ability is a burden on your body, isn't it?"

"Nah, that's not it. I messed up... sorry." Naoto turned around and stuck his thumb up with a snap.

"You see, it seems there's a sex parlor in that building over there."

"...Huh?"

"With the beds creaking and the people moaning constantly, they couldn't be more of a clueless nuisance if they tri—"

Before he could finish, Marie uppercut him on the chin, her face flushed.

"Oy, cut it out, princess!" Halter called, as Marie stomped on the back of Naoto's head in silent anger. "That brain holds the future of the world."

"The world must have gone mad, then."

"Aren't you being completely unreasonable...?" Naoto groaned under Marie's feet.

Halter sighed. "Hurry up, now. This isn't the time to be doing a comedy skit."

"R-rest assured, Halter," Naoto muttered as he stood up, tottering. He adjusted his headphones and brushed the dust off of his clothes. "If we're together, something as small as a metropolis of forty million people is putty in our hands."

"Hopefully, you're right," Halter grumbled, rubbing his head.

The four of them ran down the building's emergency staircase and stepped outside. Passing the three crashed and burning helicopters, they headed towards the roundabout in front of the station.

A giant display hung on the outside of the station building, playing an emergency news broadcast. Reporting in-depth on this unprecedented act of terrorism.

"Well then," Halter said, stopping in the midst of the chaos of evacuating people. "The princess and I will wait for you guys in the workshop as planned after we evacuate the clocksmiths, all right?"

"We're leaving AnchoR to you," said Marie. "Don't screw up and die, got it?"

"You don't need to worry about that," Naoto said with a gentle smile.

"No," RyuZU suddenly interjected. "I am terribly sorry for asking this, but could you come with us, Mistress Marie?"

Marie tilted her head. "You...want me to come, too?"

"RyuZU?" Naoto asked, perplexed.

"It is impossible for me to beat AnchoR solely on my own," RyuZU admitted meekly with downcast eyes. "Master Naoto provided a suggestion that could make it possible, but... if anything were to happen to him, I suspect I would never be able to operate again."

"..."

"As such, I would like to ask you to accompany us to guard against that disastrous, albeit unlikely—possibility. Just in case, Mistress Marie." RyuZU bowed deeply.

Marie's eyes widened. *To think that RyuZU of all people would lower her head to me when, even without her abusive verbal filter, she has unfailingly treated everyone except Naoto like an insect.*

Marie gulped, then slowly nodded. "Very well. I don't think I can do anything against AnchoR, but even so, I'll accompany you if you would like me to. Win or lose, we'll be together to the end."

RyuZU raised her head with a composed look. "Your resolve is admirable, Mistress Marie."

Marie turned around and looked up at the bear of a man beside her. "Halter, you'll be fine by yourself, right?"

"Yeah. After all, Dr. Konrad will be with me," Halter said flippantly. "That grandpa is no amateur himself. He'll be able to handle the evacuation."

"If you're disrespectful towards Dr. Konrad...I'll strangle you to death later, you know?" Marie glared at him menacingly.

"Hey, Konrad is that old guy, right?" Naoto cut in. "Will he really be okay?"

"Yes, he should be fine. He may look feeble, but..." Marie shrugged. "He can hold his own against a dozen lightly armored automata with just a screwdriver."

"...What, really?" Naoto groaned, reluctant to believe it.

Halter backed up Marie's claim, grumbling, "To be honest, I'm allergic to the guy. The way he asserted that he could easily pin me down by twisting my arms, just because he has full knowledge of the structure of my artificial body, is just..."

"No no no... you two are just trying to trick me. You're exaggerating, right?"

"Nope. It's the whole and unadulterated truth," Marie asserted flatly.

Naoto still looked suspicious. "I doubt that this could be the case, but... does everyone from Meister Guild think 'might is right' like you?"

"Now *that's* impossible. At its core, Meister Guild is a gathering of intellectuals, you know?"

"Of course... I should have known better! Phew..."

"It's just that, since repairing clockwork is a test of stamina, everyone does some sort of basic body training," Marie continued. "Incidentally, Dr. Konrad is the one who taught me self-defense, you know."

"You...call those nasty techniques of yours self-defense?" Naoto recalled Marie's footwork in taking down two soldiers. The muscles along his spine trembled. *No matter how you look at it, that technique was designed to kill.*

"Well, you know," Marie said smiling. "When trouble arises with the local military, we have to be able to crush them easi... I mean, at the very least, we have to defend ourselves."

"You said crush just now, didn't you?!" Naoto cried, but Marie only gave him a sweet grin.

The three of them parted from Halter and got moving. They headed towards the train station's underground parking lot. It fulfilled their requirements for a wide and deserted space that they could use to lie in wait for AnchoR. They took up a position where they could monitor the entrance.

"Will she really come?" RyuZU muttered.

"She'll come."

"She'll come."

Marie and Naoto both asserted, but for different reasons.

"Our actions should have caused them to deviate from their plan," said Marie. "After all, there's no way that they would have accounted for terrorists hijacking the city mechanisms. Now that things have come to this, neither side can ignore us. And the only one who can stand up to RyuZU... is AnchoR."

"She'll come to you. To be precise, she's coming *to be destroyed* by you, but..." Naoto narrowed his eyes as he gazed at RyuZU. "I won't let it happen that easy. Both of you will be unharmed. So, RyuZU... I'm counting on you. Please stop AnchoR-chan."

"Yes. If you say so, Master Naoto. Besides," RyuZU paused, placing a hand on her chest. "Hurting my sister is, to put it mildly, something I would like to avoid as much as possible." She voiced her true feelings with her eyes cast downward.

Immediately after, AnchoR showed herself at the entrance of the parking lot.

The air was still in the dimly lit space. The pandemonium outside seemed far away. Two Initial-Y Series faced each other thirty meters apart. That distance could be covered in an instant by either of them.

AnchoR was a young automaton child wearing a formal dress of red and white. RyuZU, a silver-haired automaton girl wearing a formal dress of black and white.

Behind them, Naoto and Marie watched, and didn't dare move. AnchoR paid them no mind, her eyes focused solely on her elder sister.

"Can you hear me, AnchoR?" RyuZU began with a gentle voice.

There was no reply. However, RyuZU paid it no attention.

"Your voice reached my master. I can understand your humiliation at having your will trampled upon by that odious apparatus on your face, but..." She paused, taking a breath. "I will not destroy you."

AnchoR remained silent. Narrowing her eyes, RyuZU scrutinized her.

"As both your elder sister and a follower of my master, I shall save you. As such, you ought to fight for yourself as well, AnchoR. Listen only to yourself, break free of that fetter."

AnchoR didn't reply. The cube dangling by her chest came off its chain, quietly floating up in front of her.

RyuZU took a step forward in answer to her challenge.

"Subjugating." The word escaped her lips. It wasn't her usual airy singsong voice. RyuZU spoke—announced—in a mechanical, businesslike tone. "Definition Proclamation: the First of the Initial-Y Series, RyuZU YourSlave."

"Definition Proclamation," AnchoR replied in kind. "The Fourth of the Initial-Y Series, AnchoR, The One Who Destroys."

Both of them began to transform. While Naoto and Marie watched on, the two Initial-Y Series charged straight into a territory that the humans could never fathom.

"Inherent ability: 'Dual Time'. Initiating start sequence."

"Inherent ability: 'Power Reservoir'. Initiating transformational sequence."

They both declared their defiance of the natural law. Together, they were saying: right now, from this moment onward, *I shall break the laws of physics.*

Naoto struggled to breathe. RyuZU's hidden power manifested, a function antithetical to the laws of this universe. At the same time, there was the resounding noise of gears meshing into place...

Like dominoes toppling over, RyuZU's black dress changed in a flurry. The naked, pale skin of her arms was laid bare, and her face was adorned with a fluttering veil. A bride with her dainty torso wrapped tightly in a pearl-white wedding dress, her golden eyes flaring to a brilliant, ruby red.

"Commencing shift from first timepiece, 'Real Time,' to second timepiece, 'Imaginary Time.'"

"Enemy threat level: Category Five. Initiating Shift to Twelfth Balance Wheel of Differences."

"No way," Marie gasped.

Did AnchoR say "twelfth" just now? Marie knew nothing about AnchoR's inherent ability. She couldn't grasp it by intuition like Naoto, but she could at least make an educated guess.

When we first encountered her in Mie, she definitely said "third" back then. I'm sure my memory is correct. If it refers to her output of energy, or a limiter of some kind, then the twelfth would be...

As Marie shuddered and AnchoR transformed, the cube floating by her chest twisted and began turning at the speed of light. Her glamorous black hair was stained blood red, and her pure white armor blackened and swelled from the crimson lines snaking over her like a nervous system.

The angelic ring of two half-gears above her head split into the horns of a demon, and a crackling sound came from the black mask that covered the girl's face.

"Chrono Hook. Jumping from normal operation to imaginary operation."

"Chrono Hook. Initiating output of imaginary power by means of the Perpetual Gear. Materializing."

RyuZU and AnchoR simultaneously stepped forward. More than just a mere physical movement, their steps indicated that they had entered states that should be absolutely impossible. As imaginary time spread, sealing the area, infinite heat welled to the despair of the universe.

AnchoR announced dispassionately, "Executing orders. Declaring: I shall destroy the target 'RyuZU' before me."

RyuZU smiled. "Come at me with all that you have, 'AnchoR.' I shall do you a kindness and teach you to respect your older sister."

The sisters called out each other's names as they faced one another. Then RyuZU pinched up the hem of her skirt and curtsied, while AnchoR simply dropped down onto all fours. Like a wedding vow and a cry of despair respectively, they spoke the most heretical, blasphemous words in this world:

"...'Mute Scream'..."

"...'Bloody Murder'..."

The two legendary automata clashed, and what occurred after was beyond anything that Naoto and Marie could grasp.

•••●•••

RyuZU dashed through imaginary time. The moment hung frozen. The domain between zero and a second later belonged to her. It was a fictitious domain that shouldn't exist. A contradictory gap formed by a breakdown in the laws of physics. As long as she was in this state, she was untouchable. Her scythe was absolute...

However, her little sister was also an irrational existence, in mutiny against this universe.

AnchoR's blood-red hair traced an arc through the air as she evaded RyuZU's unobservable attack with a leap into imaginary time. Simultaneously, she stomped and swung her right hand down. Trying to tear both RyuZU and imaginary time itself apart with her enlarged, enormous hand and its sinister claws.

"..."

RyuZU's face showed no surprise. She evaded AnchoR's claws with a composed and elegant maneuver, putting some distance between them. This much was within her expectations; she had already known beforehand that AnchoR was capable of this.

Even if RyuZU could move unfettered by the restraints of time itself, AnchoR could keep up through sheer force. Her infinite heat distorted the universe, wrenching open small holes in space-time.

RyuZU gracefully danced through the frozen world, while AnchoR violently burned through into imaginary time. The two of them defied the natural flow of time with completely different methods.

RyuZU raised her arm.

The first of the Initial-Y Series, RyuZU, YourSlave. Envisioned as a servant, she was armed only with the two scythes extending from under her skirt. Compared to AnchoR, designed for battle with her innumerable armaments, you could even call RyuZU weak. As such, RyuZU called herself the weakest of her own accord. In her own words, she was "the one least suited for combat among her sisters."

However...

"That does not mean...that I will lose."

The black scythes cleaved at AnchoR from both left and right as she charged towards RyuZU. Her swings were not only swift but skillful, the scythes flashed through the air. RyuZU gracefully ripped everything before her to pieces, neither breaking form nor revealing her aberrantly powerful blades for more than an instant.

However, the sharp blades were blocked by something, and metal rang out against metal as they were repelled.

"...?!"

RyuZU shifted her center of mass and, twirling to the side with a light step, dodged AnchoR's barreling charge. She noticed there were ripples in the empty air where her scythes had been. The cube floating above AnchoR's head twisted and changed shape.

"So it was her spatial manipulation...!"

Spatial manipulation: the basic ability of the weapon called AnchoR. She had created small spatial distortions in the path of RyuZU's scythes to shield herself. It was impossible for RyuZU to break through.

"...gh!"

RyuZU swung her scythes again. Expecting another block, she prioritized speed over accuracy—hoping that AnchoR wouldn't be able to react quickly enough from the overwhelming flurry of attacks.

"—!!"

They were all repelled. Ripples appeared, and AnchoR grunted with a distorted voice. Everywhere RyuZU swung, her attacks were neutralized. RyuZU dashed away in uneasy retreat, and AnchoR chased right after.

Although they were nearly equal in speed, RyuZU was slightly faster. The field of imaginary time itself gave her an advantage.

No matter how much AnchoR accelerated, her spatial manipulation ability was restrained by imaginary time. The fact that she was only relying on spatial manipulation for defense, and not tapping into her armory of countless weapons, was proof of that.

In other words, AnchoR would have to take RyuZU down with just her bare hands.

"...gh!"

AnchoR swung her claws. It was a close call, but RyuZU evaded it with a jump to the right. However, as those claws cut through the air, space-time jarred and twisted furiously. The car behind RyuZU was annihilated. Blown into smithereens without a trace.

The heat AnchoR possessed, enough to wrench open gaps in time, was pouring into the claws of her right hand. If even a single claw touched RyuZU, her body would be helplessly disintegrated.

AnchoR defeating RyuZU with just her bare hands? It was a

very real possibility for "The One Who Destroys." Not being able to use her weapons didn't even count as a handicap for AnchoR.

To begin with, RyuZU's attacks couldn't penetrate her defense. Even if RyuZU could use her speed to prolong the battle, eventually her spring would unwind and she would shut down. That, or she would be caught and smashed to pieces.

That was the conclusion. The near future that would soon arrive. The end to this duel.

However...

"Just as expected, or rather, *just as planned*," RyuZU muttered as she evaded the claws tearing through space-time around her.

There was no fear in her eyes. This was what she already knew would come to pass.

Three days ago, at the strategy meeting, Naoto and RyuZU had spoken about it.

"If I were to battle AnchoR head on, our chance of victory would be zero," RyuZU asserted.

"You don't necessarily have to win, you know?" Naoto replied with a troubled expression. "If you could just destroy that mask—"

"It is the same thing, Master Naoto. The differences of combat ability are simply insurmountable."

"Even if you use your inherent ability?"

"Yes. Even if I were to access imaginary time, AnchoR would be able to follow me into it through sheer force. She has an infinite reservoir of heat energy that makes it possible."

Naoto nodded. "In that case, there's only one answer."

"What would that be?"

"It's simple," Naoto said. "Just make me into your shield."

"That is out of the question." RyuZU glared at him, immediately cutting down his proposal. "It's not even worth considering. Do you truly understand what you are suggesting?"

"There's no other way, is there?"

"There is. We can just avoid an engagement with her altogether," RyuZU said, her gaze below freezing. "I shall be blunt. Compared to exposing Master Naoto to danger, AnchoR being enslaved is a trivial matter.

"Even if Tokyo collapses, and several hundred million members of the esteemed human race fall to the bottom of the planet because of it, I do not care..."

It was the one line that RyuZU would absolutely not cross.

"...gh"

RyuZU kicked off the ground, flying into the air. Hooking on to a pipe with her scythes, she used it as leverage to swing her body upwards. With that maneuver, she narrowly escaped AnchoR's claws yet again.

Glancing behind, RyuZU saw her little sister rushing towards her without a single moment's pause. With all the heat she had stored up, AnchoR was distorting space-time around her just by existing. An ominous shimmer enveloped the child's body, as if she were on fire.

RyuZU twisted and kicked off against the ceiling. She launched herself and, using her scythes and feet, remained elegantly airborne by vaulting through the sealed space of imaginary time.

She tried to slip past AnchoR with a maneuver resembling the trajectory of a pinball, but AnchoR didn't move. The shape of her cube changed in non-Euclidean geometry.

"...?!"

A large spatial distortion unfolded towards RyuZU. One of her scythes was caught up in it and crumpled like scrap paper. The force caused RyuZU's body to jolt off course. She lost her balance, thrown by the shockwave.

Just before she hit the wall, RyuZU cut off her broken scythe with the remaining one. If it couldn't fulfill its purpose, it was nothing but a burden. Regaining her freedom of movement, RyuZU landed perpendicular to the wall and immediately reversed her trajectory, rebounding with a leap.

The wall she had kicked off of disintegrated in a blast.

She recalled...

"Even if I were to agree to such a ridiculous plan, pardon my bluntness Master Naoto, nothing would be resolved by someone as measly as you laying down your life. A human body would not even serve as an anthill before AnchoR's power." RyuZU looked down and asked in a weak voice: "Master Naoto, do you think that it is fine for you to die?"

"Hm? Why do you say that?" Naoto replied, laughing jauntily. "You've got it all wrong, RyuZU. I'll risk my life, but I haven't the slightest intention of dying. Nor do I have any intention of sacrificing you. And of course, I won't be giving up on AnchoR-chan, either."

Casting her golden eyes downward, RyuZU sighed. She shook her head.

"That is an impossible luxury. Frankly, it would be a mad endeavor."

"Well, that might be true. But for some reason, I don't get the feeling that we're going to fail." Naoto winked one ashen eye. "I'm not gonna die, and AnchoR-chan's not gonna kill me, either. I believe that you'll be able to pull it off for us, RyuZU. Besides..."

She had lost one of her weapons.

That meant her options had become significantly more limited. The number of times she could attack in a set amount of time, her methods of evasion, and the maximum permissible damage she could bear... her very chances of survival had been reduced.

Even so. "There is no problem." RyuZU turned her timepiece, her crimson eyes burning.

Quickly. Swiftly. Rapidly. And more deftly!

She would master herself. She would command time and space. She would maintain the initiative and control the battlefield. RyuZU understood she was capable of this, that she could win if she just saw it through.

She had lost one of her weapons in large-scale spatial interference but had gained some distance between herself and AnchoR. The space between them was paltry. AnchoR could cover it in less than a second, even in imaginary time, but even so, it was an opportunity.

Keeping her eyes on AnchoR, RyuZU leapt over her. AnchoR turned around and gave chase.

There was no point in considering their difference in abilities and strength. Her own master had said that she could do it. Naoto believed in her abilities, so RyuZU would believe in them, too. More than anyone, RyuZU believed in her own little sister.

Her master had said: "After all, AnchoR-chan can't kill humans, right?"

RyuZU didn't refute those words. She simply asked, her expression unchanging: "You do realize that she is being controlled right now?"

"But she's desperately resisting." Naoto asserted, looking into RyuZU's eyes. "She didn't attack either me or Marie in Mie. She only targeted you and old man Halter the whole time."

"It could simply be that she had chosen her targets by their threat level."

"That could be true," Naoto admitted, but he immediately shook his head. "I don't think that's the case. I'm sure of it. I'm okay with risking my life to save her and prove that I'm right.

"Besides," he continued. "That child asked her dear older sister to save her."

"……"

"AnchoR-chan can't kill humans. So, if you use me as a shield and create an opening that way, you'd be able to break her mask, right?"

RyuZU didn't answer. Thinking about things logically, she couldn't accept Naoto's plan. It was too risky. But neither could she bring herself to lie and say that it was impossible, so she remained silent.

Naoto smiled gently as if he knew what she was thinking.

"Yeah, in that case: this is an order, RyuZU. Make me a shield and save your little sister."

Hesitating would be pointless.

She determined the proper timing by eyeballing the distance between herself and Naoto, and then the distance to AnchoR. AnchoR looked like a small meteor—charging towards RyuZU, distorting space-time around her.

"AnchoR," RyuZU said. "I believe in you."

She couldn't see AnchoR's face through the mask, but she was closing in—her body an avatar of destruction.

RyuZU finished her calculations. She could picture the maneuver in her mind. She smiled gently and lowered her speed slightly. Through that alone, she entered AnchoR's attack range. AnchoR raised the massive claw of her right hand. A crushing blow came straight at RyuZU.

She jumped straight up. She couldn't evade the attack like this. Considering the time and the distance between them, AnchoR's strike would smash her body into pieces in midair.

However, that was only *if* AnchoR accelerated.

The instant RyuZU jumped and AnchoR saw who was before her, she flinched. AnchoR abruptly decelerated. Like the core of an exhausted nuclear reactor, she lost the massive amount of heat that allowed her to warp space-time.

In other words, she entered a completely frozen state inside imaginary time.

RyuZU smiled bewitchingly.

"You did well."

She dispatched her scythe. Its single black edge turned in countless flashes as it brushed past AnchoR's mask, again and again. She halted the mask's gears, severed its wires, and dismantled it down to its very last screw.

She brushed aside the massive claws that had been hovering over *Marie's* head, and whispered.

"Rest for a little while. Master Naoto will repair you right away."

RyuZU returned to normal time, and AnchoR's was blown back by the crushing force of the explosion.

• • ● ⬤ ● • •

Naoto and Marie couldn't tell what happened in imaginary time.

The only things they could perceive were a thunderous roar, a burst of wind, a shockwave, and some marks of the battle left behind.

Additionally, it appeared that RyuZU was falling asleep and AnchoR had been blown backwards.

It happened instantly. All at once.

"—?! AnchoR-chan!!" Naoto cried, seeing the young automaton girl slam forcefully against the wall.

He rushed to her side and held her up. She wasn't moving at all.

AnchoR's condition was, frankly, awful to behold. She had returned to her original appearance—an angel instead of a devil. It was clear even at a glance that she had taken massive damage. It looked like a truck had hit her, or she had fallen under a gigantic hammer.

In reality, the explosion had come from herself. Feedback caused by abruptly halting her energy output. Like forcefully stopping an engine that was accelerating out of control. With no means of release, enough energy to wrench open pockets of imaginary time turned against AnchoR herself.

"Ah... h-her inner parts are still moving at least... thank goodness," Naoto sighed in relief.

Sounding out AnchoR's condition by listening to her, he knew her inner mechanisms were still functioning.

Marie nodded. "In that case, wind RyuZU's spring. While you take care of that, I'll see to AnchoR's emergency repairs."

"R-right. I'm counting on you, Marie...!"

Marie took on the task of repairing AnchoR until RyuZU rebooted. But even if her spirit was willing, there still wasn't much she could do. Marie simply did a quick inspection of AnchoR's whole body and disengaged any mechanisms that were burdening her. Truly fixing her up would require a workshop full of equipment, and Naoto's ears.

Finishing AnchoR's first aid, Marie sighed.

"Really... to think that this worked! I couldn't believe it when RyuZU agreed to using you as her shield, but..."

There's no way that RyuZU would expose Naoto to danger, she had thought. And indeed, that should have been the case.

While a normal automaton wouldn't be able to defy its master's orders, that didn't apply to RyuZU. If she deemed it necessary, she could ignore Naoto's orders. Even so, it had happened.

"That is because I believe wholeheartedly in Master Naoto," a cool voice said from behind. Marie turned around to see RyuZU standing there, her spring rewound. "Master Naoto, who exceeds so much of mankind, said that he believes in me. I have a duty to repay his faith. Similarly, if Master Naoto says that he believes in AnchoR, then I must believe in her as well."

And, judging by the results, Naoto's plan was a great success. AnchoR was in terrible condition, but she could be repaired. They had overcome a battle that they absolutely shouldn't have been able to win. They'd accomplished their goal. It was more than enough of an achievement.

Naoto had believed in RyuZU and AnchoR, and RyuZU had believed in Naoto's belief in her. RyuZU and AnchoR had risked their lives to answer his faith. Marie genuinely thought it was beautiful.

"Yes... you two have a wonderful relationship, don't you? Really, I see both of you in a whole new light."

"I suppose I am thankful to you for accompanying us, Mistress Marie. While it goes without saying that I believe in Master Naoto, a pragmatic concern still daunted me, so it was necessary for me to procure some insurance."

"Hm...? Aren't you putting that rather strangely?"

Clueless that she had been just a few centimeters away from death in imaginary time, Marie tilted her head.

"Oh...?" Naoto said in a small voice, having taken off his headphones.

"What's wrong? Did you hear something?"

"Well, I just heard a tremendous sound from below. It...

appears that the fight between Tokyo and Mie is over as well. The enormous weapon has stopped making any sound."

"Well, that's good news. Looks like it was worth raising hell," Marie said, standing up. "Now then, how about a change in scenery? Let's get AnchoR to a workshop and fix her up."

• • ● ● ● • •

I feel really sleepy...

The girl had been walking inside a sweet, white fog. Or swimming, perhaps. She might have even been flying. Everything felt ambiguous, fluid, haphazard, vague... but even so, there was no mistaking the glittering light floating in front of her eyes. The warmth she felt inside her heart.

I wonder what this feeling is.

I've felt something like this before, sometime, somewhere...

She quickly came up with the answer. *It was simple...*

Ah, it was when I was born.

I felt like this when I was born. In that very warm, pure white room full of wonders.

There were people there, I remember they would tell me stories.

But... it's strange.

I can't remember the details of our conversation at all...

The stories they told me, they should have been fun. Why can't I remember...?

She became immensely sad, and even felt like crying. But she heard a voice that sounded familiar...

"I'm telling you, that's just how it is."

"Don't mess with me!! First an imaginary mechanism and now a perpetual one?! How am I supposed to fix that? Are they picking a fight with the universe?!"

"Ugh... I'm saying that you don't *have* to fix that! There's a zero-friction escapement inside her, right? It's fine if you only fix up the gears that are meshed against it."

"How can gears mesh against something with zero friction? Can you describe that in words that a human could understand?!"

Their voices sounded familiar, yet they were foreign to her. Still, the girl felt happier, and her head grew warm. Something locked into place inside her. A dense lump of energy, small enough to be scooped up by a spoon and eaten, oozed from the depths of her heart.

"Argh! Fine, I'll fix her then! Lend me your screwdrivers!"

"Hah?! Wh-what's up with your hands? They're shaking! The way you're holding that screwdriver is crazy. Hey, do you want to break her or something?!"

"I'm only doing this because you're taking so long, you know?!"

"That's not... y-you... fine! Give me some proper instructions on what to tamper with and how, since I'm going to be doing exactly as you say."

"I've been telling you that there are three gears to the right of the 40,325,831th resonance-linked circuit, haven't I?!"

"Where are you counting from to get that kind of number?! If you don't cut it out I'm really going to hang you!!"

Really, how nostalgic...

The energy seeping out of AnchoR's heart diffused through her whole body, bit by bit. Things that had felt vague and murky, began to take on form. The first thing she recalled was her own name. Indeed, she would recall this if nothing else. It was the name she had received while everyone was celebrating her birth.

It was a precious name, a vow.

"What's up with this cryptic incomprehensible unidentifiable mechanism, in the first place?!"

"Allow me to explain it in a way that Mistress Marie's regrettable brain can understand."

AnchoR batted her eyes.

I know that voice. There's no mistaking it. It's the voice of someone I truly love. My older sister!

"AnchoR's inherent ability is Perpetual Gear. In other words, she uses the energy from her self-winding spring as a driving force without expending it. All of that energy is converted into heat and stored inside this cube.

"So, her spatial manipulation and storage, as well as summoning armaments... they're all just expressions of her ability to create and utilize infinite heat.

"The function of her body is simply to operate perpetually. Do you understand now?"

"How can I understand that?! Would you be so kind as to explain the principle behind it?!"

"Master Naoto... Mistress Marie's feeblemindedness has exceeded my expectations. Please, if you could try..."

"So it's basically this: it exists."

"Like I'd accept an explanation like *that*!!"

"He he," AnchoR giggled.

The fog inside her mind cleared like thick stage curtains lifted at the beginning of a play. She became aware that she was no longer dreaming.

Still, I remember...

Even if it was a dream, my heart clearly remembers! It was just like this when I was born...

AnchoR opened her eyes. Three faces greeted her. One of them AnchoR knew well. It was a face that had always been smiling, but that now reflected concern. AnchoR's eldest sister, RyuZU.

And as for the other two...

"Good morning, AnchoR-chan. Do you feel all right?"

"She should feel fine. Probably. Most likely."

"That's rather timid for a self-proclaimed genius, don't you think? Well, I suppose the way you admitted that AnchoR's mechanisms were beyond you is commendable at least."

She didn't recognize them, but the feeling they gave her was the same as a very important memory. AnchoR opened her mouth, but hesitated.

She didn't know how to address them.

Ahh.

Immediately, she came up with the answer. She knew the two most perfect, wonderful words.

"Father, Mother, Older Sister. Good morning."

Why...are they looking at me like that?

For some reason, the very moment she uttered those words, the three of them stiffened.

•••●•••

The safe house that Konrad and the other Meisters had prepared near Akihabara boasted a comprehensive set of clocksmithing equipment. After bringing AnchoR there, it took Naoto and Marie about three hours to repair her.

AnchoR successfully rebooted, but... on hearing her first words, Naoto, Marie, and RyuZU cringed.

"Oh, AnchoR... so the repairs failed after all," RyuZU lamented. "That is why I warned you not to let Mistress Marie touch her, Master Naoto! And yet..."

"Hey you shut up over there!!" Marie shouted. "Do you have any idea how I feel right now?! I was just implicitly called this pervert's wife, you know?! I've never been so humiliated in all my life!"

Naoto crouched until his eyes were level with AnchoR's.

"AnchoR-chan, can I have a word? Listen caaaaaarefully, okay sweetie? My tastes aren't thaaat bad. It's already been settled that RyuZU is my wife. So my tastes are good, right?"

AnchoR tilted her head with a blank expression. "I can't call you 'Father'?"

Naoto grinned widely and shook his head. "Listen, AnchoR-chan. That's fine. Completely fine. To be honest, I got chills hearing you call me 'Father'!"

"Wow," Marie groaned in disgust, her face twisted as if looking at a louse she'd crushed underfoot.

Naoto paid her no mind. "But, you see, if you call that girl over there 'Mother'... it implies the unthinkable: that we're married. My wife is RyuZU. Living out my life with that walking animal-protein landmine over there would be a nightmare. It hurts me a little that you would think that, AnchoR-chan. Do you understand how I feel?"

"Hey, it's *me* that would be stuck in a nightmare! Even if I were to play around in the future, I do have standards, you know?"

"......?" AnchoR tried to find the error in what she had said. Shaking her head, she rushed over to Marie and hugged her tight.

"Huh?!" Naoto cried out. "That ain't fair, Marie! I'm so jealous, let me take your place this instant!"

"Shut up! Don't come near me, you pervert!" Marie cursed, knitting her brows.

Freed from her mask, AnchoR's face was the very picture of an innocent little girl.

There's no problem with her movement as far as I can tell, Marie thought. *Her facial expressions probably only seem limited because of the personality she was programmed with. That also has to be why her diction seems lacking, compared to her mental faculties.*

But it's strange how emotionally attached she's become to me and Naoto, despite not having completed her Master Confirmation. It'd be weird enough for an automaton to even have the concept of parents, let alone for the imprinting process to cast her in the role of a child. What kind of a joke is this?

"What's the meaning of this?" Marie asked RyuZU. "Does she have a circuit that recognizes the people who repaired her as her parents? It'd be a different story for a cheap automaton, but for an Initial-Y Series to have such a crude Master Confirmation? Seriously?"

RyuZU frowned. "No, this has nothing to do with her Master Confirmation. It appears that she is confusing her memories. Do you understand, AnchoR? Calling Master Naoto your father is enough. That thing over there is not important."

"Hey, watch it."

"She is one of the tools that Master Naoto used to repair you," RyuZU emphasized, ignoring Marie's protests. "You understand, right?"

AnchoR tilted her head and continued to cling to Marie. "Can't I...?"

"...gh! You can! If you want to call her that, we don't mind at all, AnchoR-chan! Yeah! Let's do that much, all right? What do ya say, Mom?!" Naoto tried to bring AnchoR and Marie into a group hug.

"Gyahhhhhhhh?! Don't say such nasty things, you pervert!"

"Whah?!"

Naoto dropped. Marie had brought her leg all the way back and punted him.

"Master Naoto," RyuZU addressed Naoto as he writhed on the floor. "I advise you not to spoil AnchoR too much. Be strict with her when appropriate, all right?"

"This is weird! Can't she be fixed somehow?!" Marie cried out in exasperation. She grabbed AnchoR's shoulders and tried to pry the girl off of her. AnchoR looked up at her.

"Mother...?"

"I'm telling you that I'm not your Mo..." Marie faltered.

"......"

She looked down at the innocent little girl gazing up at her. There wasn't a clear expression on her face, but...

"......"

Ugh, she's so cute.

Wait, Marie, don't let that distract you! Get it together. She shook her head, flustered, and refocused. *I'll be no better than that pervert if I accept this. What right would I have to live then? I can't let such a farce be exposed.*

"In any case, let's do her Master Confirmation first. It just might cure her of this bizarre imprinting," Marie said promptly.

If the confirmation process overwrites her current state, then great. Even if that doesn't happen, we might be able to stop her calling me 'mother' if Naoto orders it as her master.

"I suppose. We cannot postpone it indefinitely." RyuZU nodded, and turned to face the girl still clinging to Marie. "AnchoR?"

"What, big sister?"

"Allow me to confirm: No one is currently registered as your master, yes?"

"Yeah," AnchoR nodded.

"Good girl. Well then, AnchoR, I have a proposal for you."

RyuZU absently lifted Naoto up by his collar, strangling him. Paying no mind to his choking, RyuZU thrust him before AnchoR.

"Allow me to introduce him. This is Master Naoto Miura. He is my current master. Do you have any interest in registering this person as your master?"

AnchoR cocked her head to the side, her expression blank.

"Does Father want to be my master?" she asked, peering into Naoto's pained face.

"Oh? Ooh, yeah! Yes, yes, I super want to be your master!" Naoto raised both hands into the air in an excited appeal for his candidacy.

"Okay, I understand." AnchoR nodded, and left Marie's side.

All sense of will disappeared from AnchoR's eyes. She was rather expressionless to begin with, but even so the change was clearly palpable. Her red eyes lost their radiance, becoming like dark glass beads. She looked at Naoto.

Shocked, Naoto choked on the air.

Without showing any reaction, AnchoR opened her mouth.

"Verifying qualifications for Master Confirmation. Question: Who am I?" she asked in a completely bland, mechanical voice.

Naoto and Marie looked at RyuZU. Acknowledging their glances, RyuZU nodded.

"This is AnchoR's formal Master Confirmation process. If you give the correct answer, you will be formally acknowledged as her master. Although... no one has managed it yet."

"Do you know the answer, RyuZU?" Marie asked.

"Yes, I do." RyuZU nodded, her expression unchanging. "But it would mean nothing if Master Naoto receives the answer from me. To borrow from what you said earlier, her Master Confirmation is not so 'crude' as to permit cheating."

"......"

"Furthermore, although this should be obvious, there are no retries. Everyone, regardless of who they are, only has the right to try once. If they answer incorrectly, even if they give the correct answer afterwards, it would be useless. The process cannot be initiated again for them."

"I see." Marie nodded. "That's why they used that mask, eh?"

She'd wondered why they'd gone to such lengths to fool AnchoR's Master Confirmation, instead of just registering her. Now she knew.

"They couldn't successfully complete her Master Confirmation. Well, given your precedent, RyuZU, it's questionable whether AnchoR would have obeyed their orders unconditionally, even if they were able to register as her master. The same holds true for Naoto, but..." *It's not like we can just leave her.* Marie turned to Naoto. "We can't afford to get this wrong, Naoto. Let's think about this carefully before we—"

"AnchoR-chan is a cute girl, right?" Naoto answered promptly before Marie could warn him, looking straight into AnchoR's eyes. "That's just common sense."

"Would you listen to what I'm saying?!" Marie cried in exasperation.

"What are you going on about?" Naoto snorted. "This isn't a trick question. AnchoR-chan is a pretty little loli-girl. What else is there to it? Ah, maybe the little sister vibe?"

This guy's hopeless. If I don't do something about him soon... Marie looked up at the ceiling. *The stakes couldn't be higher and the dumbass decides to think with his dick...*

"No... calm down, Marie. Only Naoto failed. I haven't answered, so there should still be a chance," Marie mumbled, holding her head in her hands.

Marie was still agonizing over what she should do when...

"...Confirmed."

With those dispassionate words, the light returned to AnchoR's eyes.

"Hah?" Marie gaped.

"Hell yeah!" Naoto pumped his fist.

Next to him, RyuZU nodded contentedly. "I am relieved that you arrived at the right answer without issue. As expected, Master Naoto. So quickly too, well done."

"Wait, what?! What do you mean that's the right answer?!"

"It is just as you saw yourself. Master Naoto's answer was precisely the programmed password for AnchoR's Master Confirmation. That is all there is to it."

Marie waved one hand dismissively, covering her forehead with the other.

"Shouldn't the answer to such a question be something like... the concept behind her design? Or a message 'Y' left behind?!"

How can the answer to a question... that nobody could answer for countless years... be the filth that this pervert vomited out on an impulse?

"My, is that all a mediocre pseudo-intellectual like you can come up with?" RyuZU sneered. "The truth tends to be simple. Occam's Razor. Only the wise understand that."

"Even so, for the answer to be 'a girl'?"

"AnchoR is the only one among us who was clearly designed as a weapon. Infinite violence that operates perpetually. That is her concept, but do you seriously think that curs who give such an answer should become her master?"

"That's..." Marie faltered.

"If I may be so bold," RyuZU continued with a smile. "In defining AnchoR as a girl, Master Naoto did, in fact, pick up on 'Y''s message. If you are to attain infinite force, you must not have the intention of using it."

She paused for a breath.

"An anchor can hold back a warship. If you see why 'Y' gave her this name, then the answer to the confirmation question is not so unreasonable, no?"

Marie was lost for words. Looking back towards Naoto, she asked somewhat suspiciously: "Did you give that answer after thinking so far ahead, Naoto?"

"Eh? No, not really?" Naoto answered blankly.

I figured as much.

Marie glared at him with half-closed eyes, and Naoto held up his hands in surrender.

"As you can see, AnchoR-chan is a frighteningly aesthetic, extremely sensual, agonizingly adorable automaton, right? So what if she has some rather showy armaments? She's no different from RyuZU in that respect, no?" Naoto babbled on, in his element.

"How brave of you to cheat on me with my little sister, Master Naoto," a cold voice said from behind him.

"Huh? Ah, no, that's not it! Of course you're my one and only wife, RyuZU, but! This and that aren't related... right? I meant what I said as a father!"

The radiance disappeared from RyuZU's eyes. "To lust after your own daughter... I see that you are in the terminal stage of your disease..."

"Ah, is that jealousy I sense? Miss RyuZU is seriously cute..." said Naoto, floored.

Then AnchoR, who had remained silent until now, spoke.

"Your orders, please."

"......?" Naoto got up abruptly, looking perplexed.

"Your orders, please," AnchoR repeated.

"AnchoR-chan?"

"Yes, I am the Fourth of the Initial-Y Series. AnchoR, The One Who Destroys. I recognize you as my master, Naoto Miura. Your orders, please."

Although not quite at the point of sounding like an automated reply system, her voice still sounded dry. Like a machine. Her expressionless face and voice were the same, but she didn't seem like a little girl anymore.

Naoto turned around in a fluster. "RyuZU! AnchoR-chan seems strange! Could she be bugging out?!"

"So that answer was wrong after all," Marie muttered.

"Hahh, are you kidding me?! How else could that question be answered?!"

"No, AnchoR is operating normally, Master Naoto,"

Naoto turned around. "What's the matter with her then?"

"The answer is simple. AnchoR is denied free will once her Master Confirmation is complete."

"……"

Naoto's expression fell away. He turned to face RyuZU. "What? Why…"

"As I stated earlier, AnchoR was the only one of us designed to be a weapon. If she had a will other than her master's, she could not be considered a weapon. As such, she is programmed to cease self-determination once she acquires a master."

"Didn't you just say that her confirmation question is designed so that her master won't be someone who intends to use her for violence? What's up with that then?!"

"AnchoR was designed to trust all of that to her master," RyuZU replied dispassionately.

"Wait up," Marie cut in. "In that case, what status was she in before her Master Confirmation?

"When she is without a master, she possesses enough free will to find a suitable master who can manage her overwhelming strength. She has a significant restriction put in place during that time period."

"Which is?"

"She must not harm humans. That is all."

"I…see," Marie nodded.

When AnchoR doesn't have a master, her safety is her own free will. Once she finds a suitable master, she functions purely as a weapon.

That is how she was programmed.

"Well... considering common sense can't be applied to an automaton with free will to begin with, I guess you could say her system is well thought out..."

"Well thought out? Are you freaking kidding me?! Just what part of such a system is well thought out?! I didn't save AnchoR-chan because I wanted a weapon! RyuZU, why didn't you tell me about this?!"

"Master Naoto," RyuZU replied meekly, eyes downcast. "I had expected that you would become angry. However, surely you have not forgotten, have you? AnchoR and I are automata."

"......"

"I understand that you treasure us, for your own reasons, but we are not human. We possess inherent abilities in line with our designs and are charged with an eternal duty. Acquiring a master and putting our abilities to good use are how we derive meaning in our lives."

"But, in that case, RyuZU...!"

"I was born as YourSlave. It is only natural that the way to use me would be different from AnchoR, who was born as The One Who Destroys."

Naoto nearly shouted something... but changed his mind. He bit his lip, as if enduring it, and lowered his gaze.

"Even so," he muttered. "How am I supposed to accept this?"

"I trust you to *treat AnchoR kindly*, Master Naoto."

"......"

Naoto didn't reply. He looked downward and clenched his fists.

"Naoto…?" Marie asked timidly, seeing how crestfallen he was.

"…I don't like this."

"Huh?"

Naoto raised his head. Frowning, he glared at RyuZU, Marie, and AnchoR in turn.

"I don't like this one bit. This isn't what I wanted. A girl happens to be an automaton, so she doesn't need her own free will? That really pisses me off! In the first place, if I'm her master and my orders are absolute, then she should obey my orders goddamnit!"

"As she is right now, she will obey your will a hundred percent, Master Naoto," RyuZU replied promptly.

"That's not what I mean! It is, but it isn't! Argh! In any case, I won't be AnchoR-chan's father like this."

"Calm down a little," Marie said, amazed as his behavior. "You're all over the place, you know?"

"Shut it, stuuupid." Naoto turned to face AnchoR again. He stared right into her red eyes. "AnchoR-chan."

"Yes. Your orders, please," the weapon replied dispassionately.

"What do you want to do?"

The weapon froze, then answered.

"Error. The content of the order is unclear. Requesting further details."

"Tell me what you would like to do, AnchoR-chan."

"Yes. I would like to serve adequately as AnchoR, The One Who Destroys," the weapon answered clearly.

"Master Naoto," RyuZU said gently. "I know I am repeating myself, but AnchoR no longer has her own will."

"She does," Naoto asserted curtly.

"What makes you think that?" RyuZU asked softly.

"If AnchoR-chan didn't have her own will, she would have killed me. When that mask was manipulating her: she resisted."

The strange noise that he'd heard from AnchoR when she was being controlled hadn't simply been her operating sound...

It was the proof that AnchoR had her own will.

Naoto remembered that voice well. That cry of lament.

That was how he knew.

"That is your 'mission' now, right, AnchoR-chan?" Naoto asked, staring at the girl in front of him.

"Yes."

"Aside from that, what do you like? What do you want to do?"

"Yes. Confirming: Is that a request for a disclosure of information regarding AnchoR's own will?"

"Right! What does AnchoR-chan wish for?"

"Yes. Answering: Currently, this automaton's free will has been locked."

"Okay, then let's give you an order. Remove that lock, okay?"

The weapon took a while to respond. "Yes... Confirming: is that an order for me to act according to my own will?"

"I am entrusting you to your own will, AnchoR-chan."

"Yes. Is that an order to remove all my limiters?"

"Well, I think so?"

"Should I understand you are giving permission to voice my own opinion, disengaging my emotional suppression circuit and unlocking my routine sequence of self-determination?"

"Yeah yeah! That's exactly right! I authorize that, all of it!!"

"……"

"Do you understand? You can do whatever you want. With your own will, AnchoR-chan!"

Naoto heard countless gears rearranging themselves within AnchoR. That was the signal that her rules were changing. The sound of shattering the fate that had been forced on her. Before Naoto's eyes, AnchoR trembled. A voice escaped from her quivering lips.

"Anything I want?"

"Of course," Naoto said immediately.

"...Really?"

"Without a doubt," Naoto asserted.

AnchoR's eyes fluttered. She seemed flustered and afraid, troubled over whether she should really voice her desire. Her face was largely expressionless. Only the wavering of her eyes and voice expressed her anxiety.

"I want... permission..."

"Hm?"

"I want... permission to cry."

"That's..." Marie doubted her ears.

Permission to cry? What's going on here?

Naoto nodded immediately.

"You can cry," he said, stroking her head.

AnchoR's face crumpled right up. Large teardrops formed at the corners of her red eyes and began to fall.

"I want... more permissions."

"Yeah?"

"Can I...touch you?"

"Sure." Naoto nodded.

AnchoR took a step closer and felt his chest gingerly.

"Can I apologize...?"

"You don't have anything to apologize for, but yeah, if you want."

AnchoR buried her face in Naoto's chest and sobbed.

"I'm sorry," she repeated over and over again. Her voice was soft at first, but before long it was a reverberant wail.

"Hey RyuZU," Marie whispered.

"What is it, Mistress Marie?"

"I'm going to ask, just to be sure: was this part of your calculations?" Marie peered suspiciously into RyuZU's eyes.

Although Marie's gaze was like that of an inquisitor, RyuZU smiled gently.

"I said so just a little while back, did I not? That I trust that Master Naoto will *treat AnchoR kindly*."

Marie sighed and grandly dropped her shoulders. Crossing her arms, she stared at RyuZU. "You've got a nasty personality."

RyuZU didn't argue.

"Yes, I imagine that it would appear that way to someone with a regrettable brain like yourself, Mistress Marie. But," RyuZU continued with a sunny smile. "I am YourSlave. It would not be appropriate for me to say too much or take the lead. I simply *believed* that Master Naoto would arrive at the truth without the help of a mere servant like myself."

That was the truth. Seeing Naoto meet her expectations, RyuZU smiled with pride.

Seemingly convinced, Marie sighed. "Could I ask one more question?"

"What is it?"

"I've been wondering: on what grounds did you determine Naoto worthy of being your master?"

RyuZU raised her eyebrows. "Dear me, I thought I had already informed you plenty of times, but... no, excuse me. I should not expect anything from your memory, which is as deficient as your breasts, but..."

"......."

Marie silently fumed, and RyuZU continued.

"It is because Master Naoto is the most outstanding individual in the pathetic, even pitiful thing known as humanity." She paused for a breath, then smiled. "Because he made me believe that where he is going, I should follow."

"Is it... okay... if I don't break anything anymore?" AnchoR asked, her words broken apart by sobs. "Is it okay... if I don't kill anyone anymore?"

"Yeah. There's no need for any of that." Naoto nodded, and held her tightly.

The cube dangling around AnchoR's neck twisted and let out a groan. A single giant ripple swept through the room. It was a hole that led to an "armory" that didn't exist anywhere in this universe. As before when AnchoR had pulled out her armaments, something was slowly revealed... and tumbled to the workshop floor.

Clockwork Planet

• Interlude / 04 : 30 / Outbreaker

"A...CYBORG?"

It took Marie a while before she realized that she was looking at a man. It wasn't that his mechanical body deceived her. It was simply that the object in front of her didn't look human anymore.

He was missing parts all over the place. Limbs had been torn off, and there was a large hole where his abdomen should be. By Marie's estimate, nearly half of the man was completely gone. The only things that still retained their original shape were his head, his torso, and his right arm.

Naoto's eyes widened, and his jaw dropped. He still had AnchoR in his arms. "What's up with this old man? He seems like he's gonna die any second now. Actually, how is he even alive?"

"A sixth generation artificial body would probably be able to endure this much damage, but..."

Marie squatted down next to the cyborg lying on the floor. She removed the parts that had been crushed and inspected the surviving mechanisms.

"Hmm... judging by the characteristic Royal Oak, I think his body was made by the Audemars, but... it doesn't seem like he's the sort of commercial model that you'd find on the market. His body was probably made to order using trade secrets."

"Ah, like old man Halter?"

"I guess, yeah. Halter's a Breguet eighth generation model though. Seeing just how tattered this guy is, I imagine he fought with AnchoR while she was still wearing the mask..."

Marie cast a sidelong glance at the girl in a red and white dress, still clinging to Naoto.

I don't think she's in the kind of state where we can get information out of her yet. Still, judging from the circumstances...

"He...was probably disassembled through spatial manipulation and has been stored inside of AnchoR's cube until now."

Marie began to offhandedly repair him through muscle memory as she gathered her thoughts. *Omit all extraneous functions and connect the surviving gears with a basic interface to his brain, which is asleep right now.*

"Can you really fix him?" Naoto asked, watching Marie's hands flow like water. "He's pretty beat up."

"Just from the neck up. What I'm doing couldn't even be called first aid. Well, he should be able to talk at least." Marie increased the rotational speed of the gear connected to the man's brain.

His artificial body jumped up, spasming.

"Gheeh—Kah."

The man woke up, and his eyes opened. His creaking voice

wasn't due to suffering, but damage to his artificial vocal cords. The spasms of his body quickly stopped as everything from the neck up began to operate smoothly.

Marie waited for about ten seconds for the man to compose himself.

"Hi, are you awake now?"

"...gh... ah... What's this about..." The cyborg grimaced, seemingly nauseous.

Marie extended her hand and snapped her fingers twice before his eyes. "Can you hear me? Who are you? Try stating your name and affiliation."

"..."

The man didn't reply, but turned his neck slightly to see Marie with his artificial eyes. They widened in slight surprise. "...Marie Bell Breguet?"

"You're awake I see," Marie nodded.

"Hah, so that means that this place is hell, right?"

"Neither you nor I have died. This is reality."

"So, like I said, hell." The man flashed a cynical smile. "I'm Vermouth. Nice to meet you, princess."

"Is that your real name?" Marie asked with a suspicious gaze. "Or your code name?"

"My code name, of course. Forgive me, but wouldn't a real name be too luxurious for scum like me, after everything?"

"So you're a spy I see. Do you belong to the Audemars?"

"Good question, do I?" Vermouth played dumb, continuing: "Well, I've probably been fired for a while now, so there's no point in hiding my affiliation. But hey, even scum have their pride, so I'll beg your pardon."

"Fine... I suppose. It's not a big deal anyway."

"Can I ask a question? Where is this, and what's today's date?"

"This is Akihabara Grid in Japan. It's February eighth, just before daybreak."

Vermouth frowned, taken aback. "Hmm... February eighth, in Tokyo? I can't figure out how I'm still alive... but in the end, I guess everything worked out."

Marie tilted her head. "What...do you mean?"

"You're here because you received a transmission addressed to a ghost, no?"

Marie's face twisted into that of a raging horned demoness. "Ahhhh! In other words, it was you, yeah? The audacious dummy who sent that shitty prank message to the great Marie Bell Breguet."

"Precisely. To chase me all the way to hell for a provocation like that. As expected of the mad princess of the Breguets. You're just as the rumors say. Man, I'm relieved to see you did a better job than expected."

"Ah ha ha. You've got guts. I assume that you're prepared for what happens now?"

"Of course. But man, just how frustrated are you? My age is catching up to me, you know? If you want me to give it to you then, for starters, try shaking your cute little ass and begging for it."

"........"

Marie sprang to her feet. With a pure and innocent, even angelic, smile on her face, she raised one foot...and stomped down forcefully.

"Oy, mongrel," she said, digging the heel of her shoe into Vermouth's face. "Talk down to me and I'll decapitate you and flush you down a toilet."

Seeing everything unfold with cold eyes, Naoto opened his mouth. "Miss Marie, that old man is *hypothetically* on the verge of death, so don't go too far, all right? Also, this is bad for AnchoR's upbringing, so do it elsewhere, would you?"

"With his artificial body, it's possible for him to survive with just his brain circuits. There's no problem at all. Also, what upbringing would an automaton, who has been operating for a thousand years, need at this point?"

Vermouth laughed flippantly under Marie's foot. "For starters, princess, isn't your underwear a bit too childish? Either wear something a little sexier or just don't wear any at all."

"I'll really beat you to death, you know?!" Marie shouted, stamping down on his head again.

"Oy oy, princess?" said the low, hoarse voice of a man from outside the room. "What the heck is going on? Why are you howling?" Halter opened the door and stuck his head inside, peering.

"You... aren't you Vainney Halter?" Vermouth exclaimed from under Marie's foot.

"Huh...? Oy princess, who's this greenhorn? Looks like he's about to croak."

"How cold of you. I'm your humble fan. The Scarborough Fair Incident is still talked about by people in our line of work, you know."

"The Scarborough Fair Incident?" Naoto tilted his head, looking puzzled.

Halter waved one hand irritably. "You don't need to know about that. It's an old story from another time."

Vermouth smirked. "I was half-disappointed, half-relieved when I heard you took on the job of babysitting the princess of the Breguets."

"Relieved?" Halter asked, seeming perplexed.

"Encountering a monster like you during a mission would surely end with me in pieces. That's what I thought. To think of all the ways that I could've ended up meeting you! For it to be like this? Guess you never know what's gonna happen in life."

"A greenhorn who can mouth off with just his neck I see. You've got guts. If you want my autograph then keep your mouth shut."

"I won't ask for your autograph, but maybe you could save me? I feel like this princess is gonna kill me."

"That sounds good to me. Just die under her foot, thanks," Halter said curtly, then turned towards Marie. "Really now, where did this youthful eyesore come from?"

"It seems that he was stored inside AnchoR's cube through spatial manipulation. Apparently, he's also the one who sent that shitty prank message. I'm in the middle of thanking him extensively for that."

Marie struck Vermouth's head with her heel.

"Ahh," Halter nodded. "AnchoR should have just killed him. Actually, why didn't he die?"

"Oh, AnchoR-chan was restricted from killing humans," Naoto interjected, still holding the sobbing AnchoR in his arms. "I think that's probably why,"

Vermouth's eyes widened in fear. "Oy, don't tell me that that girl's the Initial-Y Series who crushed me?"

"She is. What about it? I'm saying this now, I ain't givin' her to you."

"I wouldn't take her even if you asked me to, brat." Vermouth looked completely baffled, watching Naoto hug AnchoR and assert ownership of her. Vermouth grimaced. "In the first place, you guys are telling me she can't kill humans? My entire team was eradicated. So are you saying that she doesn't consider us full-body cyborgs as human?"

"Hmm? I'm curious about that as well." Halter looked at AnchoR, scratching his chin. "When we first met, I was considered one of your targets, right? And this annoying greenhorn's comrades were done in, but here he is alive... Just what criteria do you use to determine your targets?"

Vermouth should have died. He didn't have a human body. But instead, AnchoR had stored him inside her cube, sparing him.

In that case, what was her primary factor in determining whether she was allowed to use lethal force?

Naoto looked up and let his gaze wander. "Probably from how human they were acting, I guess."

"Whah?" Halter stared at Naoto incredulously.

"I mean," Naoto continued. "At the time, you were only thinking about letting Marie escape, right? Forsaking me and RyuZU was a given, and you didn't care whether you died yourself."

"......"

Halter stayed silent. *That's true,* he thought. *I abandoned my humanity upon encountering AnchoR. I switched my heart from that of a human to a soldier who's ready to fight. To the machine I am.*

Adjusting his mindset. It was an exceedingly basic skill that Halter had learned to survive. Nothing was forbidden on the battlefield. All options were justifiable. You had to base your decisions on rational criteria. Emotion would only get in the way.

Halter's duty was to protect Marie Bell Breguet. To bring her back safely, he could easily let Naoto and RyuZU die. It wouldn't even faze him. For that matter, his own life meant nothing to him, either.

Because of that, AnchoR hadn't recognized Halter as human.

"......"

Halter looked down at Vermouth.

This guy... in sending such a message to Marie, he must have turned from a soldier to a human at the end. After all, I can't find any logic or rationality in that. Why would a spy send a transmission to the Breguet princess when she should be dead?

To do such an inexplicable thing... I see, so he must be human.

"Oh, old man, in case you misunderstood me, I'm not blaming you," said Naoto. "I understand that's your job. If anything, I'm impressed by how firm your resolve is."

"Ahh, you're embarrassing me. Jeez," Halter laughed bitterly. There was a mountain of things he wanted to say.

To begin with: does that mean he was reading my mental state at the time? Even if he could hear the operating sound of my cyborg body, my brain is human...

For goodness' sake, just what does this little fool really hear with those ears?

Shrugging his shoulders, Halter let out a deep sigh.

"I was deemed lacking in humanity by an automaton of all things?" he grumbled, stroking his bald head. "Oy, that hurts, you know."

• • ● ⬤ ● • •

5:38 AM, around daybreak.

Marie turned her head and surveyed the workshop. "Now then, with the relay broadcasting equipment taken care of, that's all the evidence gotten rid of, right?"

"Yeah," Halter nodded. "Dr. Konrad and the other Meisters have already left. We're the only ones here."

"Right, and as to the alibis for everyone involved in this incident..."

"I've taken care of that, of course. Aside from Naoto's."

"Good, good." Marie nodded, then turned around with a smile. "Your name will go down in history, Naoto. Isn't that lovely?"

"Well... I guess anything's fine since RyuZU and AnchoR-chan are safe," Naoto replied, wincing a bit at that smile of hers. "Although, all things considered, isn't making me out to be the sole instigator of this large-scale terrorist act pushing it a little?"

"Perhaps you should think about it this way instead, Master," RyuZU said somewhat triumphantly. "You will finally shed your lowly reputation in that ridiculous microcosm of society known as school and obtain worldwide recognition instead."

"Yeah, but as the villain of the century..."

"What worth is there in the subjective morality of fleas? What is clear is that you are a phenomenal individual, Master Naoto."

"Father, you're amazing!" AnchoR hugged Naoto's arm with a carefree smile.

Naoto broke into a grin. "Crap... I might achieve enlightenment from how happy I feel right now, heh heh heh heh—"

"Stop fooling around. We're getting out of here," Marie chided.

Halter knocked on the ball he was carrying under his arm, somewhat discontentedly. "Can't we just throw this guy away, princess?"

"Oy oy, isn't that a bit cold? Appearances aside, I'm a man with a strong sense of duty, you know? If you give me a new body, I'll work hard to return the favor." The ball—Vermouth's head—laughed flippantly. Despite being reduced to a state that would make children cry, his attitude was brazen.

Marie snorted. "Hmph. I'll work you to the bone, all right? So prepare yourself."

"Thank you for your benevolence, dear princess. Ahh, by the way, got a cig?" he asked.

Everyone ignored him.

Just then...

"Oy, wait a second," Naoto, who had been grinning, said suddenly.

Marie turned around looking perplexed, her eyebrows furrowed. "What, did you forget something?"

"That's not it! Oy, seriously, what's with this sound? It's...coming from underground?!" Naoto cried.

A thunderous roar pierced through the floor and the vibrations from an intense collision shook the city. The force was such that everything jolted up and down.

Unable to remain standing, Marie fell on her backside. Naoto tumbled down while covering his ears and screaming. RyuZU and AnchoR rushed to his side.

"What's happening?!" Marie yelled.

No one answered.

It wasn't an earthquake. The vibrations and deafening noise didn't die down. In fact, they became stronger and stronger. Even Marie, who didn't have Naoto's super hearing, could tell from the sensations assaulting her body that something was crawling up from underground.

"This can't be real!" Naoto yelled, gasping. "That thing... that enormous weapon is rising to the surface! Tearing through the earth!!"

"You're kidding me!" Marie cried.

"Like I would say this as a joke, you idiot!!" Naoto screamed back.

"What the hell is Tokyo's military doing?! Don't tell me they were annihilated?! There's no way!" Marie yelled, grinding her teeth.

The weapon was of the superdreadnought class, equipped with countless guns, and armor that even RyuZU's scythes couldn't pierce.

But its size made it a sitting duck. In a battle of attrition against overwhelming numbers, it stood no chance. If the army had clashed with the weapon at the base of the city, where they could fight without having to worry about collateral damage, then they should have been able to take it down. Although maybe not without losses.

That was how it was supposed to go according to Marie's plan, but...

"Oy," Vermouth shouted warily. "Don't tell me you had Tokyo's military clash with that weapon...?!"

"Shut up, there wasn't any other way!" Marie retorted with a click of her tongue.

Vermouth knit his brows as though he had a headache. "Give me a break, ghost princess. So you overlooked the most important part? You've gotta be kidding me."

"What are you talking about?!"

"Why do you think I went through the trouble of sending you a transmission through EM waves? The research conducted in Shiga—that violated the international treaty and led to the purge—was on electromagnetic technology. That monster is the culmination of that technology, you know?!"

Electromagnetic technology.

It had been used abundantly in ancient times but had since fallen out of favor. Electromagnetic waves could derail the particle-sized gears used by nearly all precision instruments...

Wait. A chill ran down Marie's spine. The countless events that she had experienced in the past week flashed before her eyes. She could excuse herself by saying she had far more pressing things on her mind, but...

Illegal research on electromagnetic technology had been conducted in Shiga Grid.

The city was purged because of the risk that the truth would be exposed.

Mie's clocksmiths had survived that unjust purge.

At the same time, she remembered those nauseating words from Mie's governor: *the federal government doesn't realize that Shiga's Technical Force wasn't created as an empty threat.*

"Why...! Why didn't I realize it?!"

The true ability...

Of that enormous weapon...

Was...

"That which governs an electromagnetic field... are you telling me that it's *an enormous electromagnet*?!"

Naoto covered his ears and let out a stifled cry.

"...ah?!"

As if masking his scream... all of the city mechanisms, along with Halter, RyuZU, AnchoR, and Vermouth... anything and everything that employed gear technology...

...Ceased functioning.

• • ● • • •

5:47 AM on the eighth of February, 1016th year of The Wheel.

The ground rumbled like an earthquake. As the phenomenon increased in intensity, the giant crowd of people who'd been evacuated to Akihabara Grid witnessed something. A gigantic pillar of blue light pierced straight through the dawning sky as the day broke.

Immediately after, a profoundly deafening roar rang out, and all the mechanisms in Akihabara Grid began to screech. Ripples expanded outward from the pillar of light, and everything clockwork in their path ceased functioning.

After a few minutes, which felt like hours… an enormous steel spider tore through the ground, making a sound like a howling animal.

• • ● • • •

Inside a narrow and dimly-lit room, a monitor covered an entire wall. It refreshed constantly with data on the external environment, as well as the status of the unit.

"We've reached the surface of the city. No targets in sight. Continuing to search for enemies."

"The main cannon's battery is 14% cooled and 3% charged."

"Recalculating the time until recharging is complete."

The man nodded with poise, receiving the reports in rapid succession.

"If it is as Your Excellency says," said his adjutant, standing next to him. "Then there should be two Initial-Y Series here, but..."

The person he was speaking to—an old man with ashen white hair and beard—answered with a tired voice. "They may be 'Y''s legacy, but even they should be powerless in this stilled world." The moss-green eyes in his wrinkled face were glaring at the monitor before him.

His adjutant—a bespectacled young man—unconsciously straightened his back. "Your Excellency, may I ask you something?"

"I don't mind. Go on."

"Your Excellency retired from active duty three years ago and have since secluded yourself underground, right?"

"Are you dissatisfied that an old hermit is butting in?"

"Absolutely not. It is my honor to serve under Your Excellency. This is merely the curiosity of a petty officer. I heard you were leaning against carrying out this operation, so I'm wondering why you chose to return to active duty."

"Because I've discovered a question I must ask."

"Eh?"

Paying no mind to the adjutant's confusion, the old man's eyes darkened and narrowed. He recalled the boy he had met underground that day.

I have no proof. No, such a thing isn't necessary. But I understood. When I saw that boy and his automaton that day, I was convinced...

That is "Y."

A reincarnation? A successor? It doesn't matter. Frankly, I don't care.

However, that gaze of his... he rejected everything in the world and asserted the truth of his own views without a trace of doubt. It was precisely like the man behind the creation of this world.

That was awfully... yes, extremely distasteful.

I once had hope for the future, but I was disappointed by history and the world threw me into despair. That's why I thought I should live out the rest of my life in resignation.

"Like I could let things end like this after that," the old man whispered in a low, hoarse voice. "I'll teach you what we run-of-the-mill men can do if we put our mind to it, you wretched monster."

Clockwork Planet

AFTERWORD (JOINT)

AT A CERTAIN LOCATION and on a certain day, Editor S said this to us with half-closed eyes: "Now then, feel free to explain why it took so long for you to finish Volume 2. I thought you two were playing catch, bouncing ideas off each other..."

"Heh heh heh... Since when did you get the false impression that we were playing catch?"

"We weren't playing catch, we were playing dodgeball. Dodgeball with an iron ball. Heh heh." For some reason, Kamiya and Himana answered this way while brazenly giggling.

"After all, now that Tsubaki is in Saitama as well, I can punch him anytime I want. Previously, the distance between us prevented me from doing so."

"And when he does, how strange! For some reason, I find myself punching back! Long live the Code of Hammurabi!"

"Can't you two keep things a bit more civil?"

"With due respect, did you know that a certain peace-loving musician with round glasses got into a fight with another band member, before leaving the band and causing their breakup? This is what happens when you get rid of national borders [read: division of labor]. Are you seeing this from heaven, round glasses?"

"In the end, everyone insists on having it their own way. In other words, to find a point of compromise, the only option is to speak with your fists. [In an assertive tone]"

"Indeed, peace is nothing but an illusion. Humans can only understand each other through fisticuff—"

"Well, it's fine, I guess. After all, it's you two who'd be caught in a financial pickle if the book never gets published, not me."

"'War doesn't leave behind anything but debt, does it?' [With solemn faces]" At their editor's words, the two, whose faces were swollen [from punching each other], nodded.

"...I just remembered something."

Sino, who had been watching from the sidelines until now, spoke up:

"Regarding a certain series of Mr. Kamiya's that was published by another publisher... Mr. S, you were the one who set up that project and also the one who made Mr. Kamiya adapt it into a manga, along with his wife, right?

"...Wouldn't it be the case, then, that you made Mr. Kamiya publish Clockwork Planet knowing full well that he would be crushed by the additional workload, Mr. S?"

Sino had realized what should not have been realized.

Indeed, as everyone fell silent, only Editor S said leisurely, "Now then, I have to get back to sending the manuscript to the printers. Please be quicker with the third volume, all right?"

Seeing him making his exit with a dark smile, Kamiya and Tsubaki both barked:

"Stop right there! If I wasn't being crushed to death by work for my other series, we could have given you the manuscript for Volume 2 a tad earlier, you know?!"

"No wonder Kamiya kept saying 'I'm busy,' when I asked him whether he had checked over the plot outline yet. So you were the culprit behind everything!"

The two of them then, like mirror images—shook hands with ferocious smiles. "The source of conflict ought to be sentenced to death 3." With that show of unity, the two chased after their editor at full speed.

Sino nodded deeply. "Wowww, conspiracies really do exist in real life."

Yep, it looks like we're still far, far away from achieving world peace, Sino muttered internally...

A character design segment despite it being Sino's afterword!

This time it's on the Fourth of the Initial-Y-Series, AnchoR.
The theme of her design is "dual nature."
I put effort into points like making her clothes asymmetric and making her look like an angel before she transforms but like a demon afterwards. AnchoR herself *is* an angel, so that aspect isn't at odds with her character (lol). She went on a rampage in imaginary time this volume, but that actually wasn't her true form. Her true form might be revealed sooner rather than later, so please look forward to it until then!

Clockwork Planet